MARVEL

THE AVENGERS

Little, Brown and Company

Hachette Book Group
1290 Avenue of the Americas, New York, NY 10104
Visit us at lb-kids.com

LB kids is an imprint of Little, Brown and Company.
The LB kids name and logo are trademarks of Hachette Book Group, Inc.

The publisher is not responsible for websites (or their content) that are not owned by the publisher.

First Edition: April 2015

ISBN 978-0-316-34085-4

10 9 8 7 6 5 4 3 2 1

CW

Printed in the United States of America

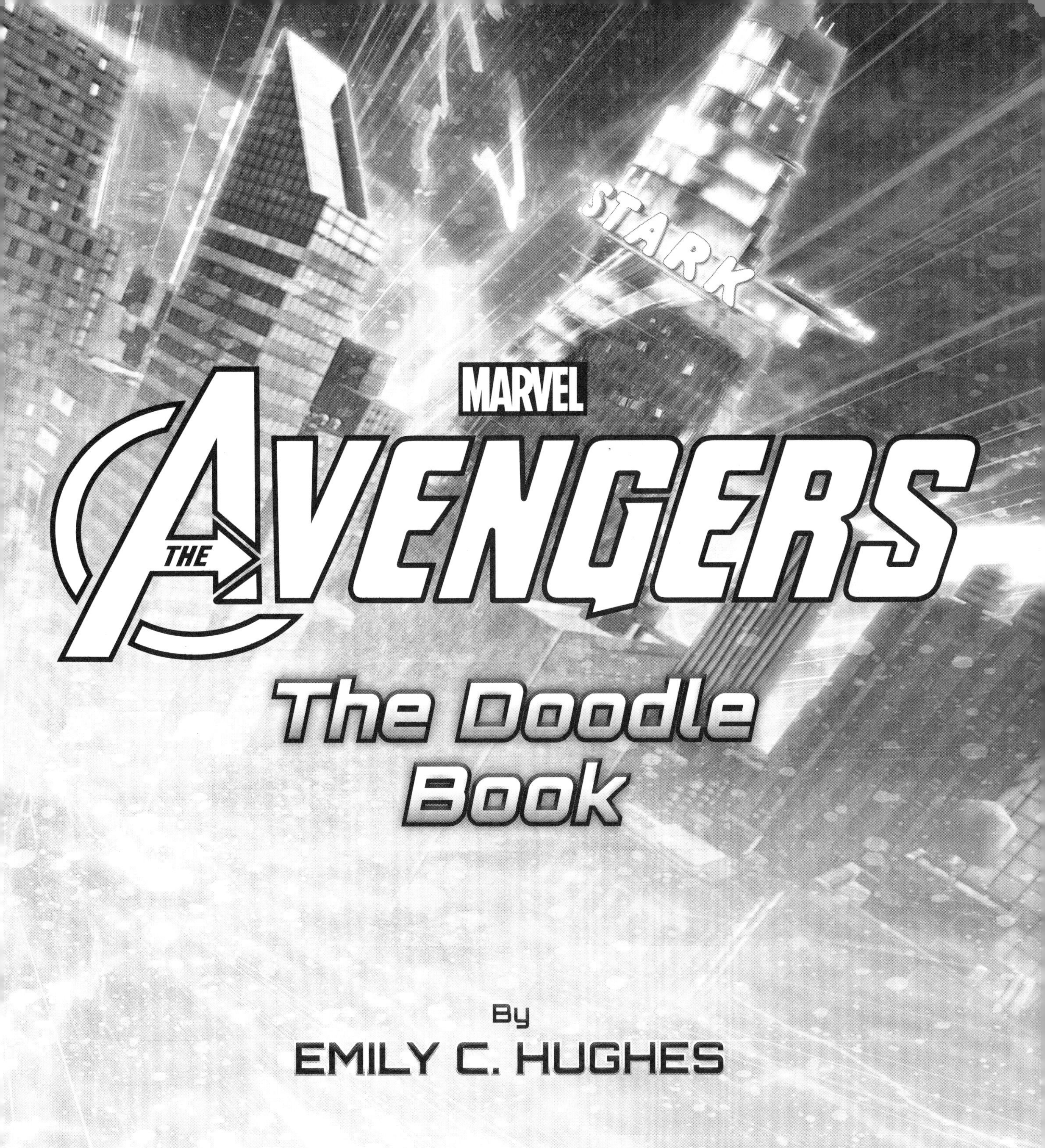
STARK

MARVEL

THE AVENGERS

The Doodle Book

By

EMILY C. HUGHES

LB

LITTLE, BROWN AND COMPANY
New York Boston

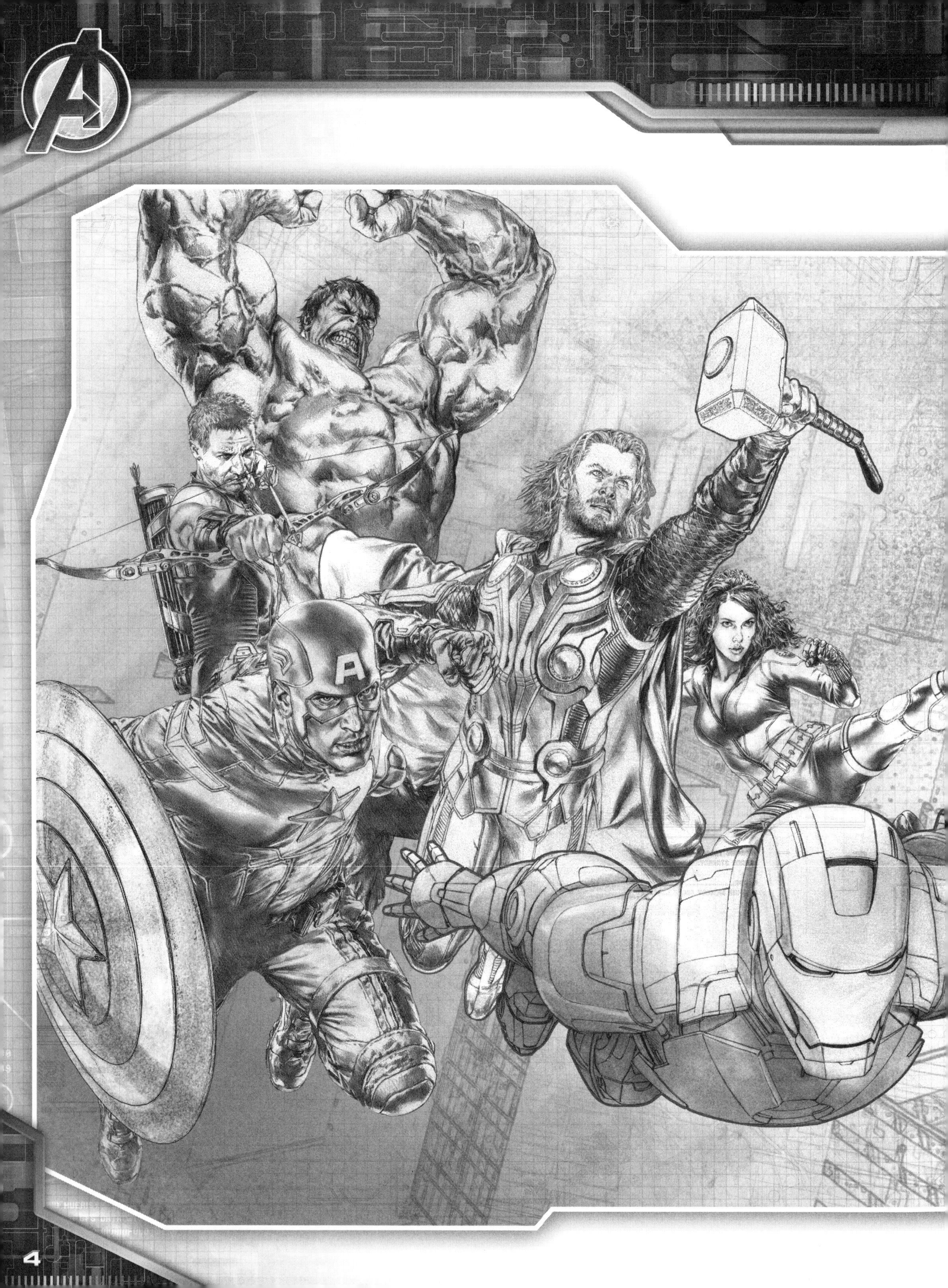

The Avengers are Earth's Mightiest Heroes! Assembled by Nick Fury of S.H.I.E.L.D. (Strategic Homeland Intervention, Enforcement and Logistics Division) to fight the foes no single Super Hero could withstand, they found themselves united against a common threat. On that day, the Avengers were born!

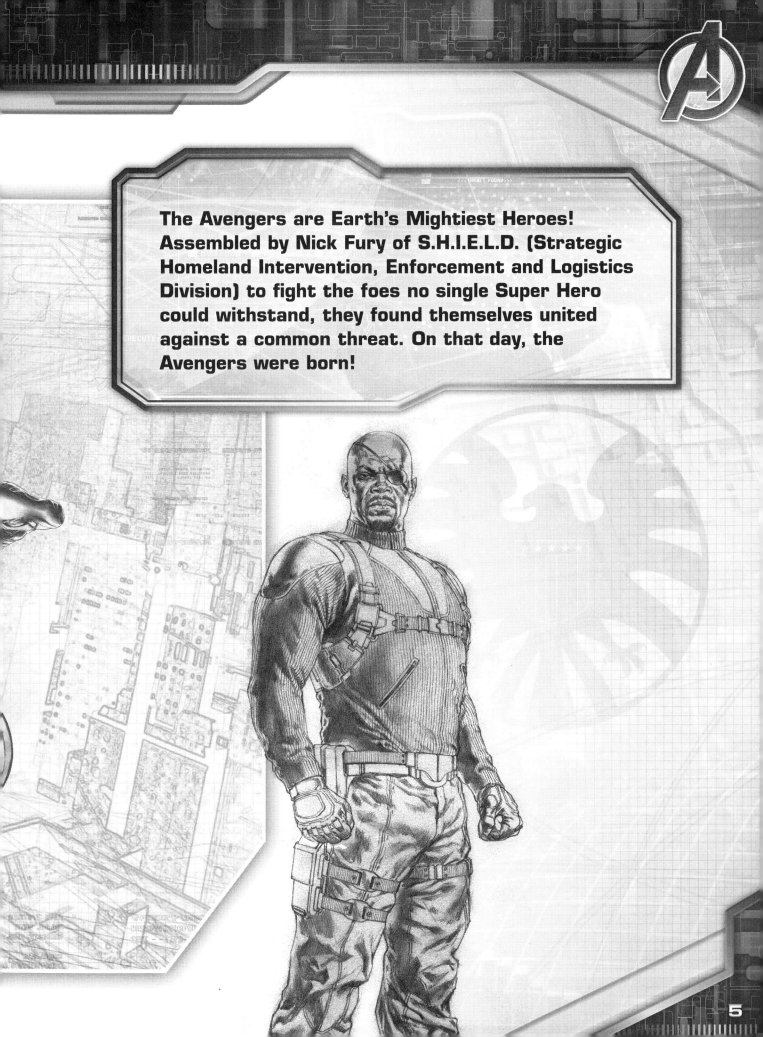

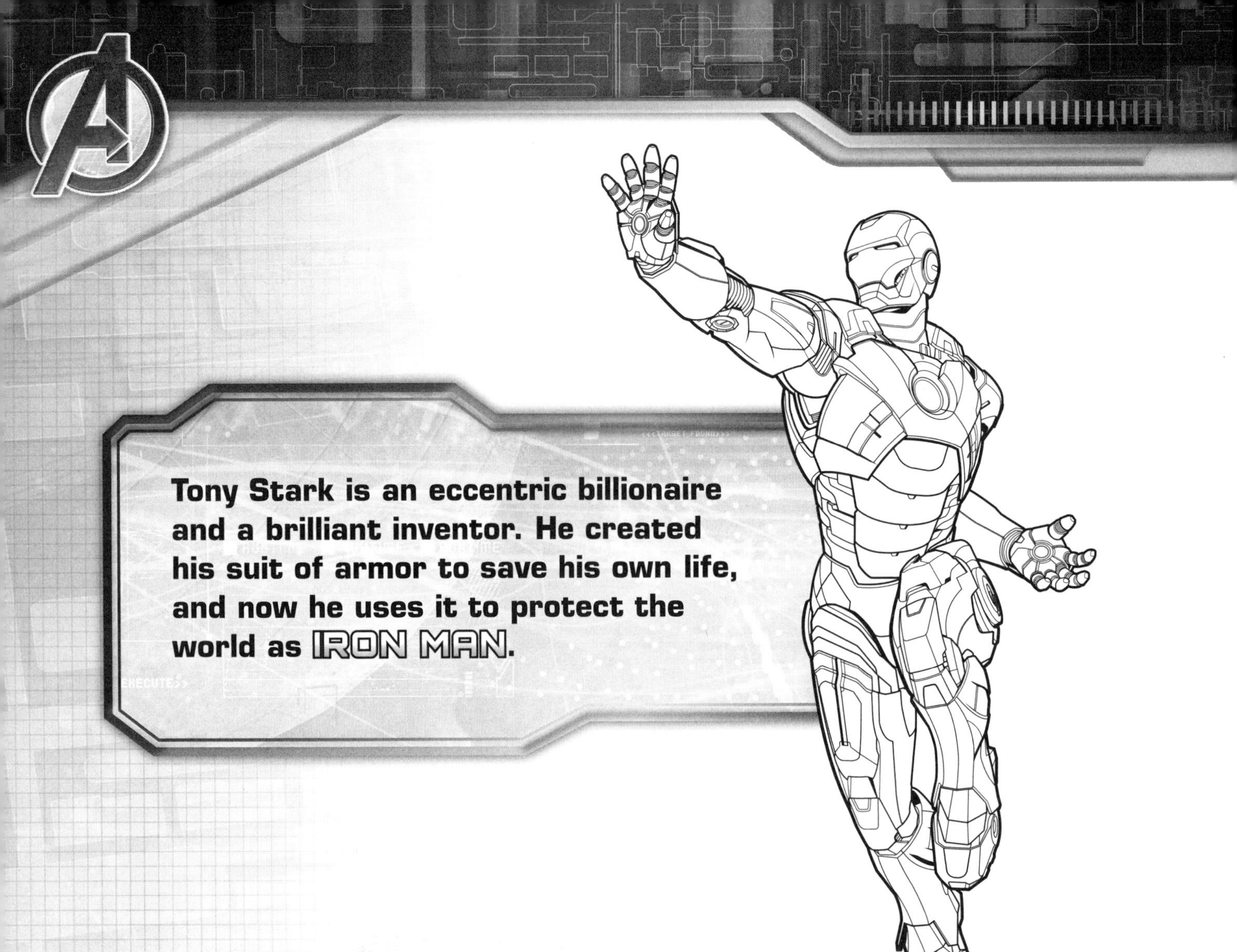

Tony Stark is an eccentric billionaire and a brilliant inventor. He created his suit of armor to save his own life, and now he uses it to protect the world as IRON MAN.

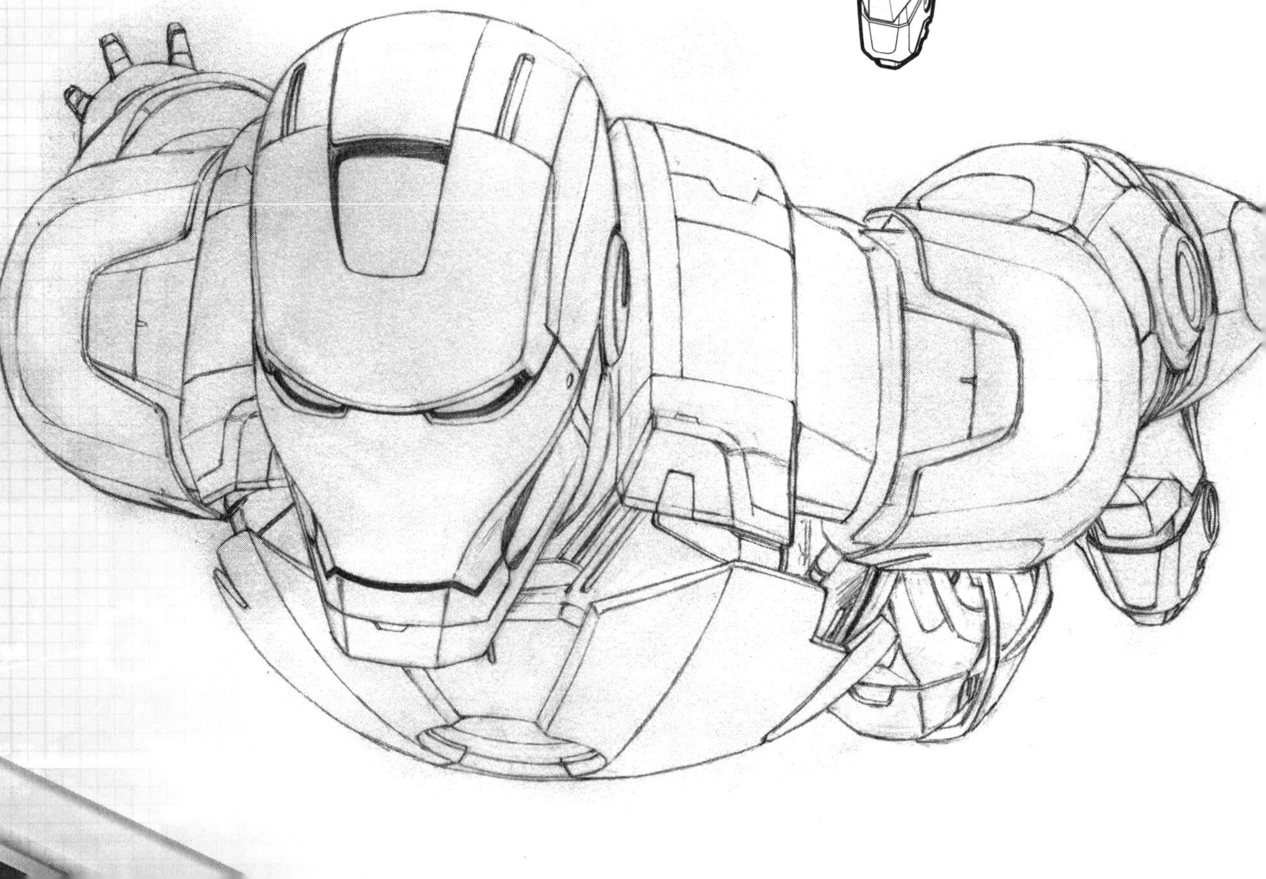

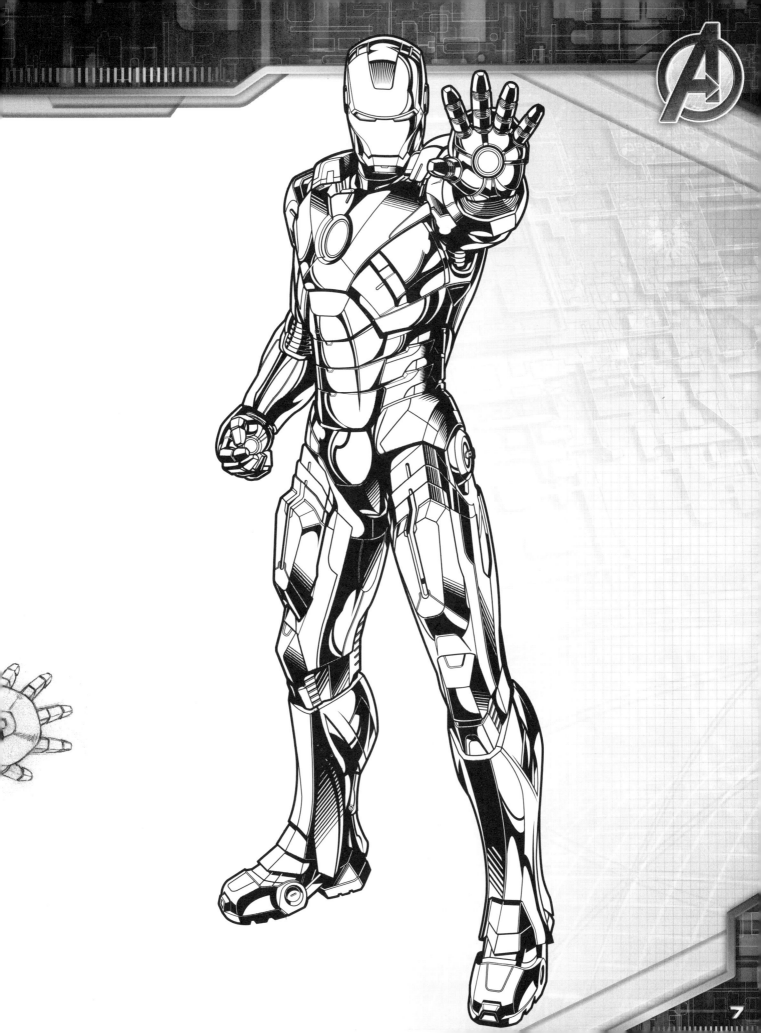

After an accident with gamma radiation, Dr. Bruce Banner turns into the monstrously strong HULK when he's angry. His superhuman strength is unbeatable!

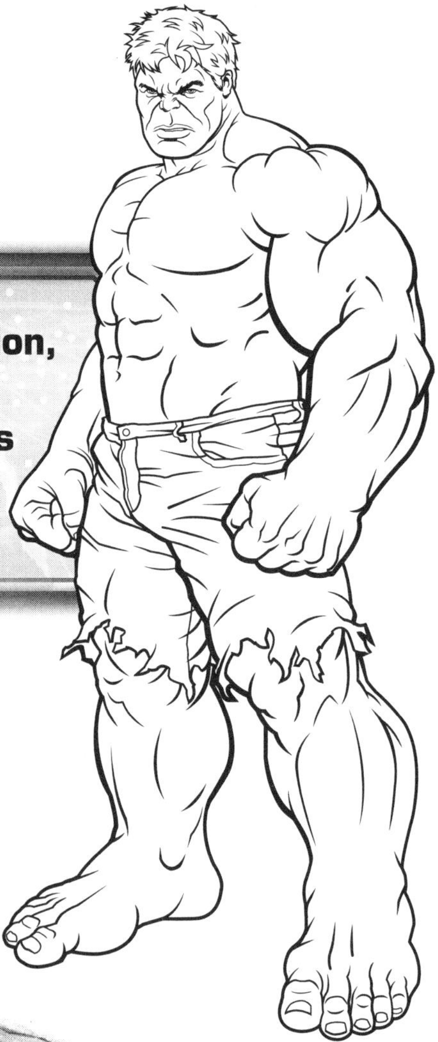

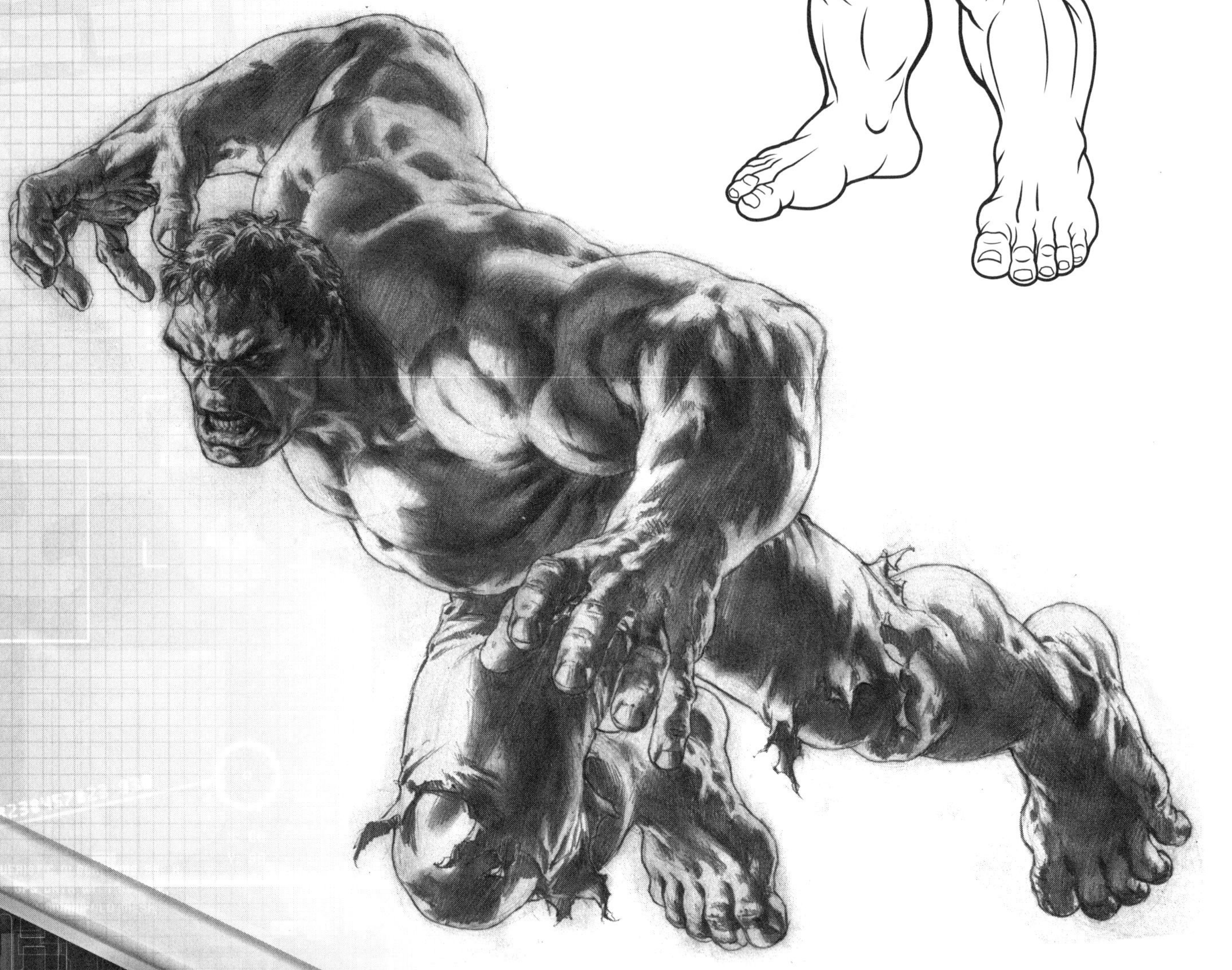

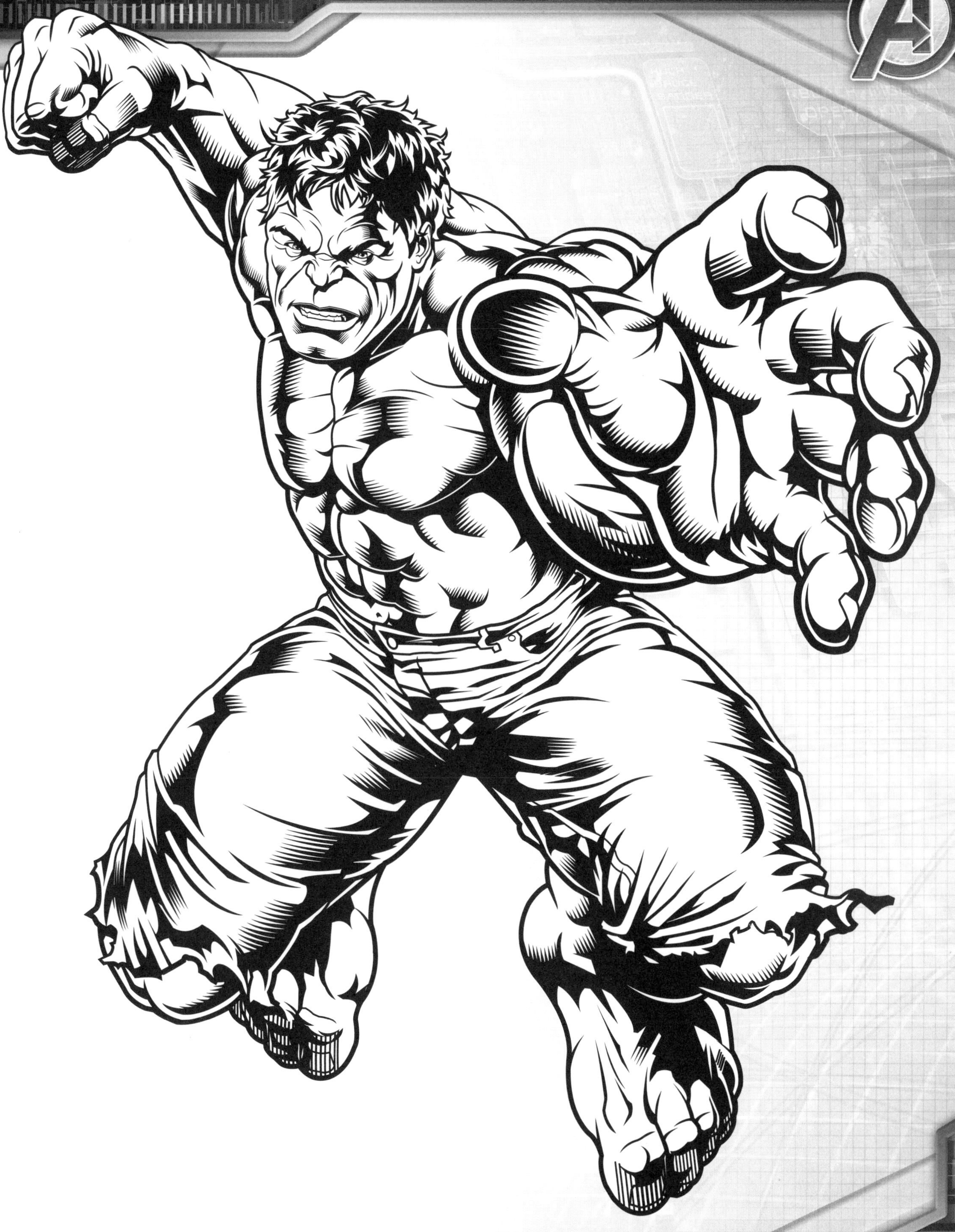

The Super-Soldier serum turned Steve Rogers into the peak of human perfection to fight America's enemies in World War II. After decades of cryosleep, CAPTAIN AMERICA is back in fighting form to protect humanity.

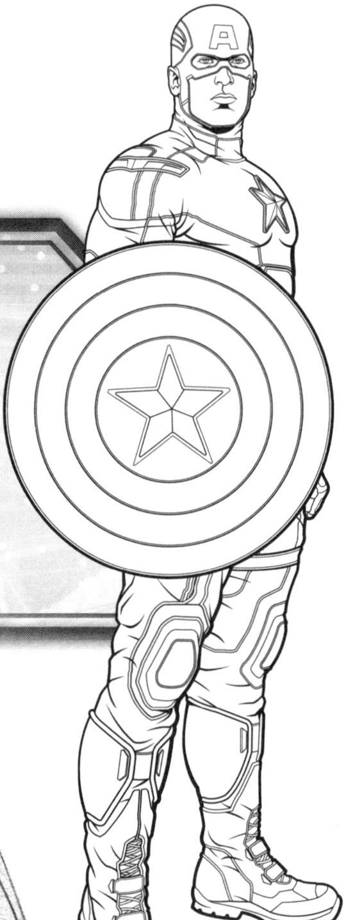

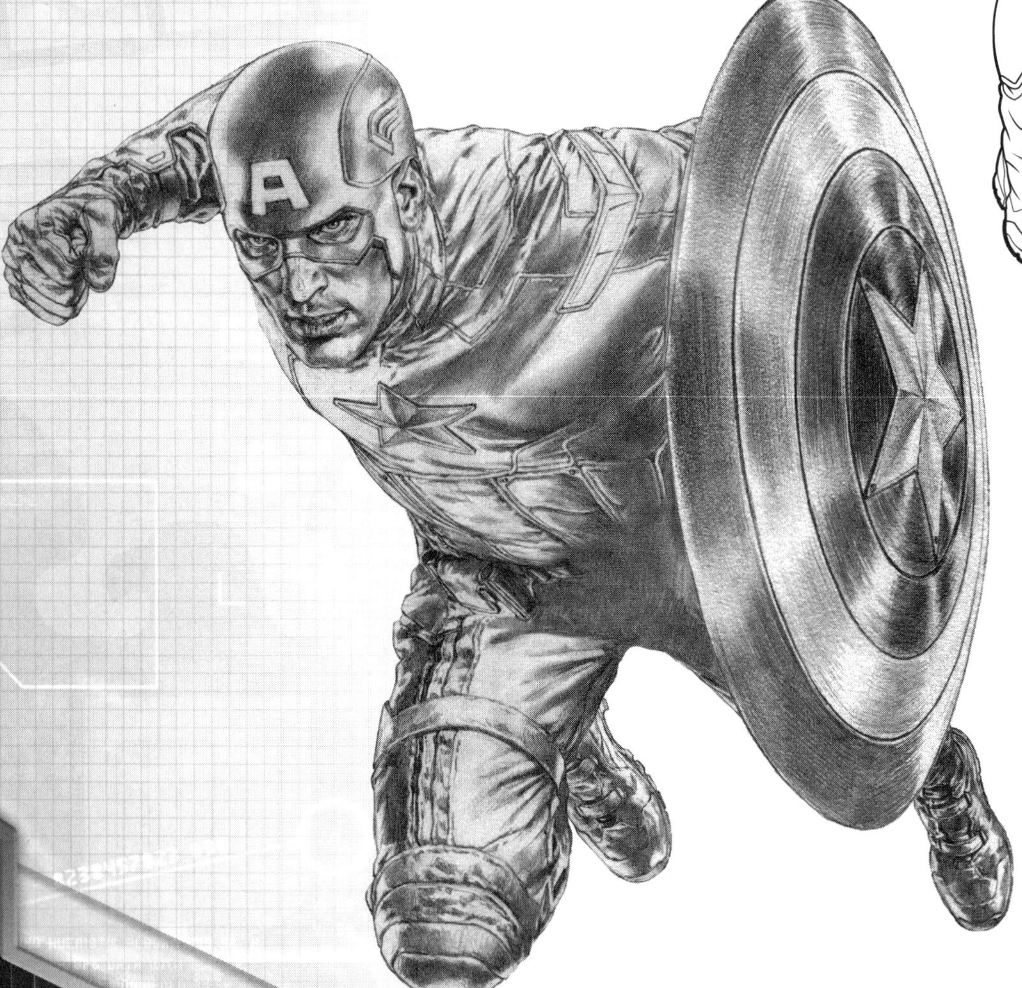

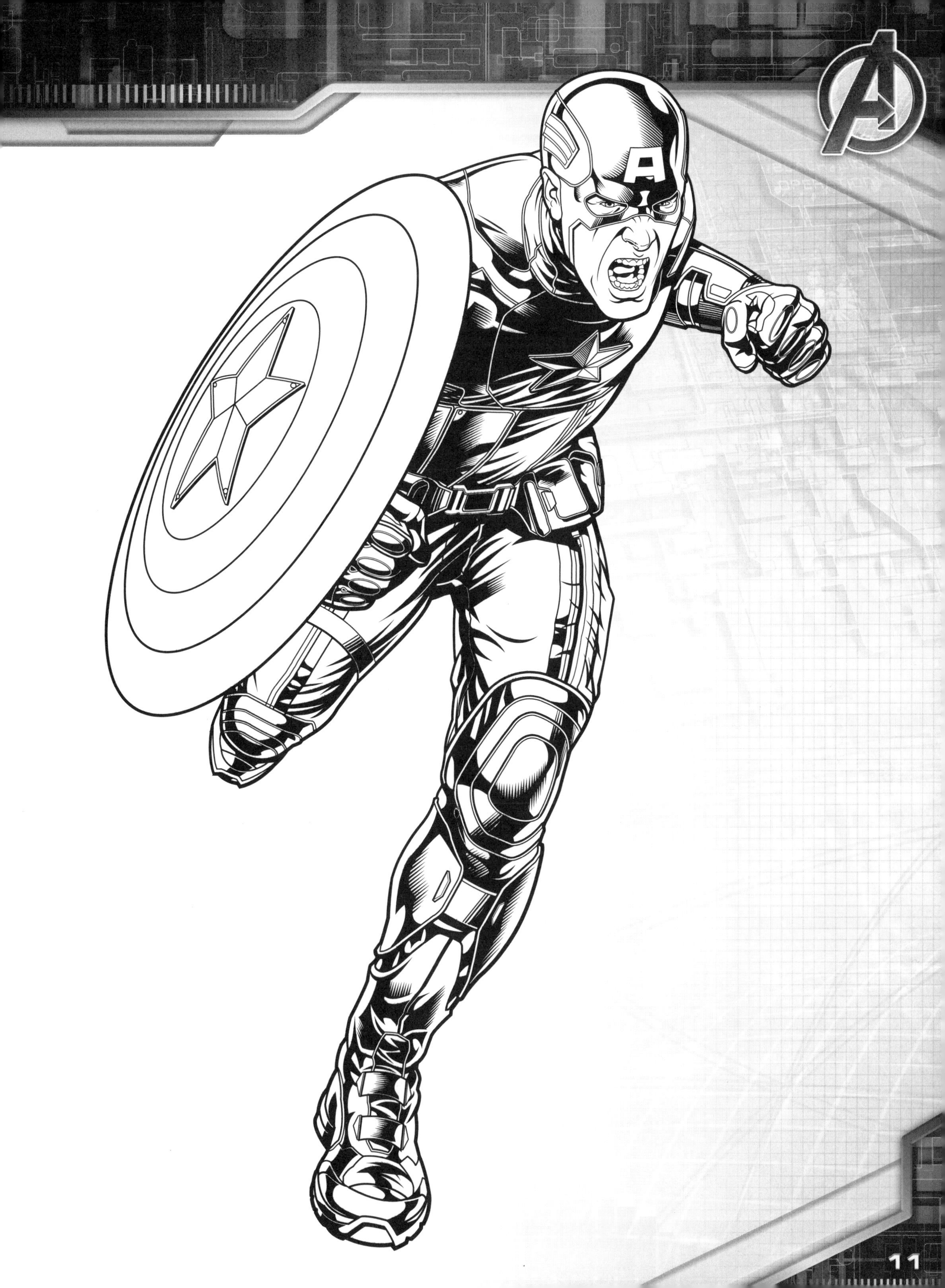

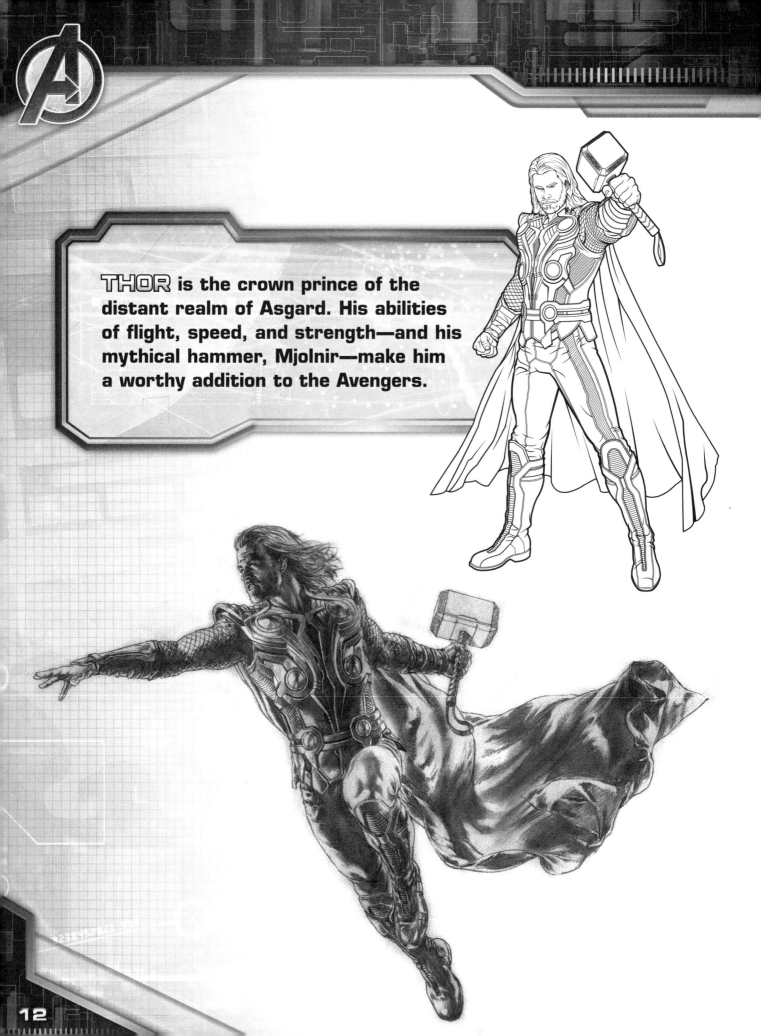

THOR is the crown prince of the distant realm of Asgard. His abilities of flight, speed, and strength—and his mythical hammer, Mjolnir—make him a worthy addition to the Avengers.

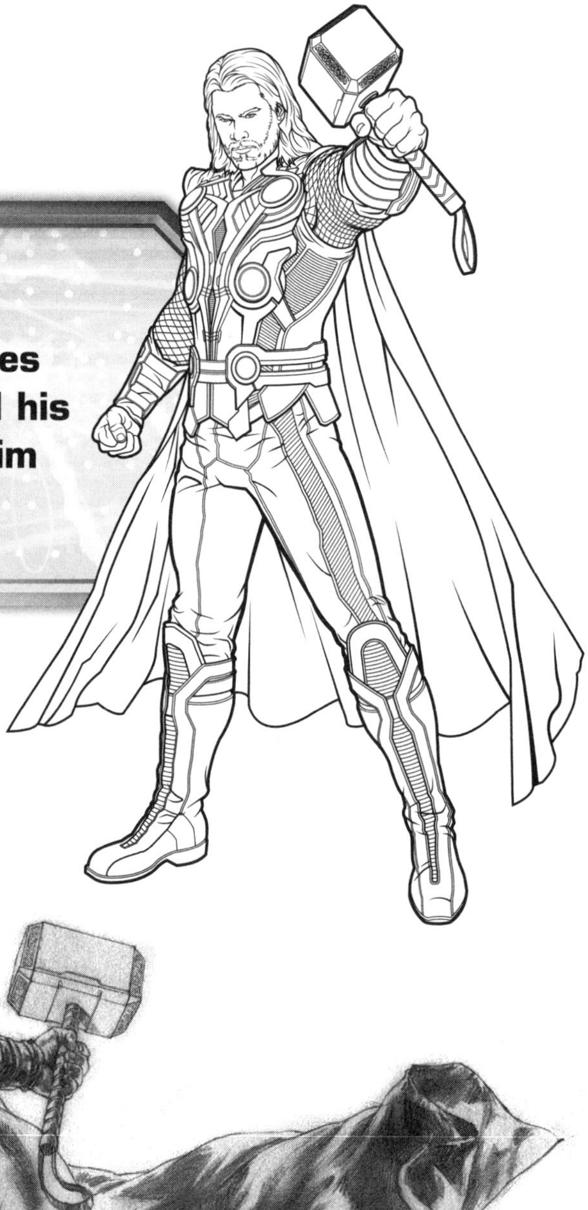

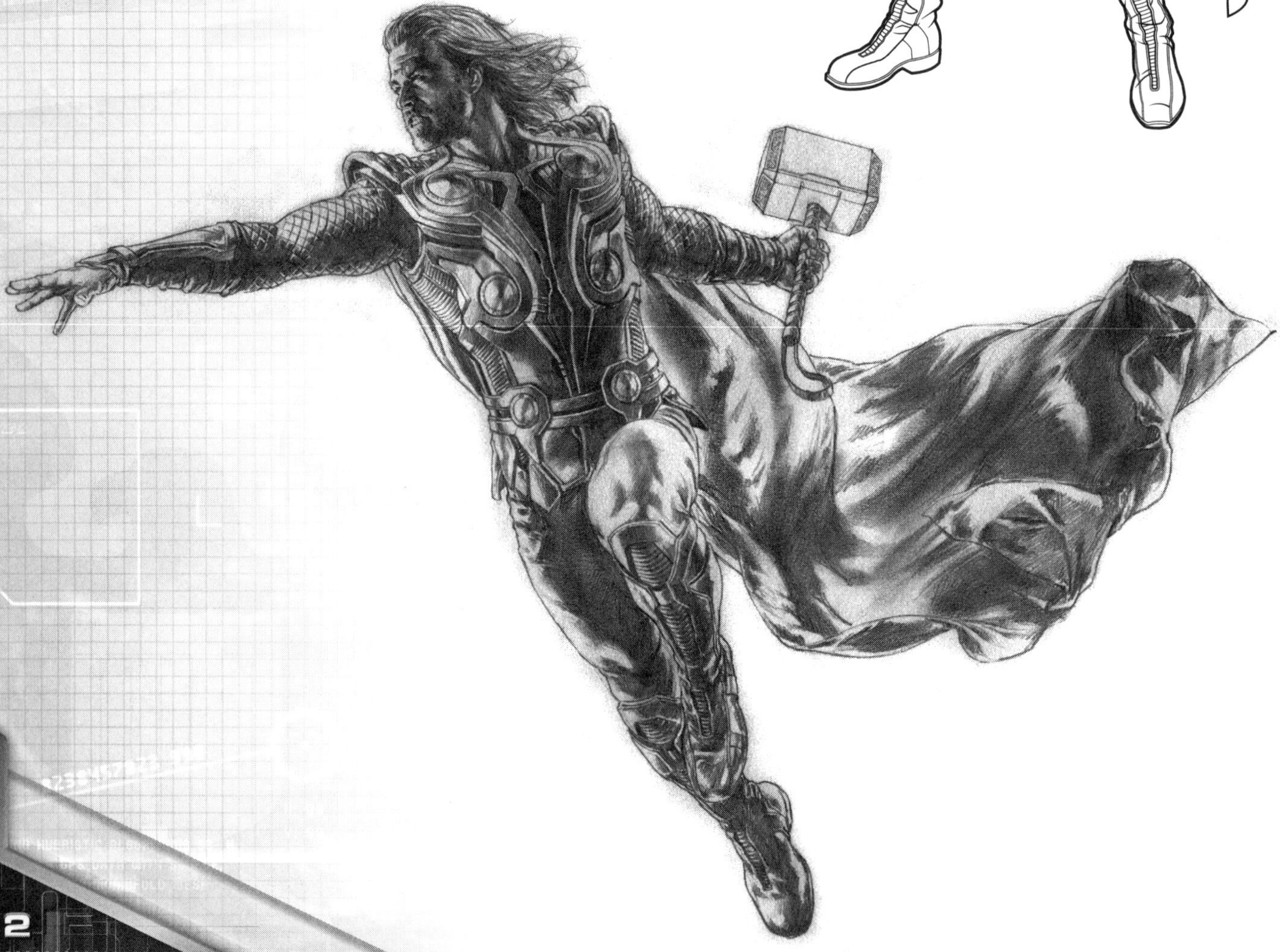

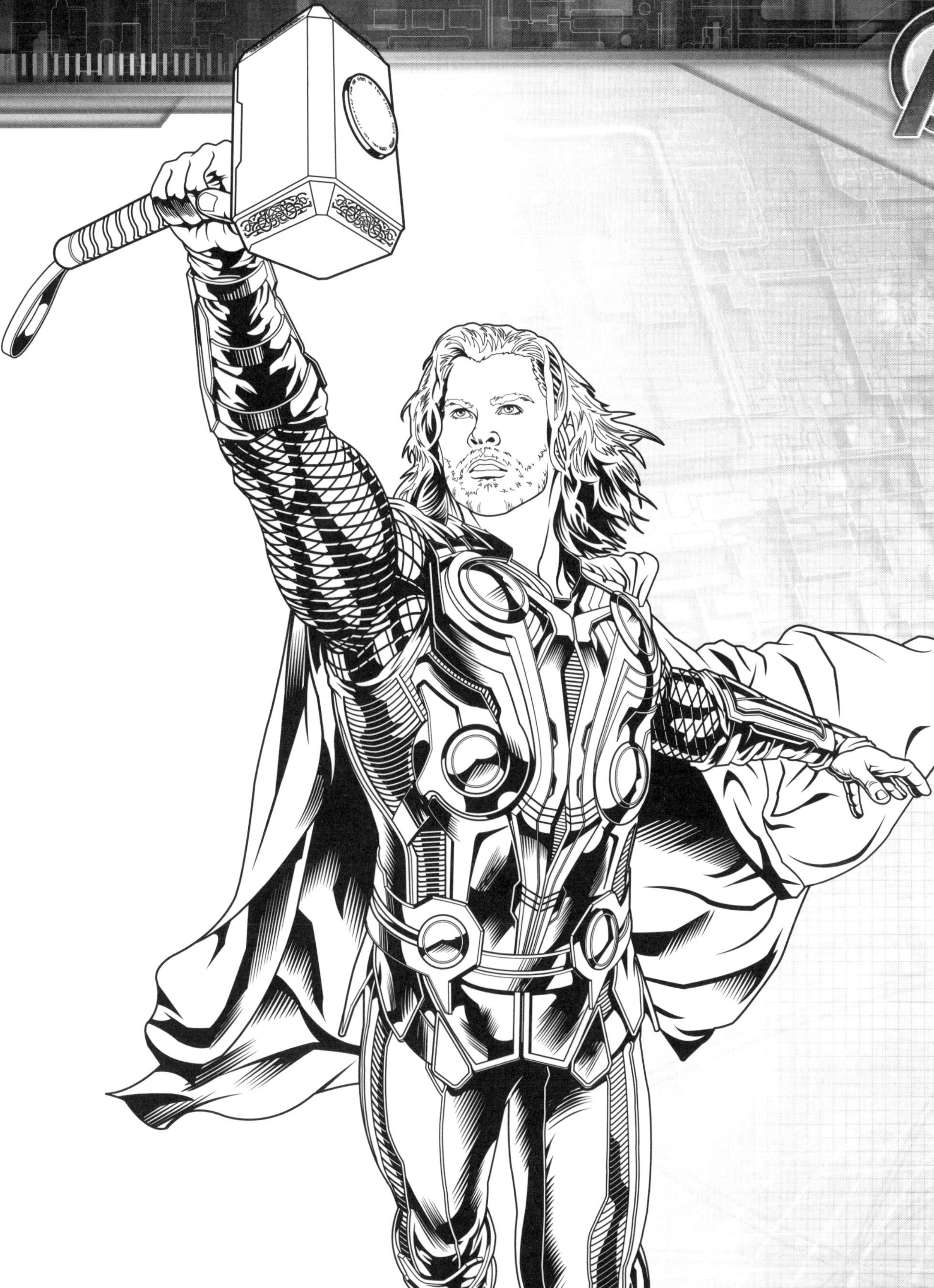

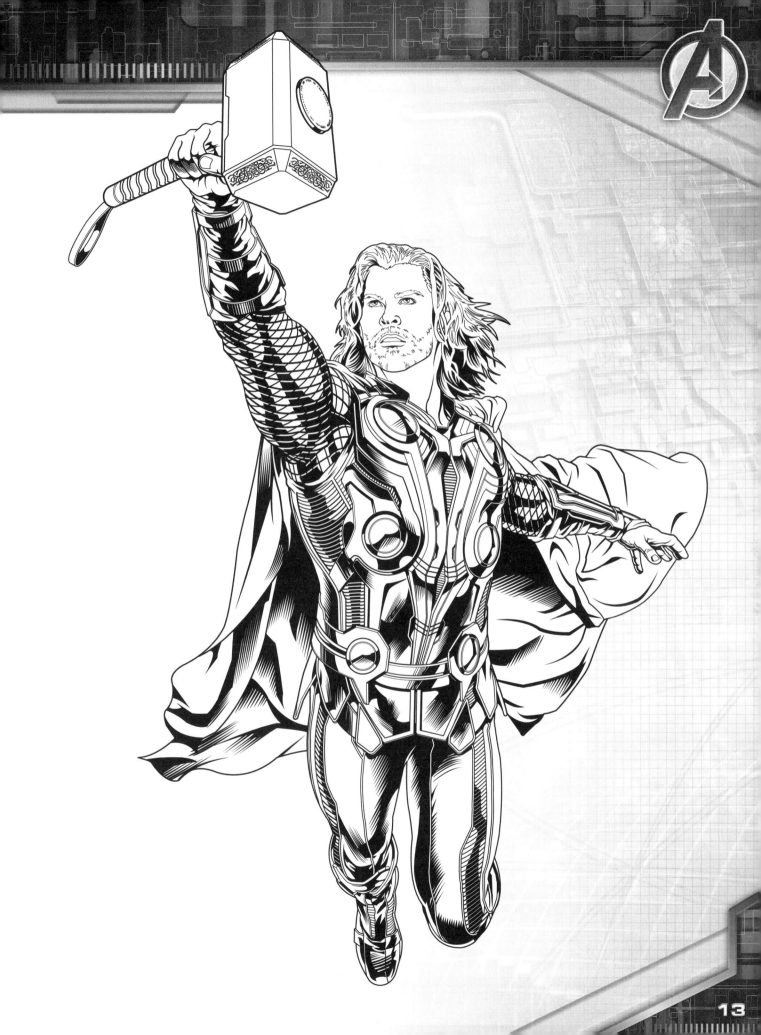

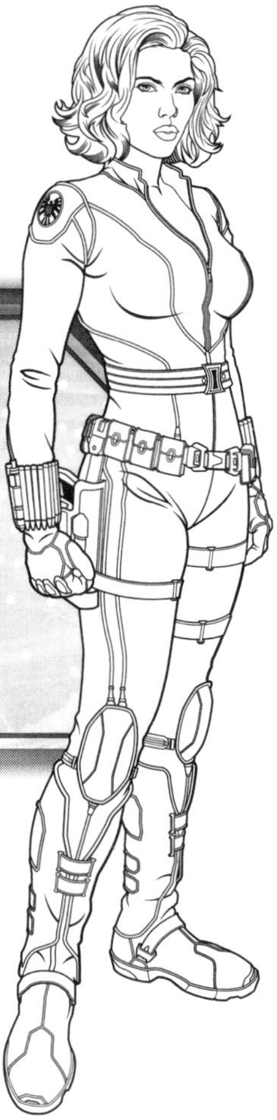

Black ops superspy Natasha Romanoff, better known as BLACK WIDOW, is S.H.I.E.L.D.'s secret weapon. Her martial arts skills know no equal, and she's a deadly asset to the Avengers.

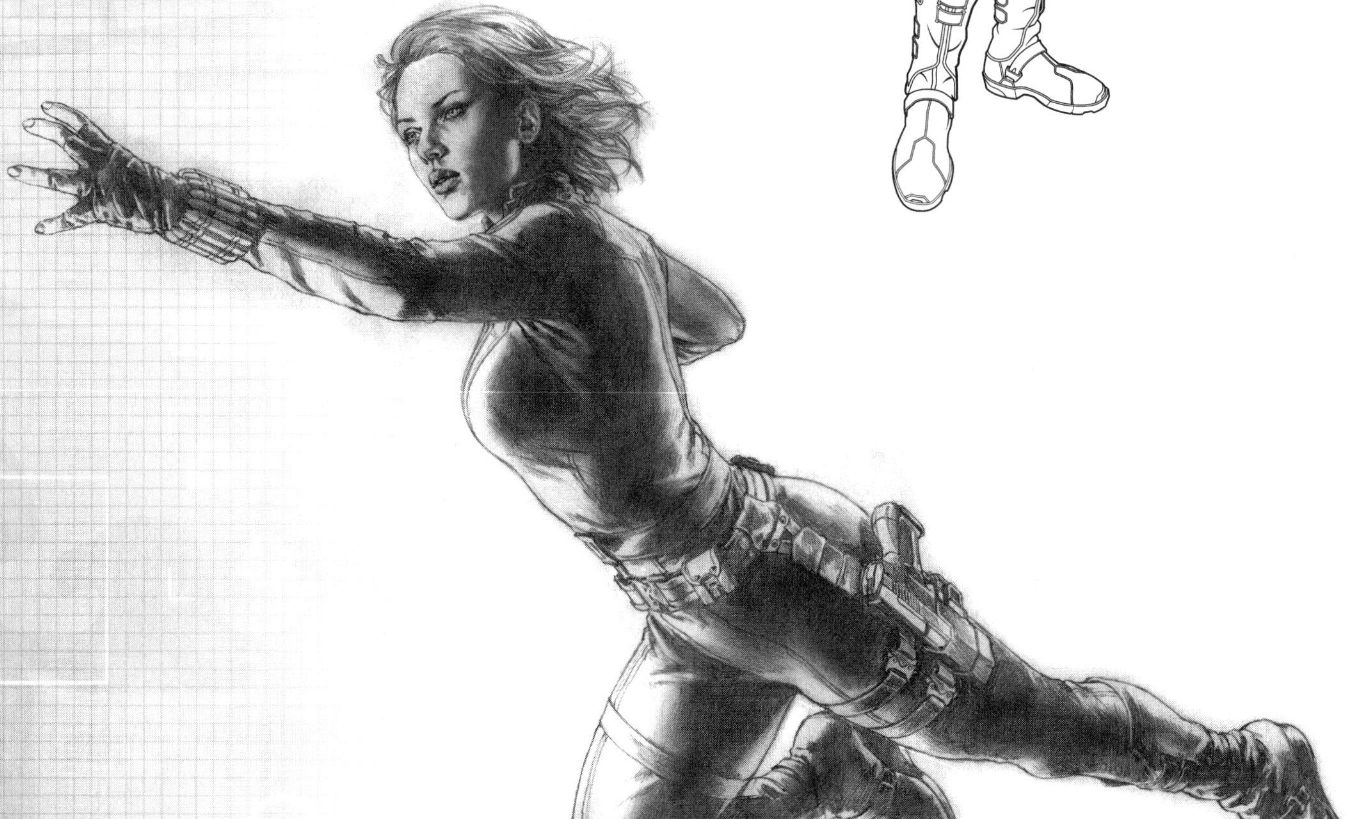

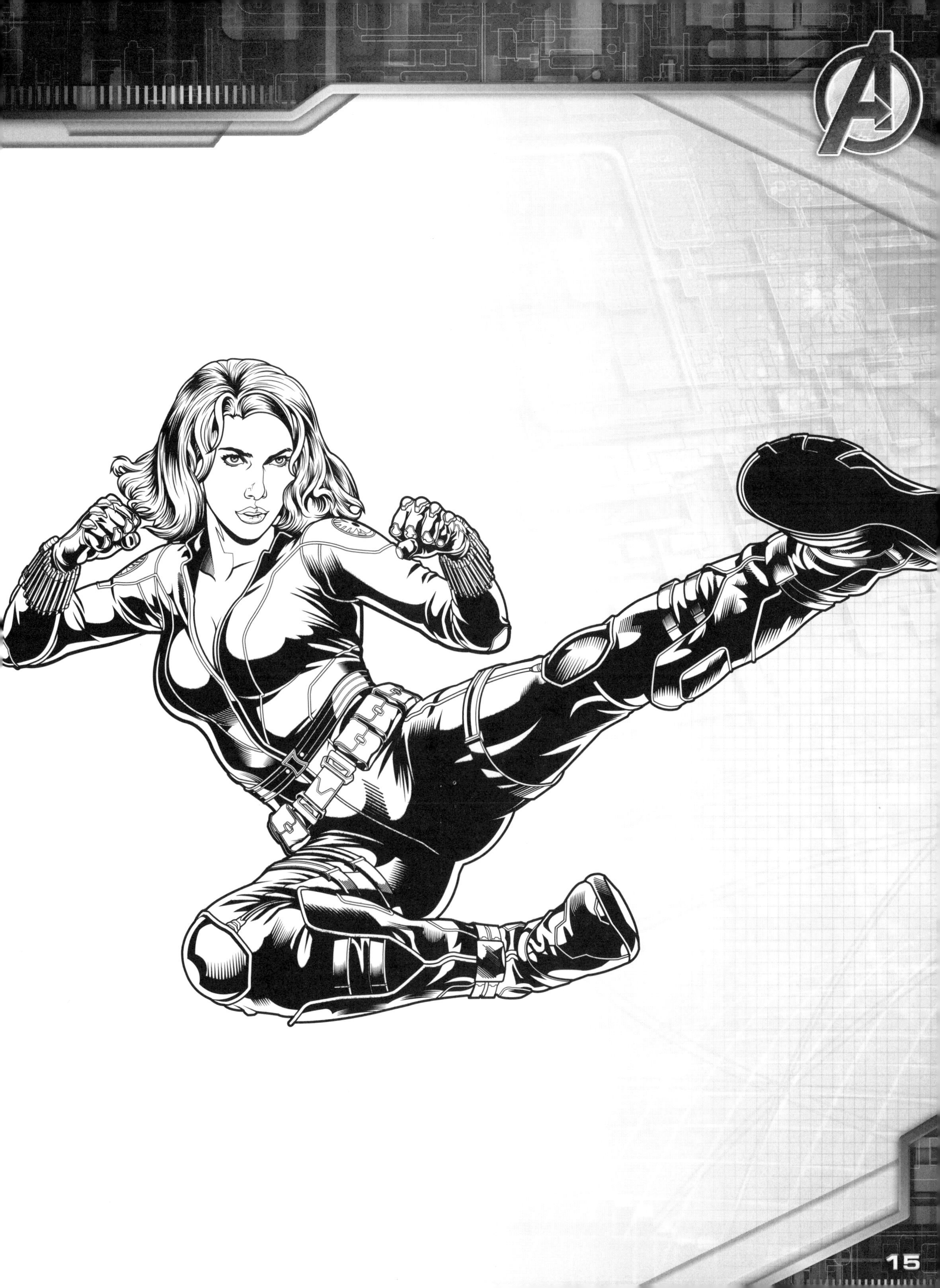

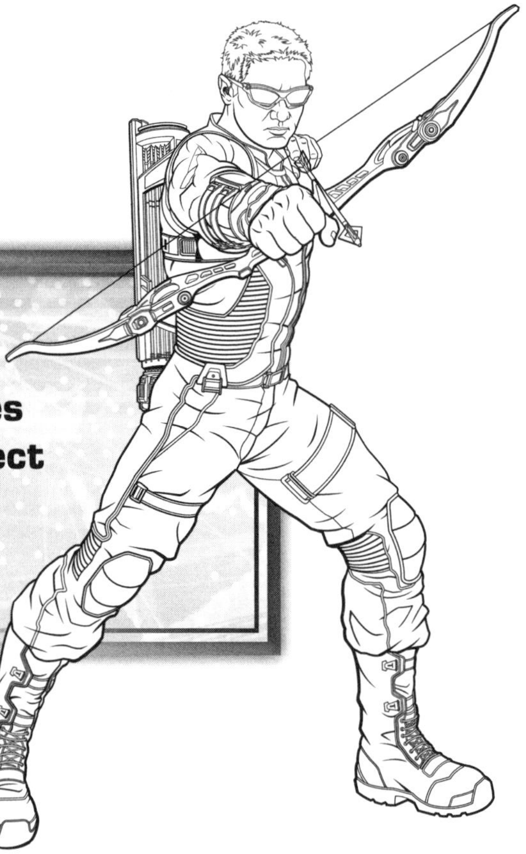

Master archer HAWKEYE fires his augmented arrows with perfect precision. He never misses.

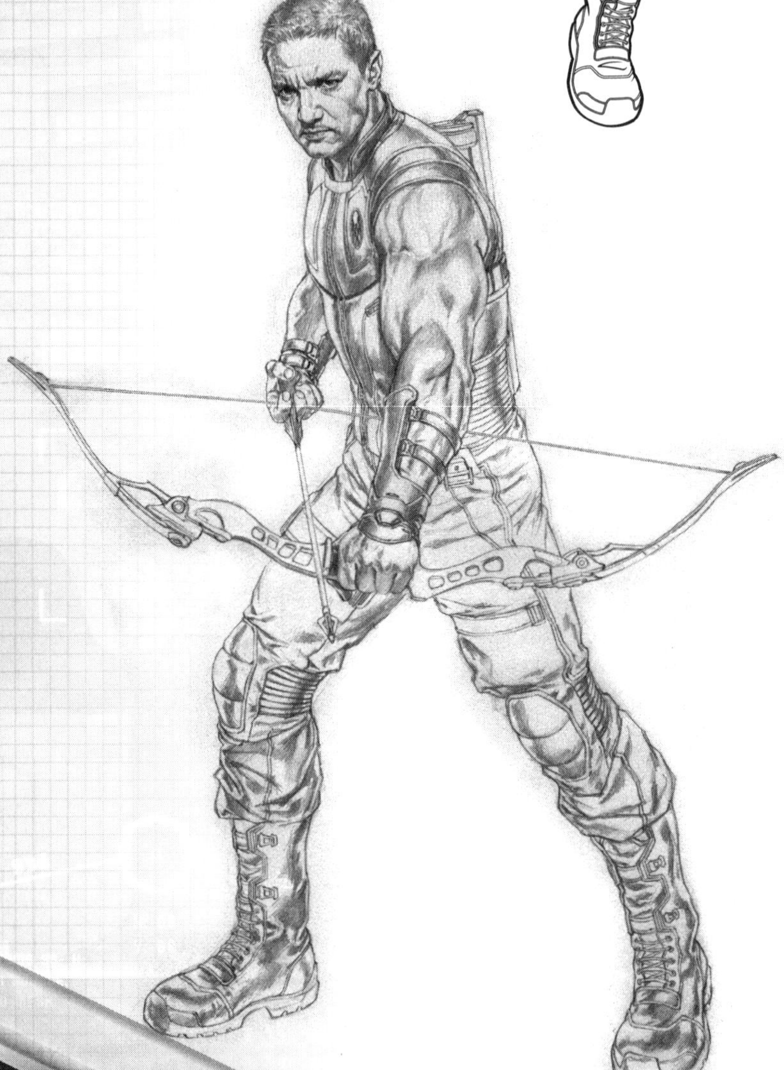

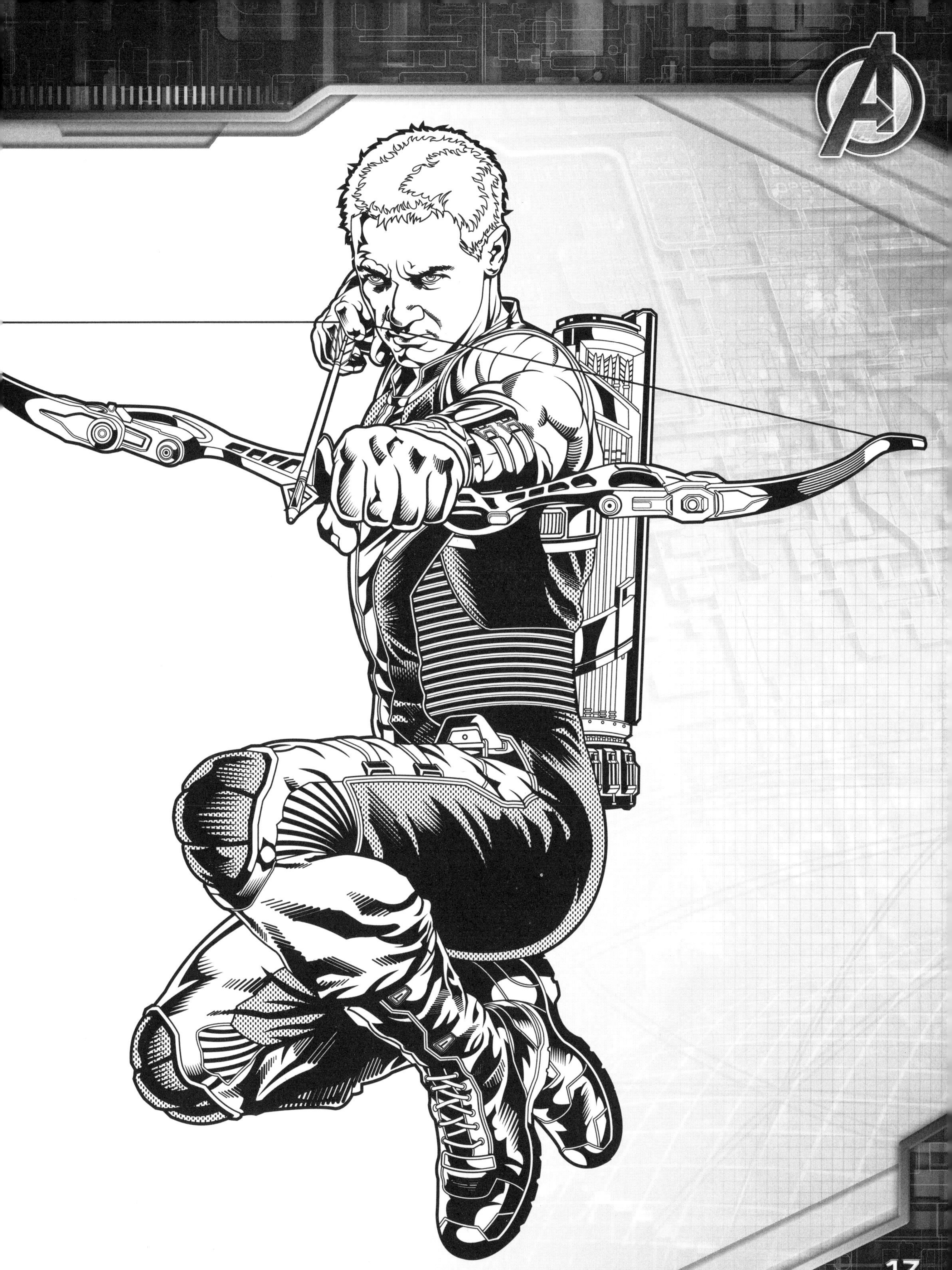

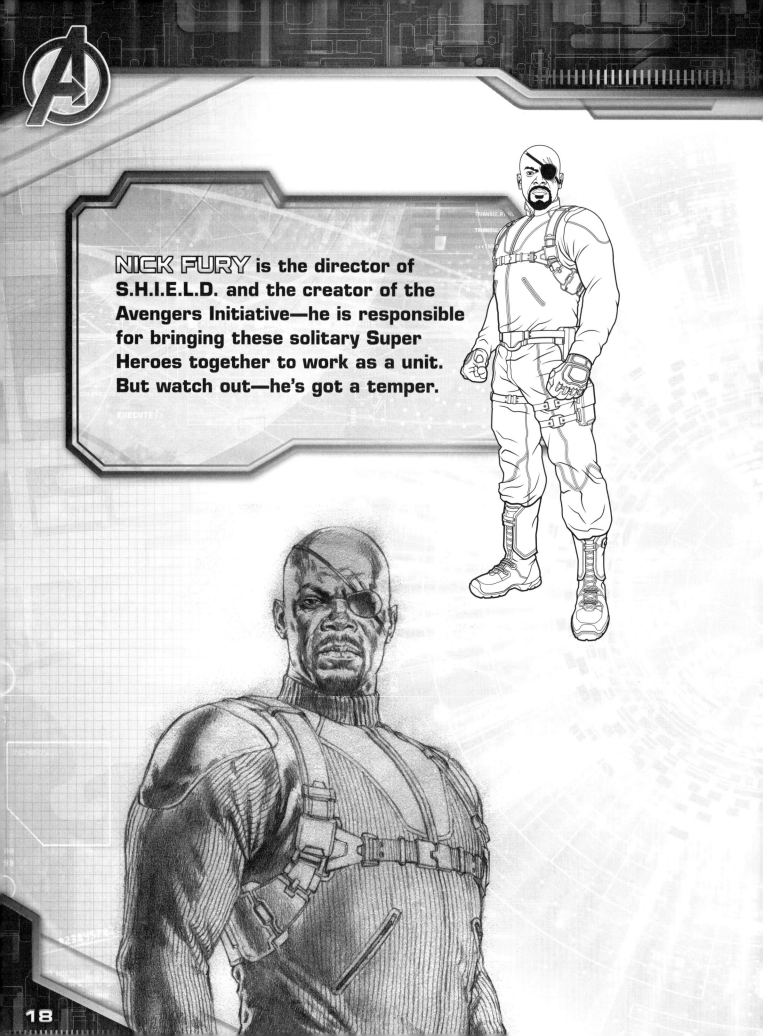

NICK FURY is the director of S.H.I.E.L.D. and the creator of the Avengers Initiative—he is responsible for bringing these solitary Super Heroes together to work as a unit. But watch out—he's got a temper.

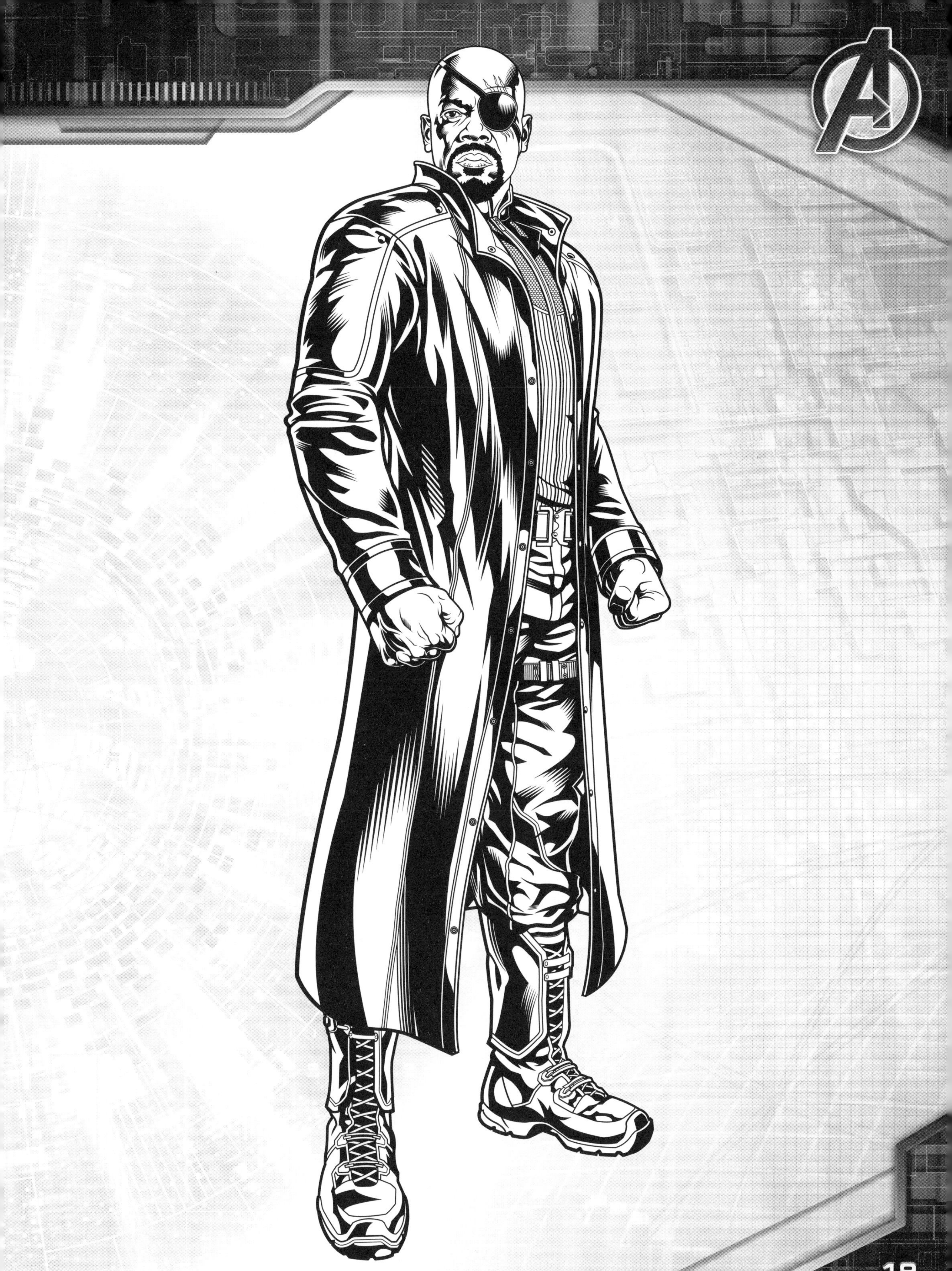

PHIL COULSON and MARIA HILL are two of S.H.I.E.L.D.'s top agents. Together with Nick Fury, they support the Avengers from their flying headquarters, the Helicarrier.

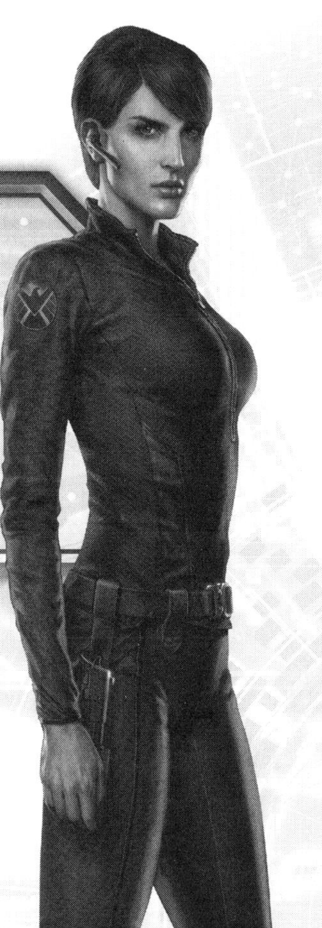

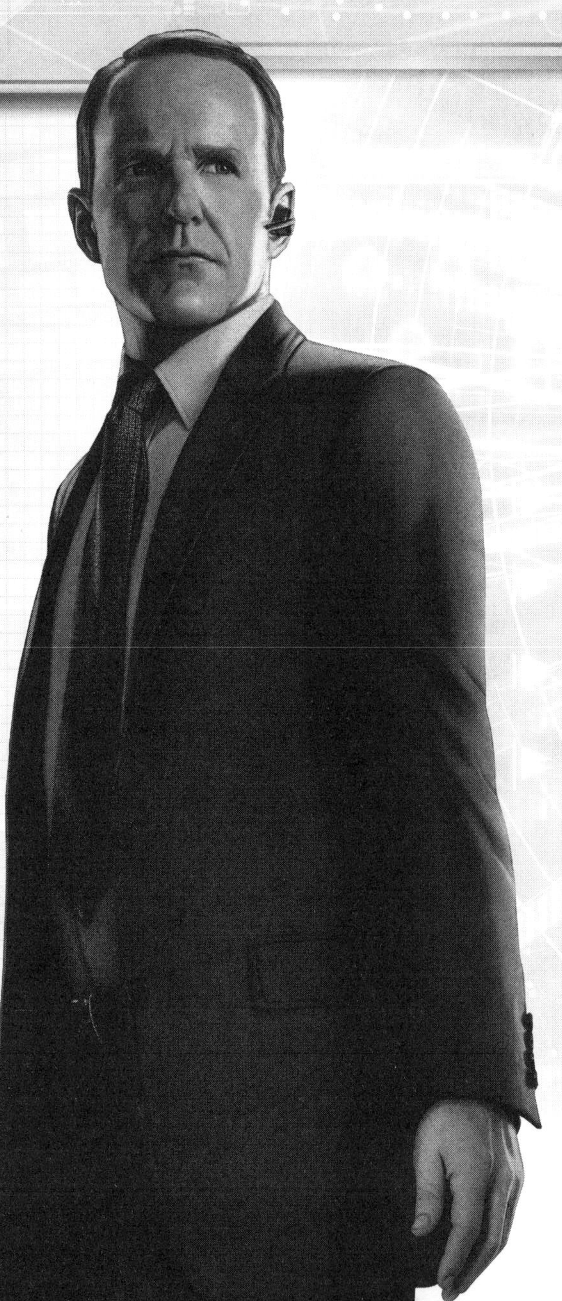

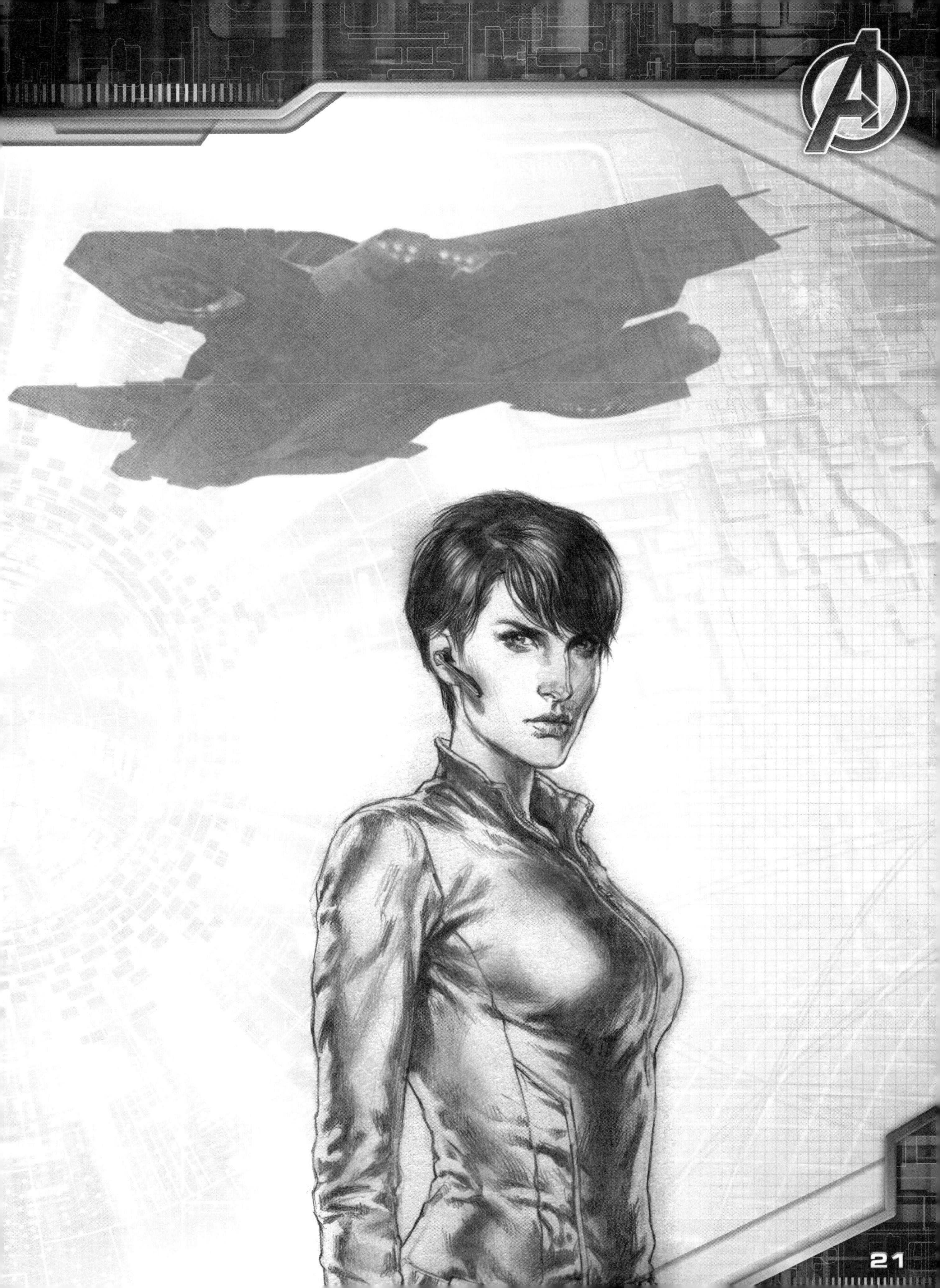

Together, THE AVENGERS are the most powerful defense the Earth has. Fill in the blanks to spell a message:

SHI_LD
Bl_ck Widow
Nick Fu_y
_esseract
Natas_a Romanoff
Agent Coul_on

Captain A_erica
Qu_njet
Steve Ro_ers
Maria _ill
Clint Bar_on
Lok_
H_licarrier
Jarvi_
_hor

_ulk
Dr. Bruc_ Banner
I_on Man
Mj_lnir
Hawk_ye
Tony _tark

_ _ _ _ _ ' _

_ _ _ _ _ _ _ _ _

_ _ _ _ _ _

Answer: EARTH'S MIGHTIEST HEROES

LOKI is Thor's adopted brother and wants to rule humankind. Finish drawing him.

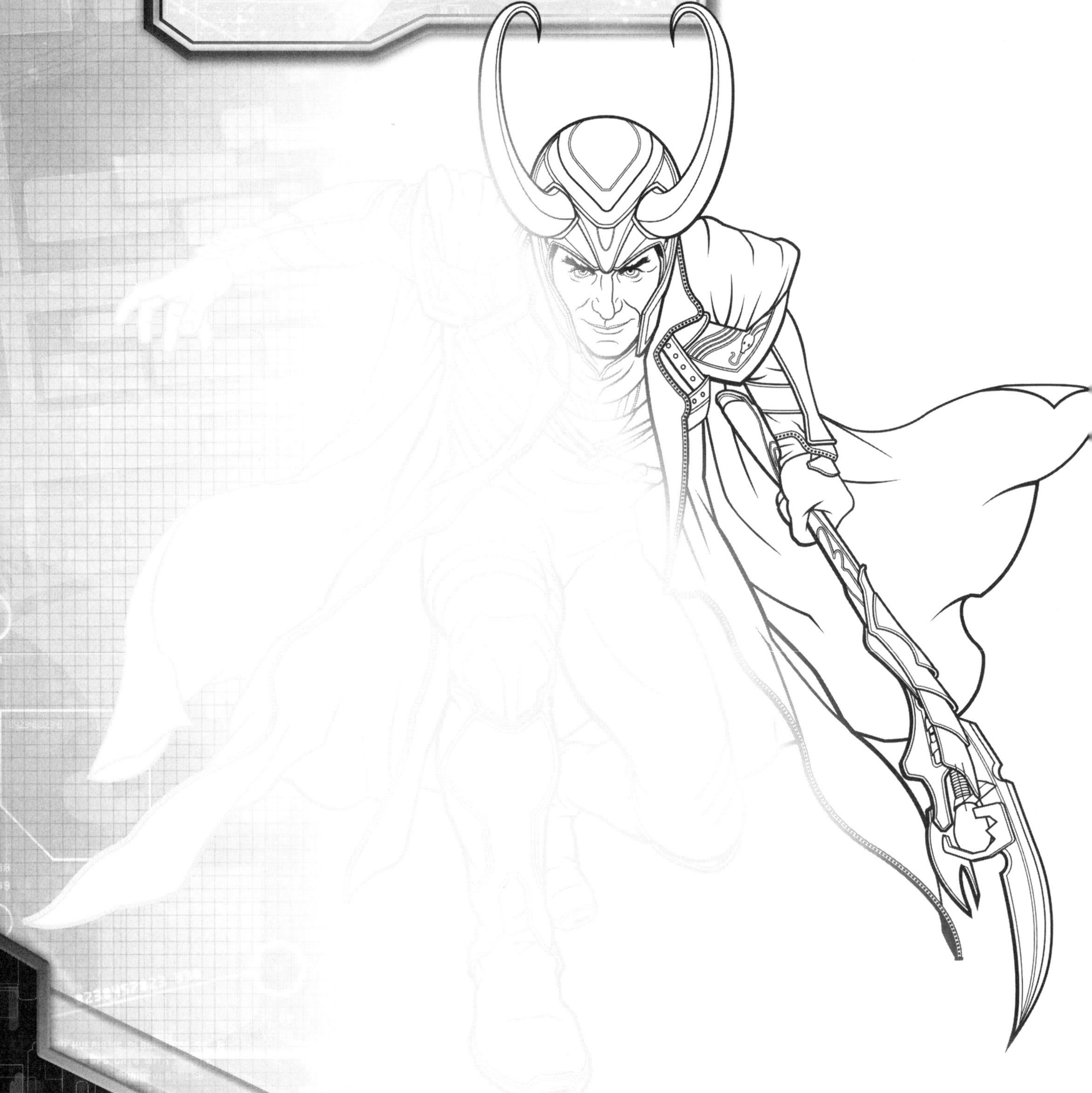

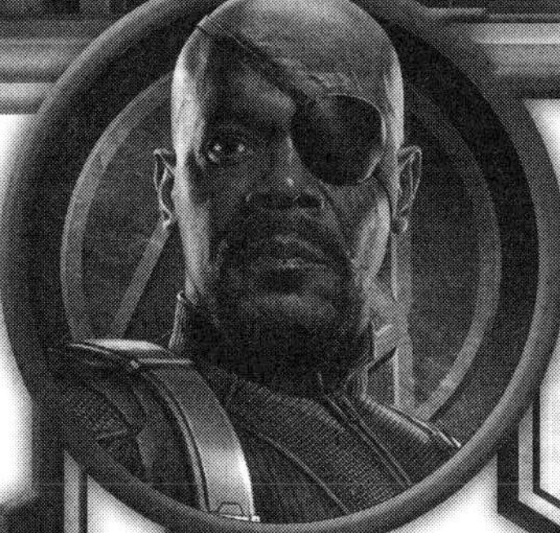

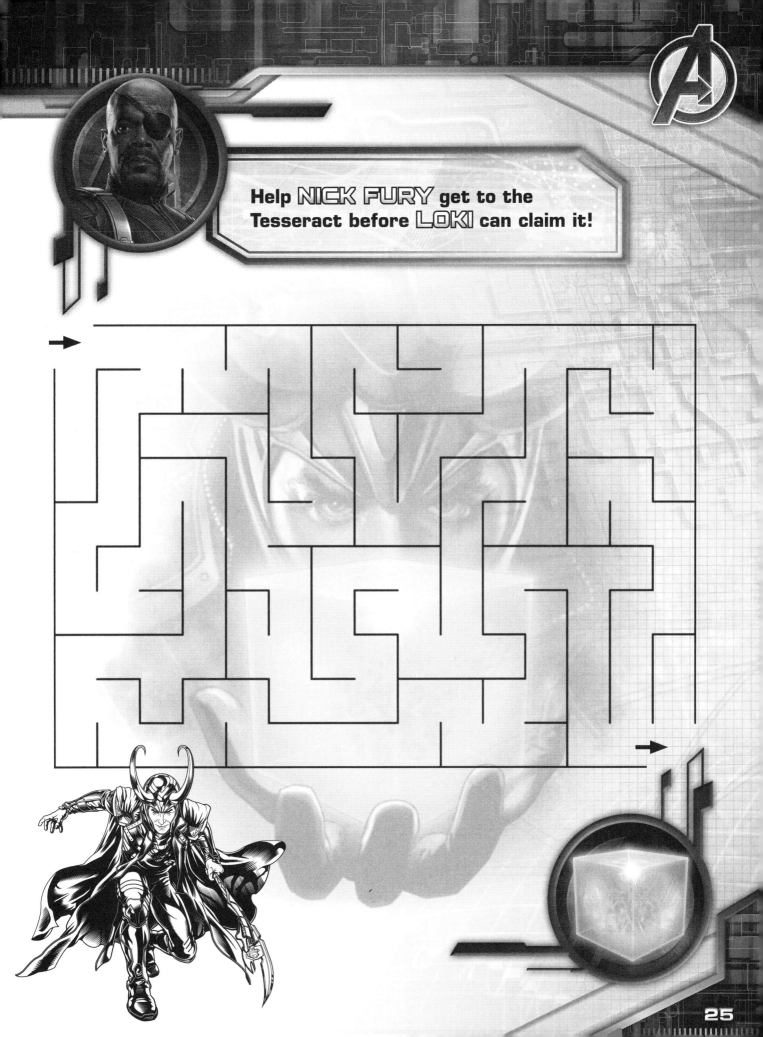

Help NICK FURY get to the Tesseract before LOKI can claim it!

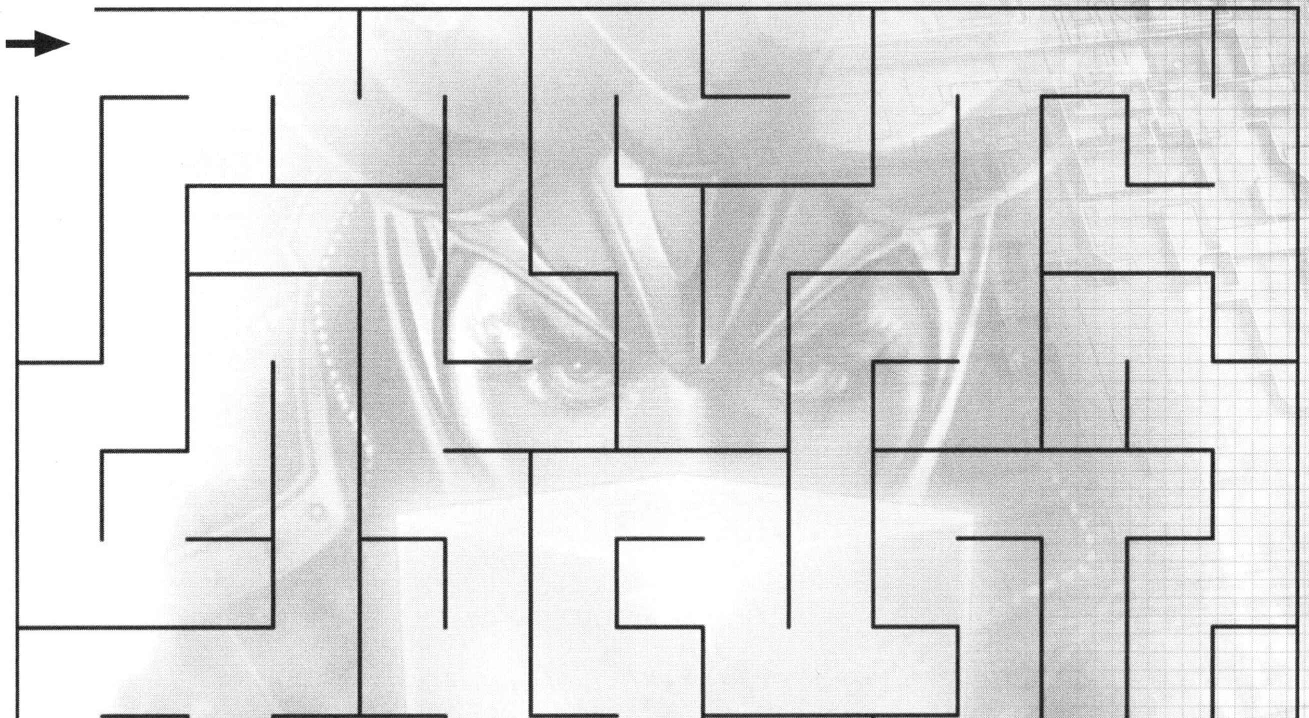

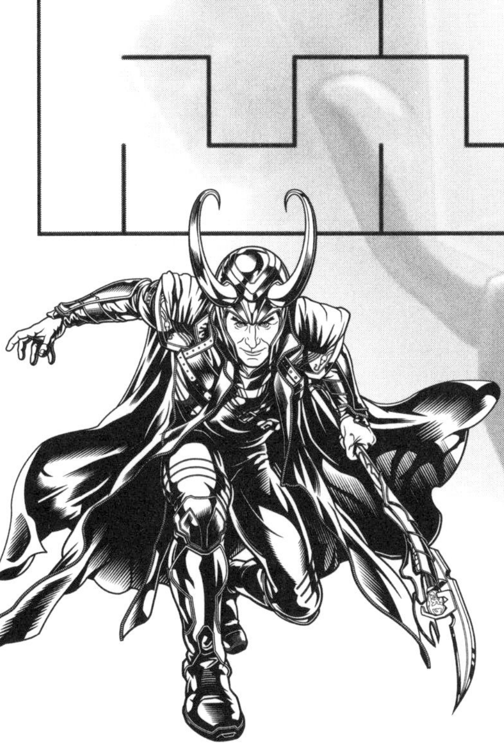

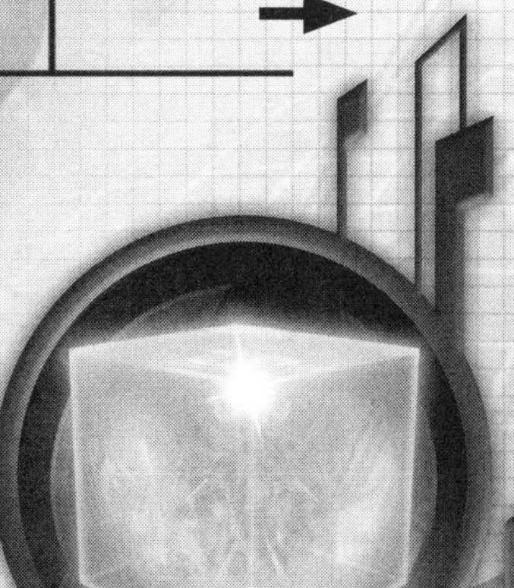

LOKI uses his staff for mind control, and HAWKEYE is his first victim. What does Loki's staff look like?

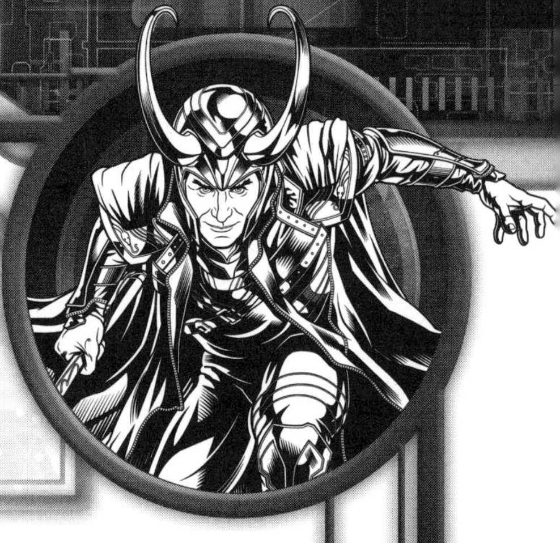

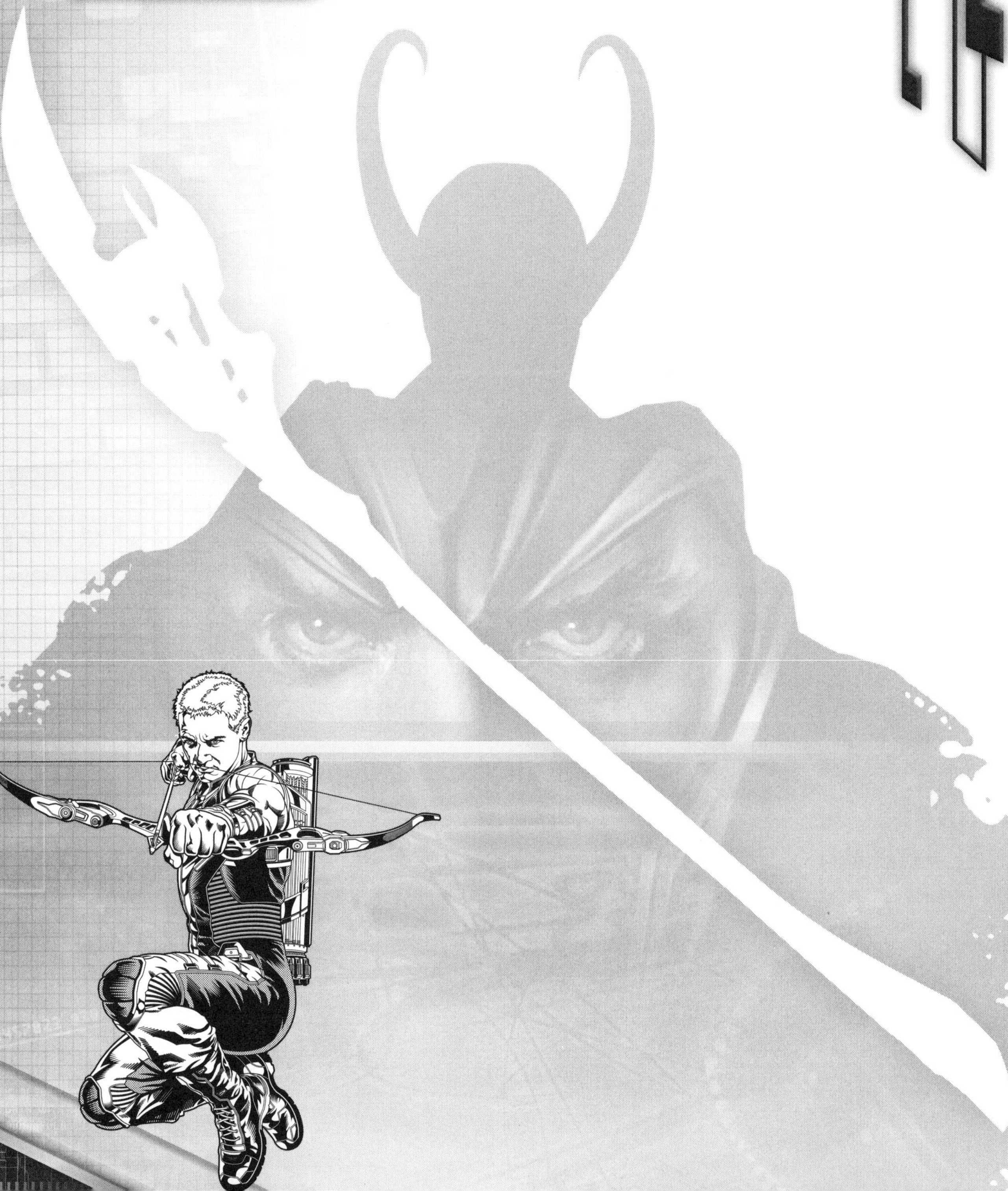

Now **NICK FURY** has to assemble the Avengers to stop Loki's evil plan and save the earth. Uh-oh! He lost his eye patch in the chase. Draw him a new one!

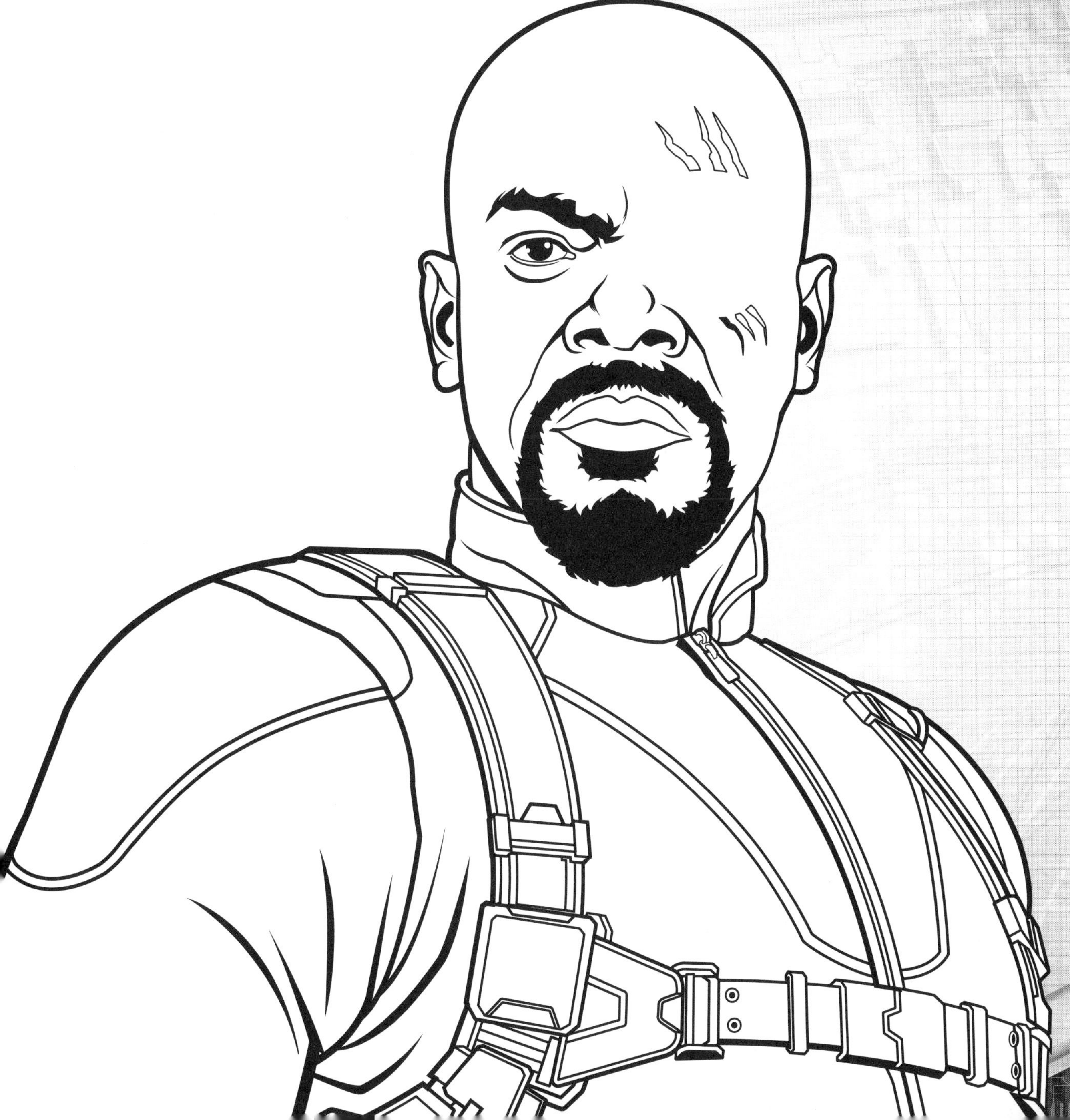

Connect the character to his or her Super Hero alter ego so **NICK FURY** knows who to look for:

NATASHA ROMANOFF	IRON MAN
DR. BRUCE BANNER	HAWKEYE
TONY STARK	CAPTAIN AMERICA
STEVE ROGERS	HULK
CLINT BARTON	BLACK WIDOW

Now match the logo with the Avenger:

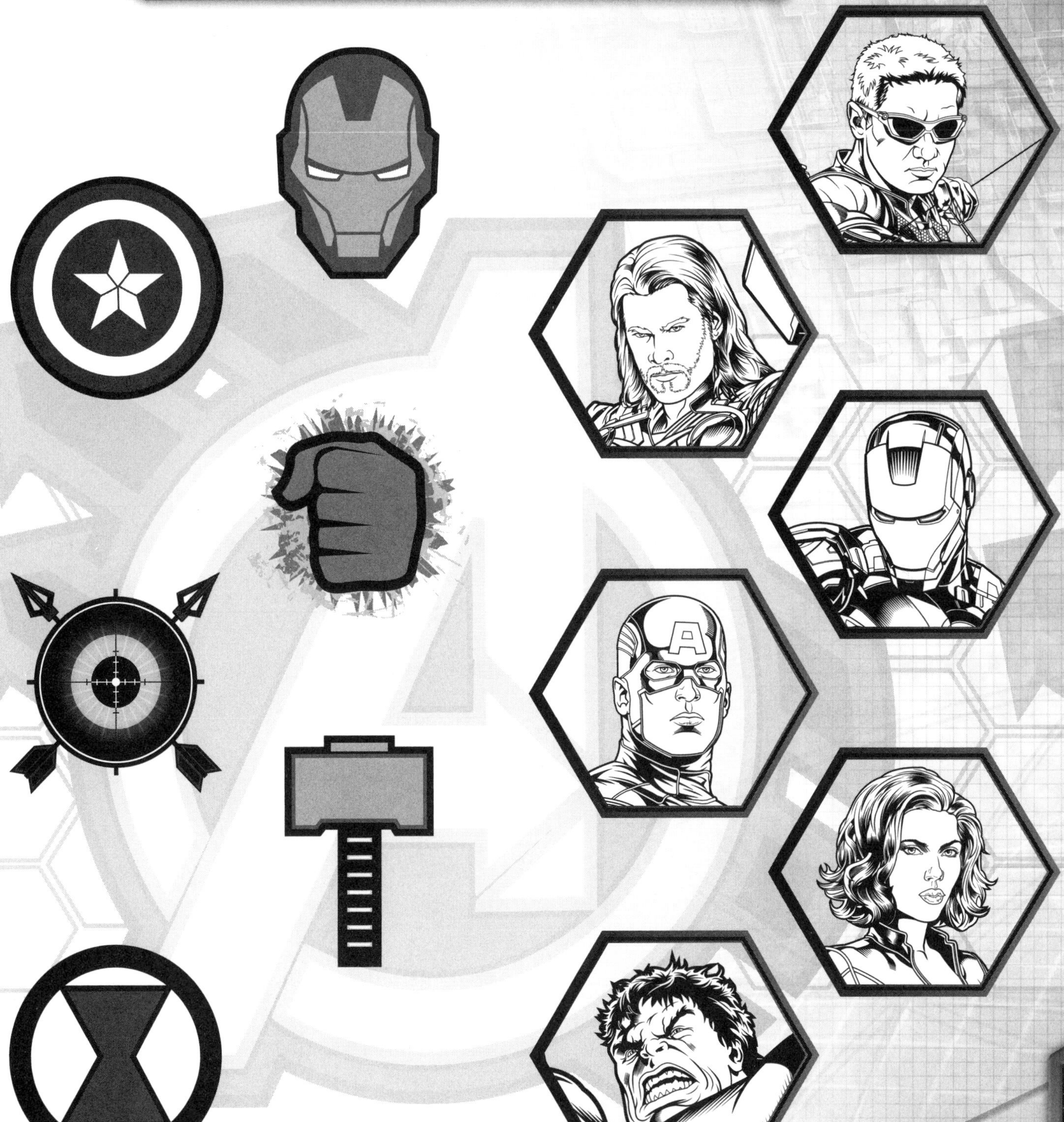

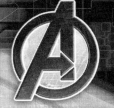

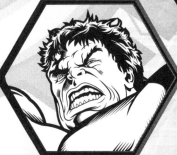

First, **BLACK WIDOW** has to escape from her captors. Who is she fighting?

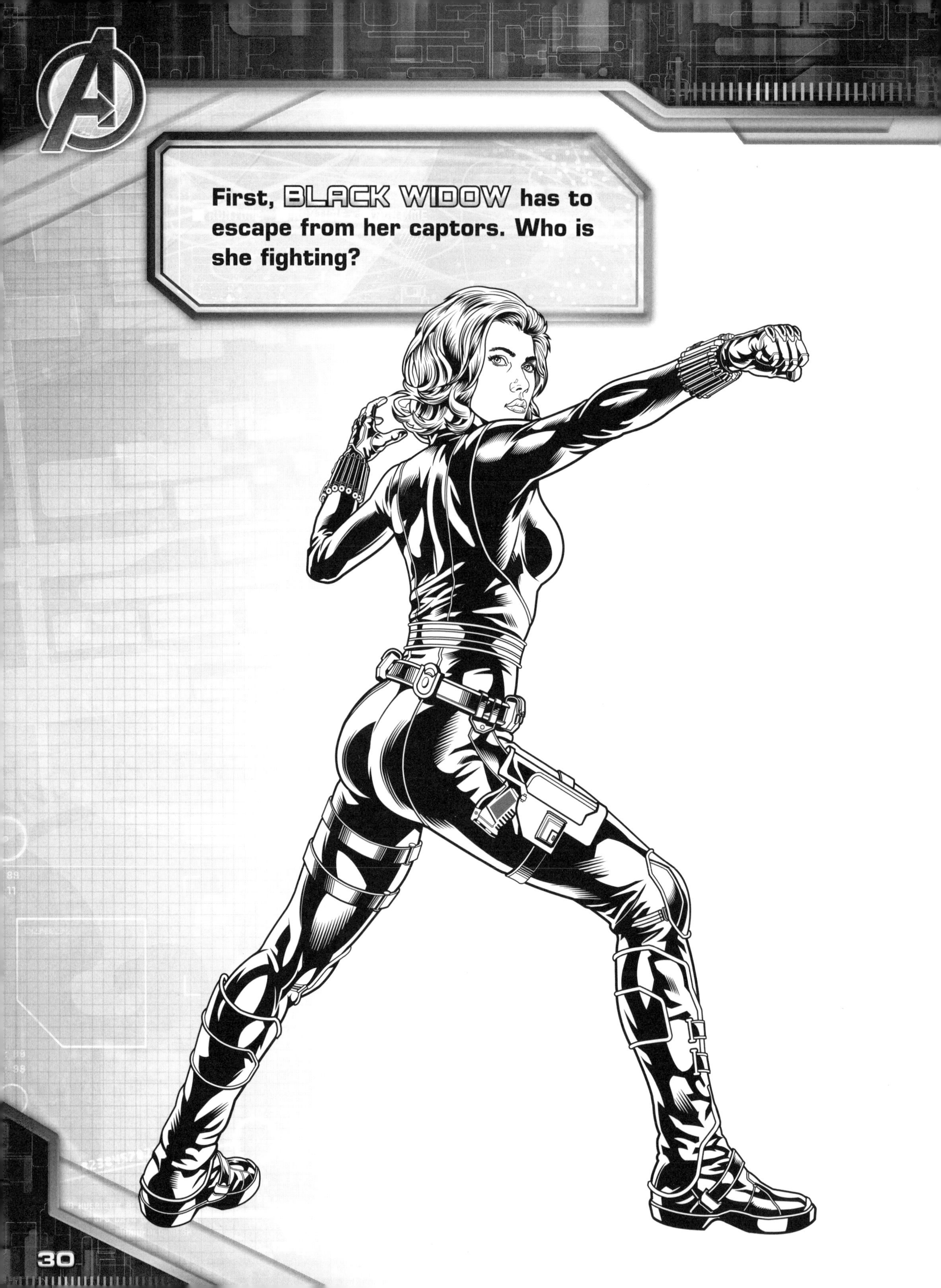

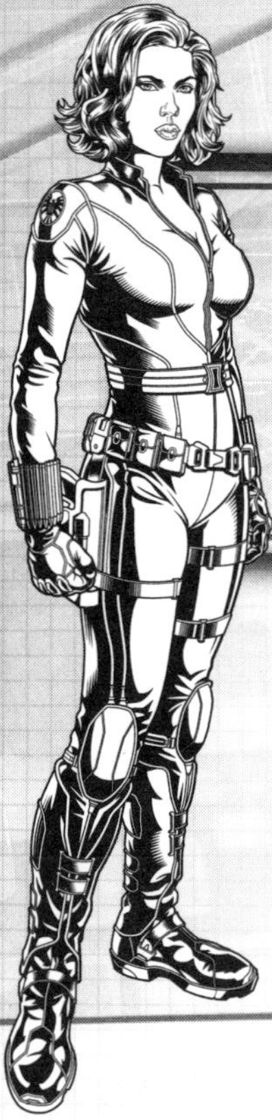

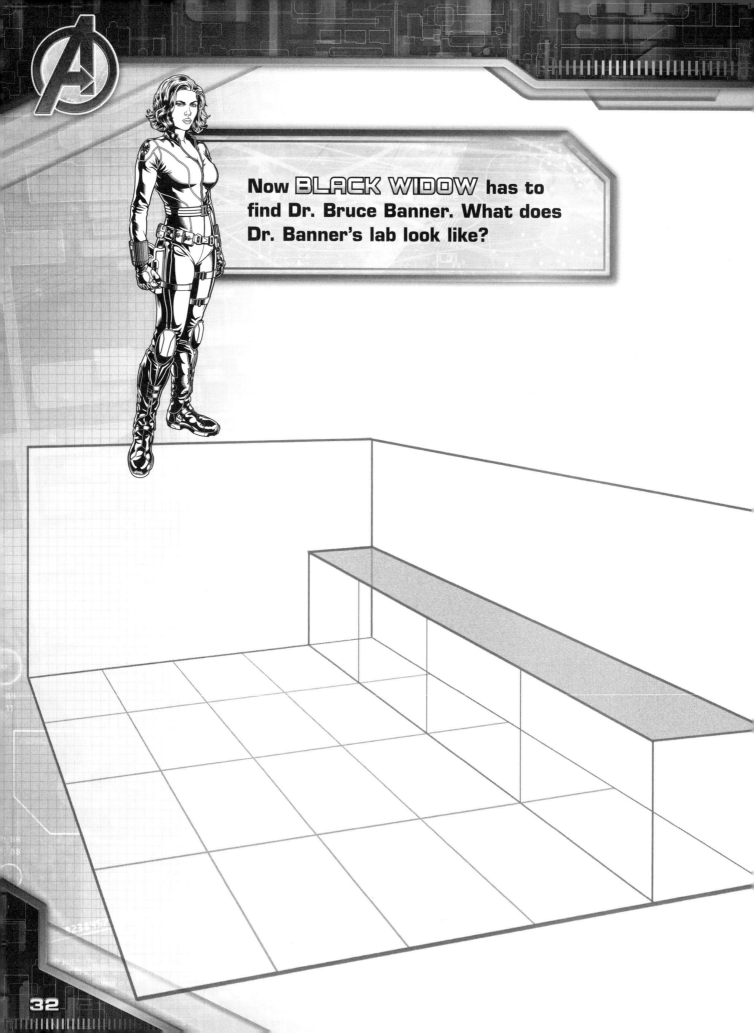

Now **BLACK WIDOW** has to find Dr. Bruce Banner. What does Dr. Banner's lab look like?

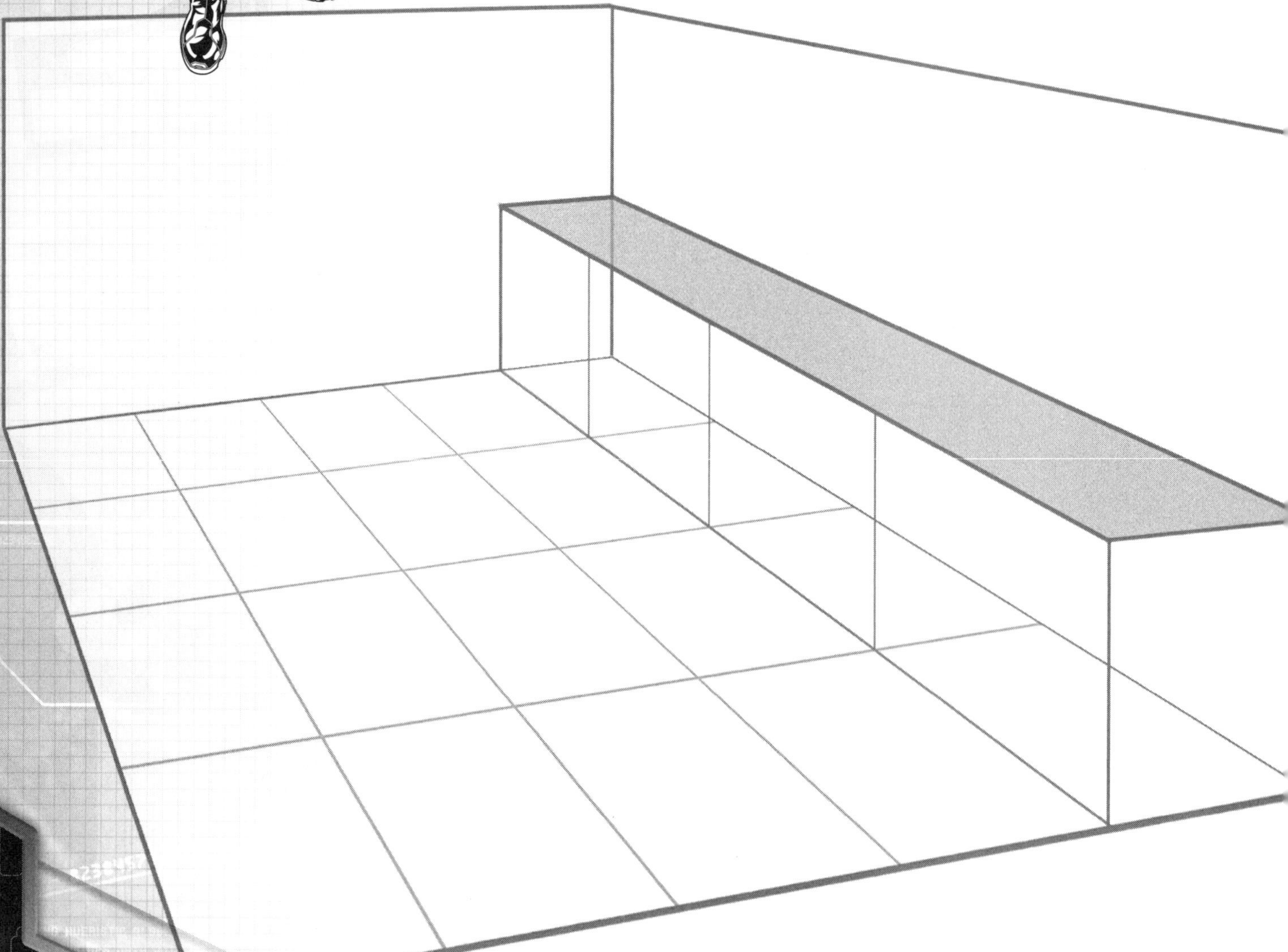

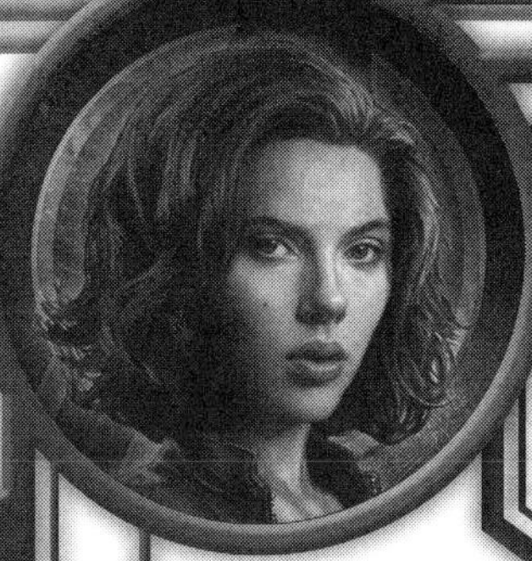

BLACK WIDOW needs to get back to the Quinjet with DR. BANNER. Help her find her way!

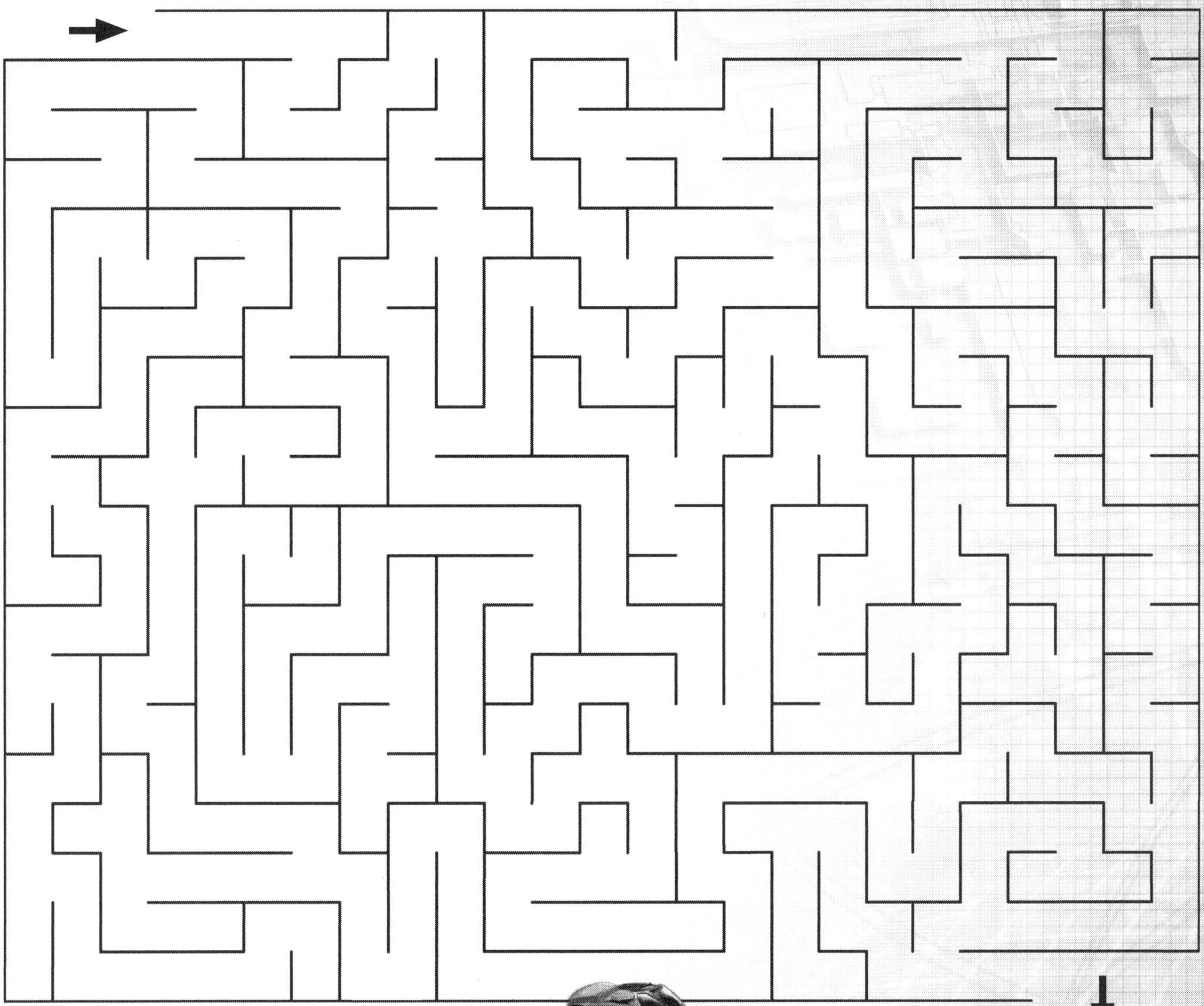

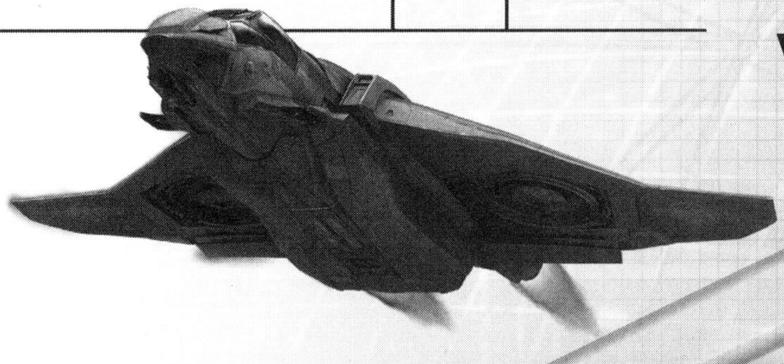

AGENT COULSON is convincing Tony Stark to join the fight. Unscramble the phrase below to decode his message!

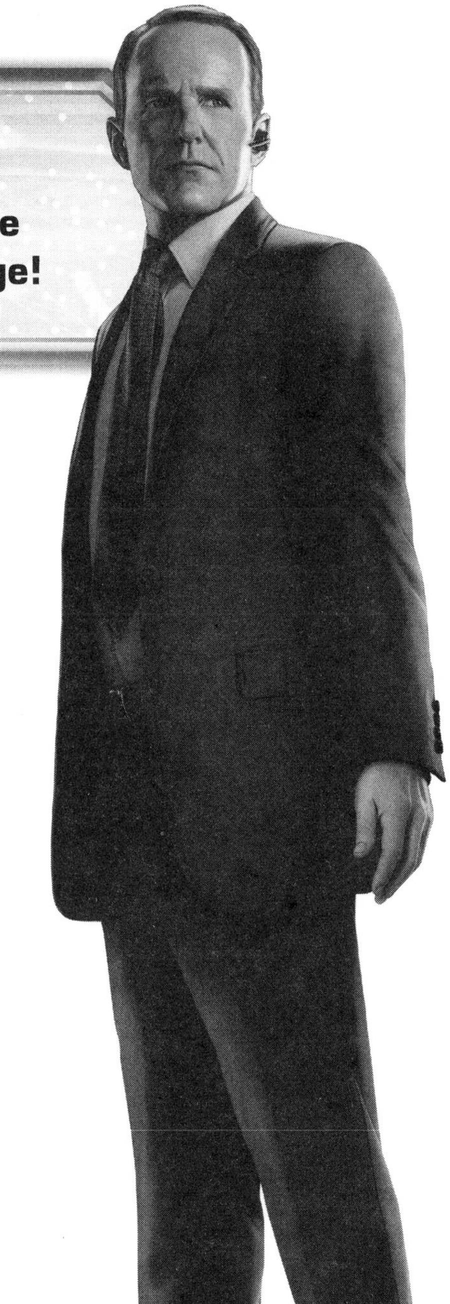

E W

E D E N

R Y U O

L P E H

Answer: WE NEED YOUR HELP

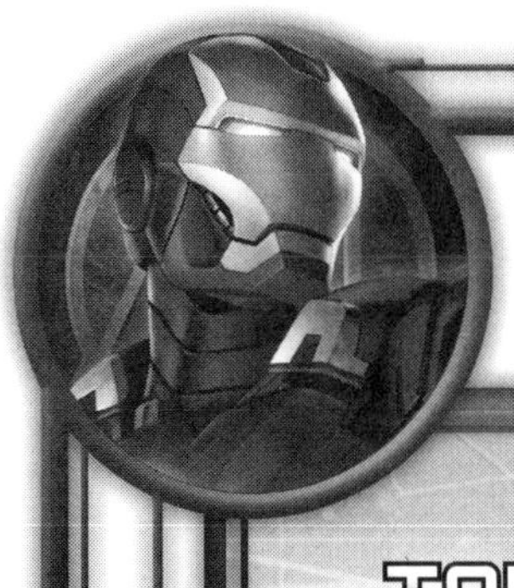

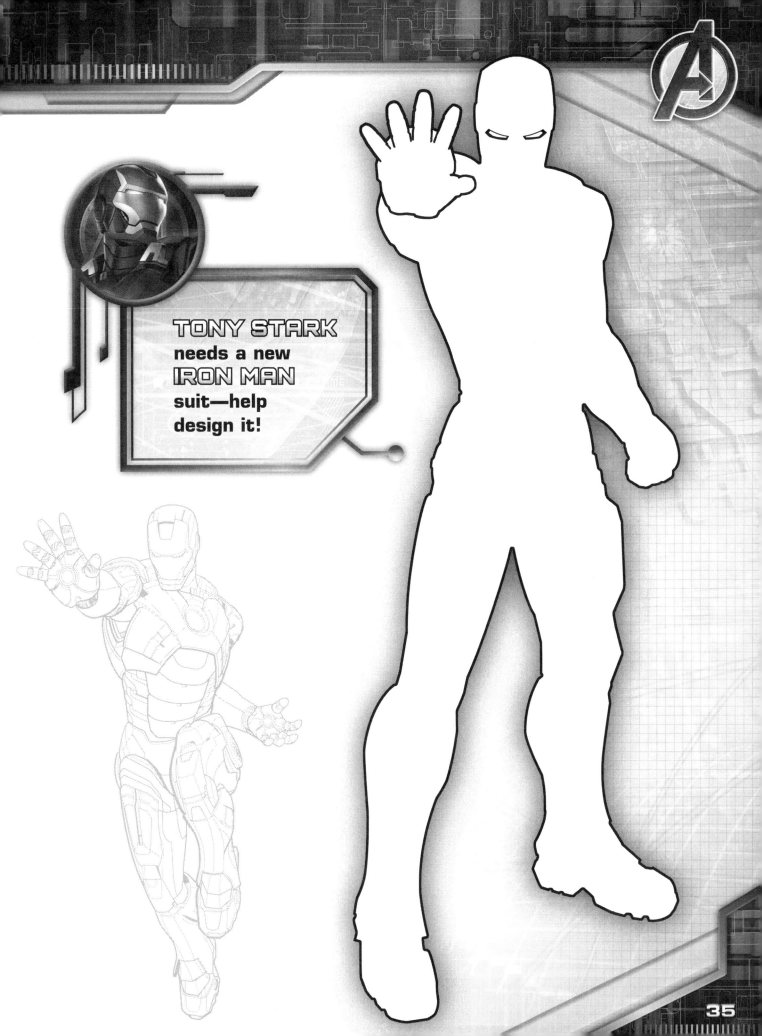

TONY STARK needs a new IRON MAN suit—help design it!

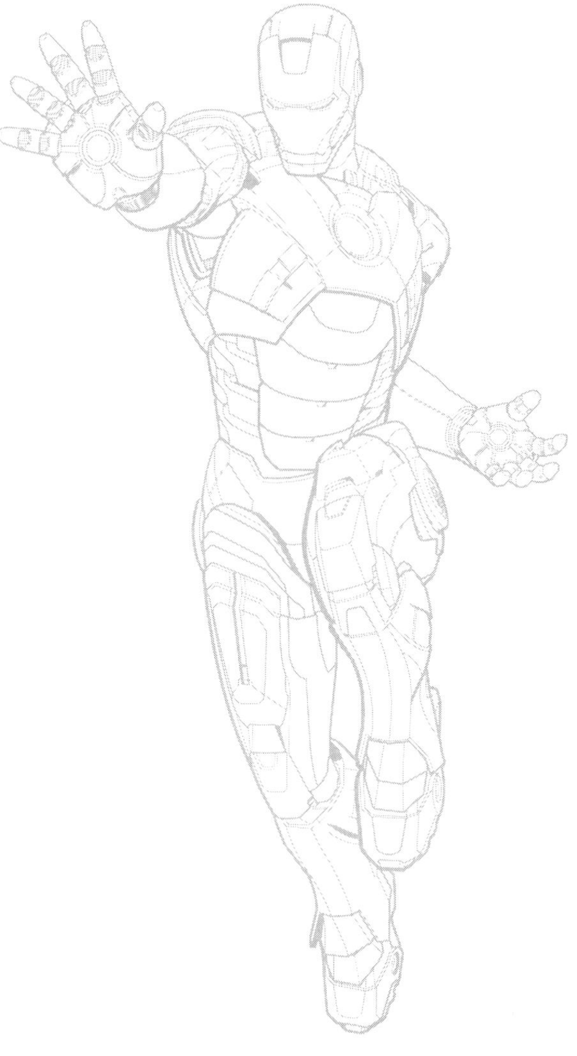

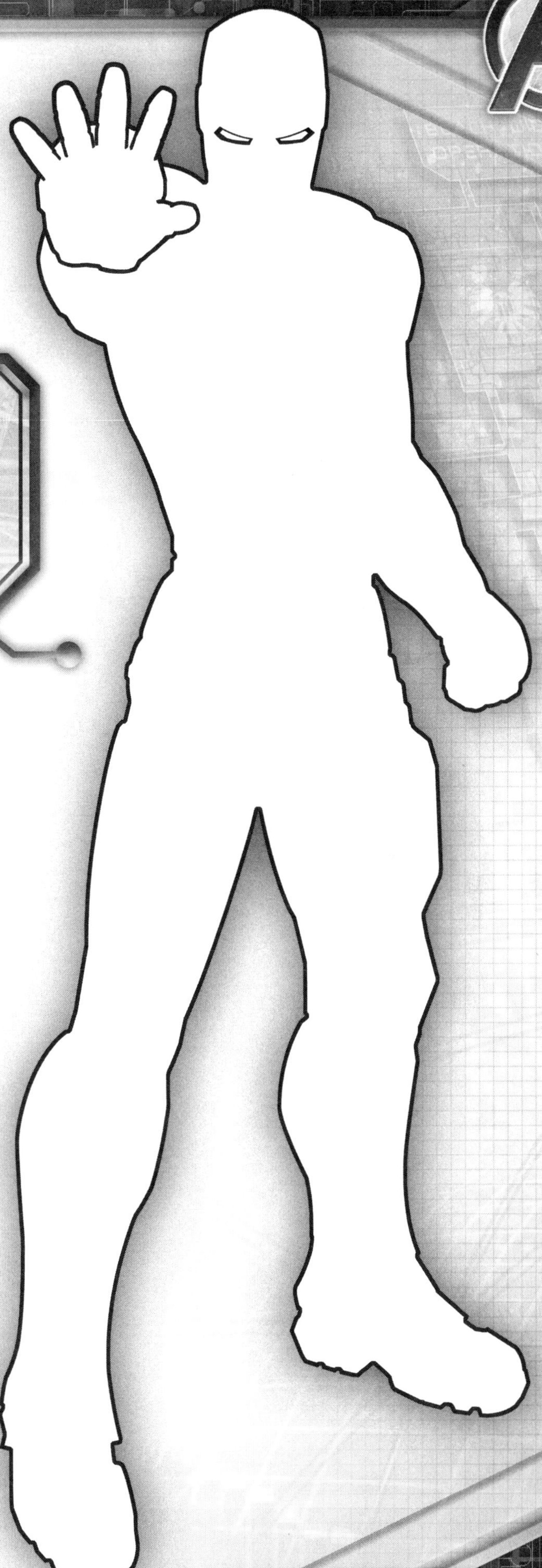

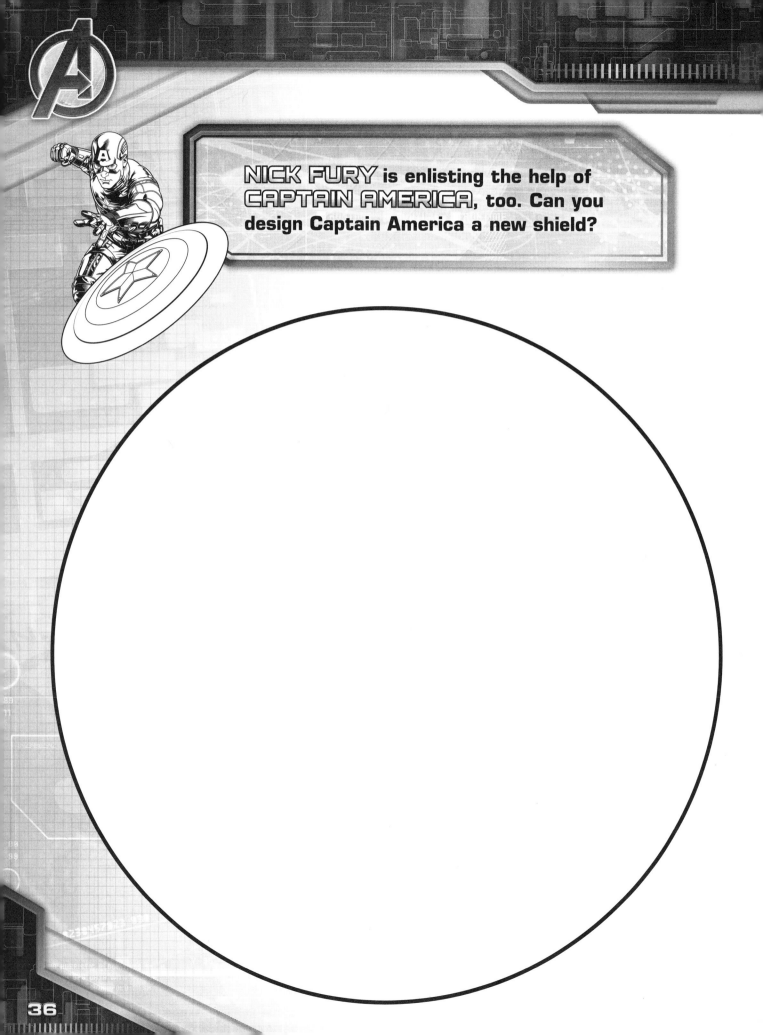

NICK FURY is enlisting the help of **CAPTAIN AMERICA**, too. Can you design Captain America a new shield?

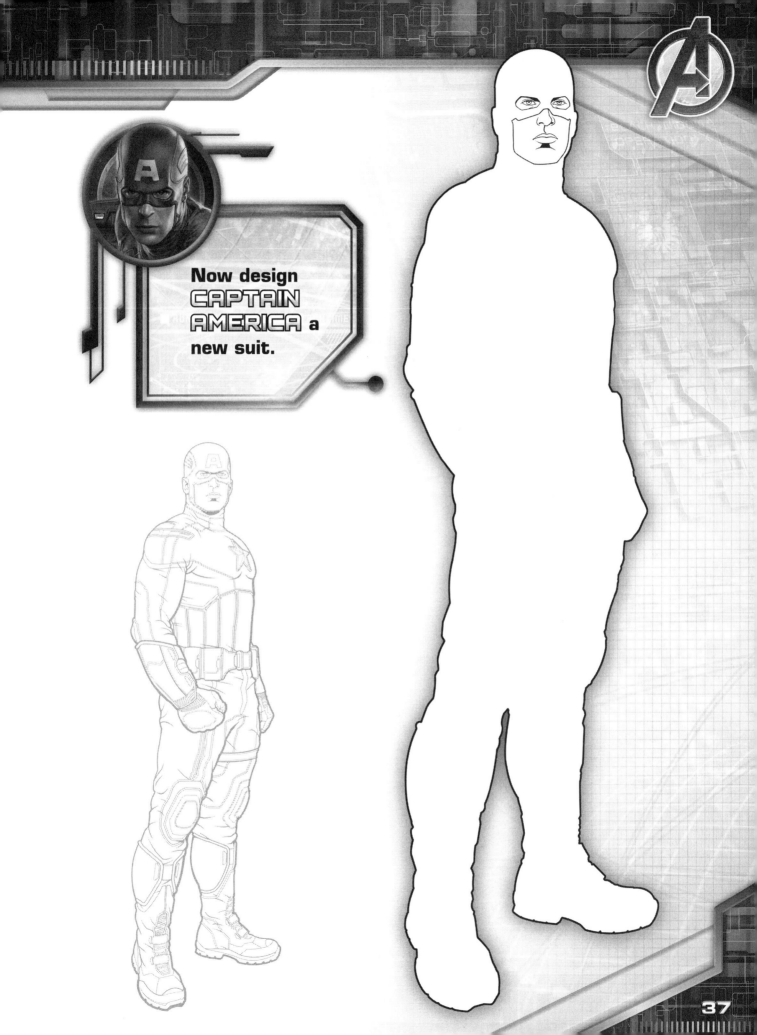

Now design CAPTAIN AMERICA a new suit.

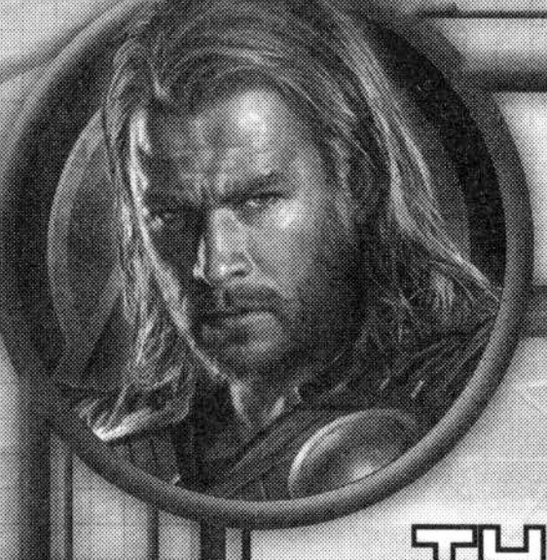

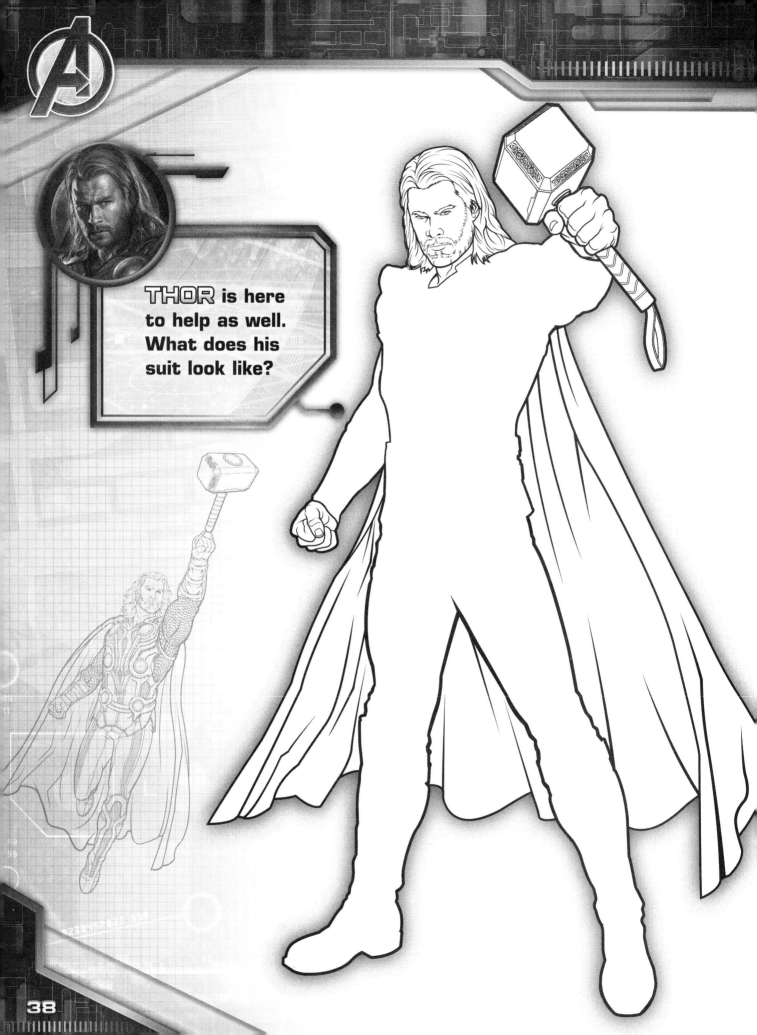

THOR is here to help as well. What does his suit look like?

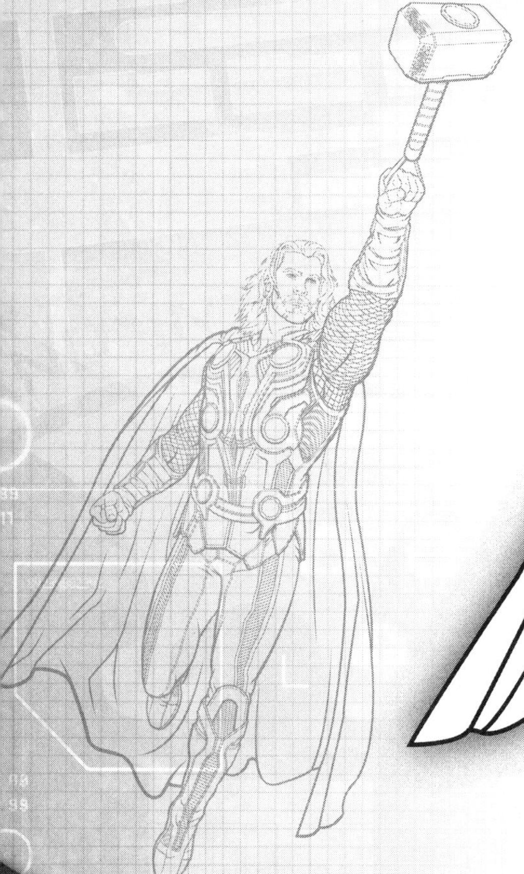

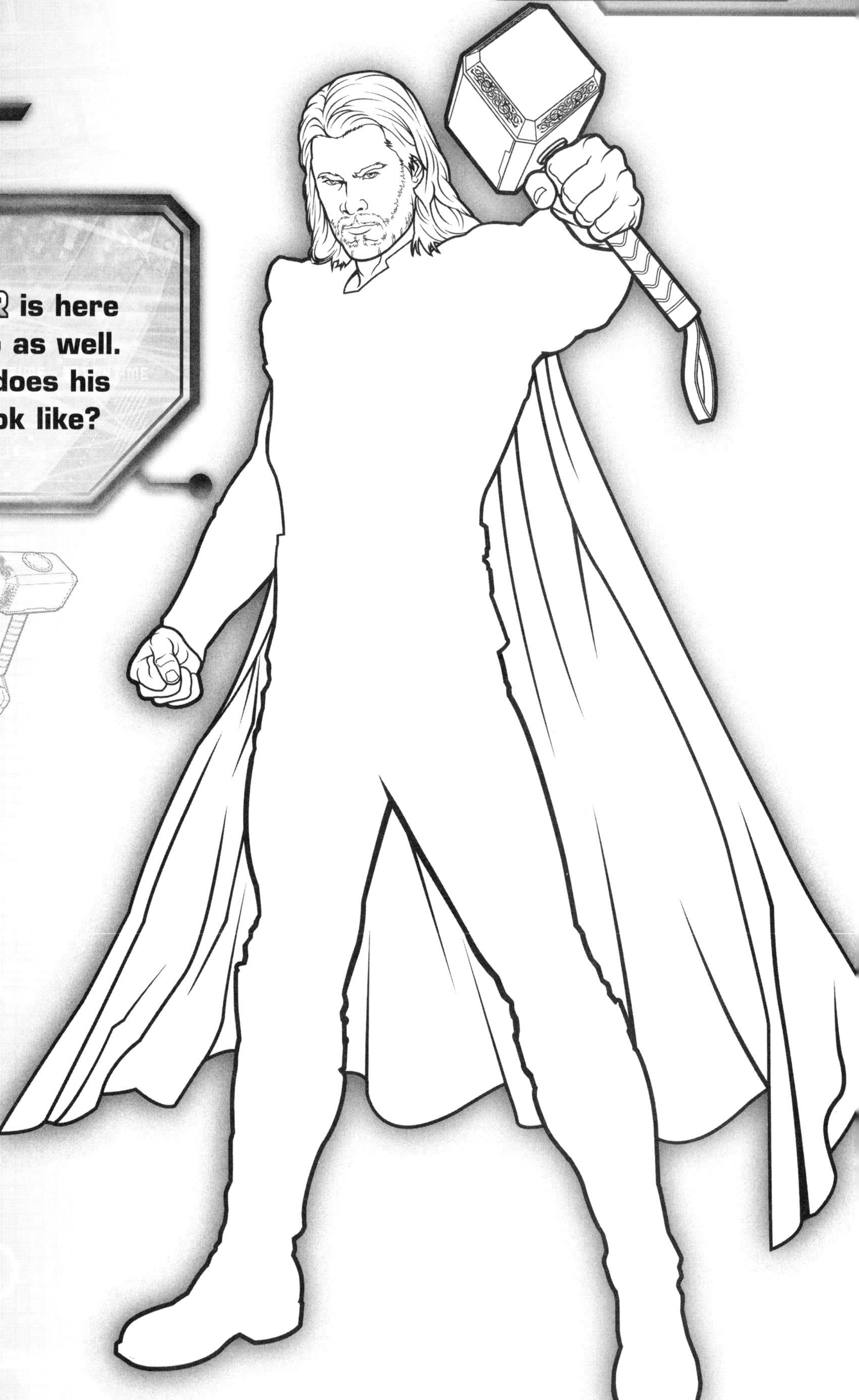

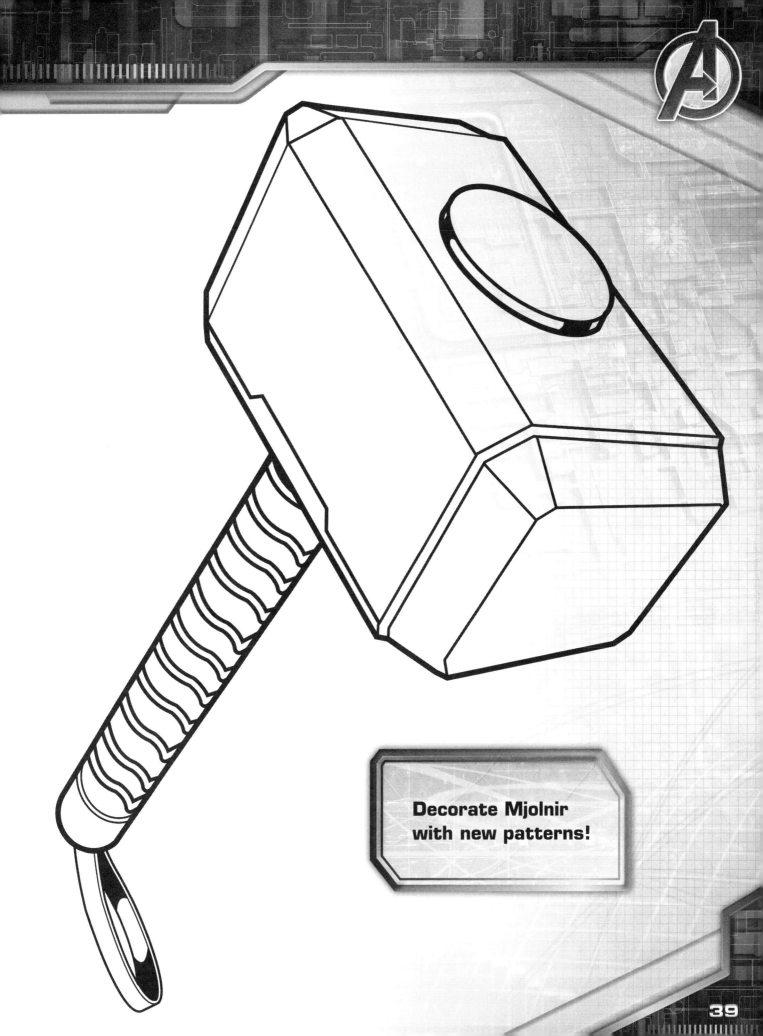

**Decorate Mjolnir
with new patterns!**

THE AVENGERS are taking the Quinjet to track down Loki and the Tesseract. Finish drawing the Quinjet!

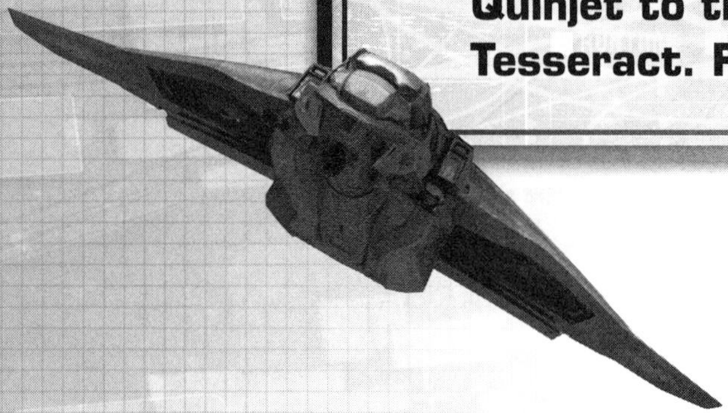

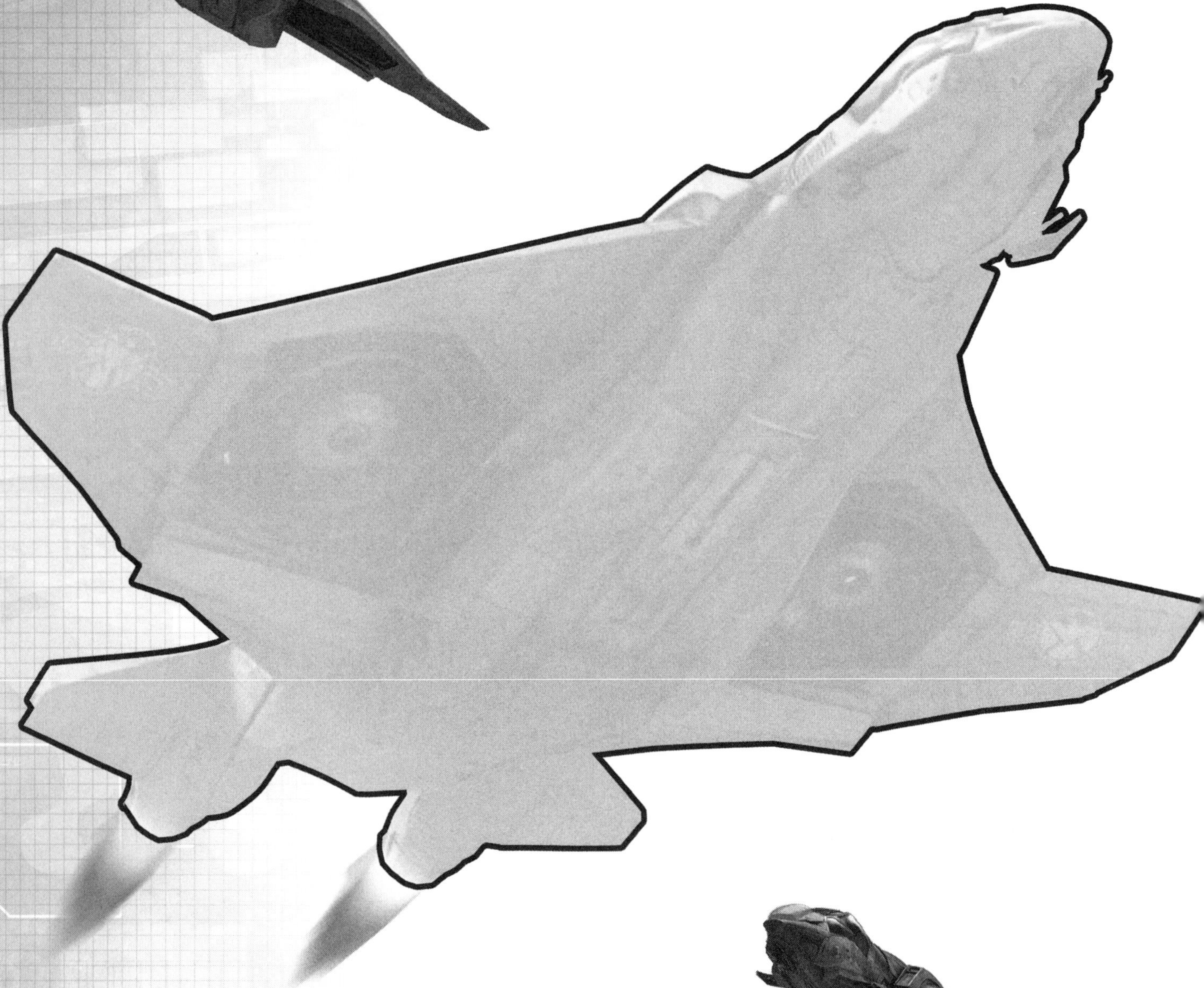

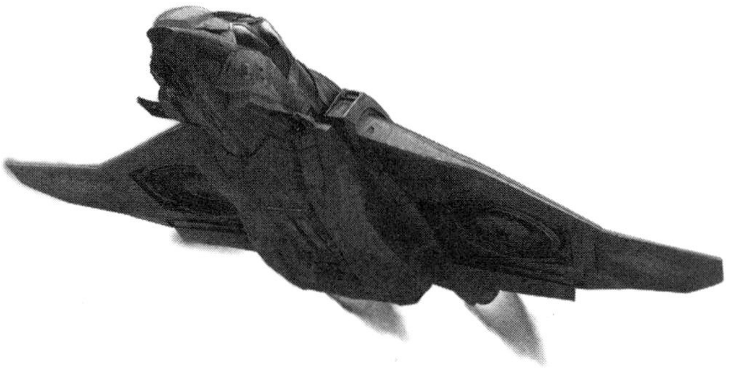

Unscramble the phrases below and match them to their Super Hero!

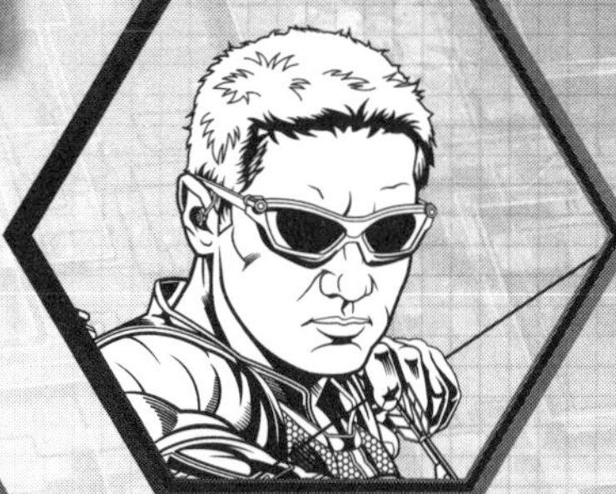

RMARO PU

_____ __

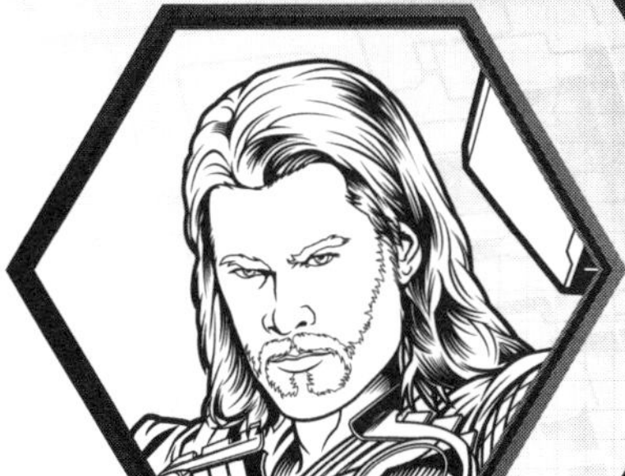

PSERU LDOSREI

_____ _______

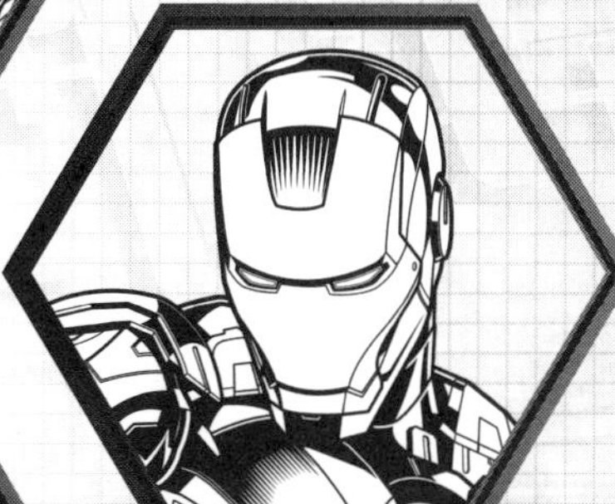

RFO SGDRAA

___ ______

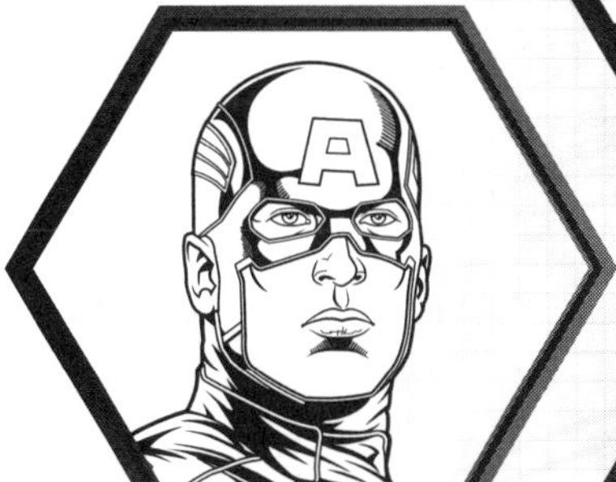

KHLU MHSSA

____ _____

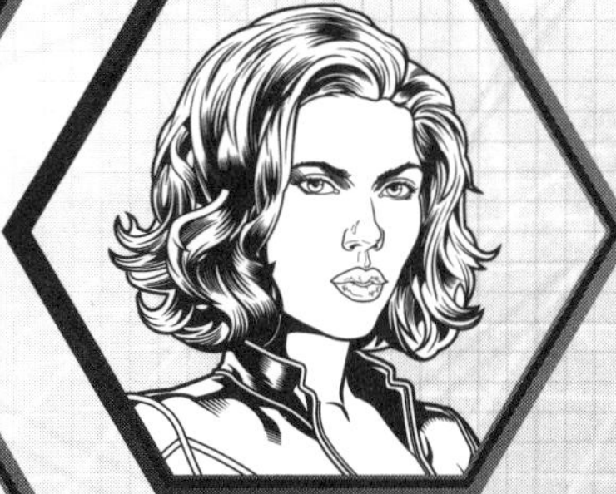

SLUEEBYL

____

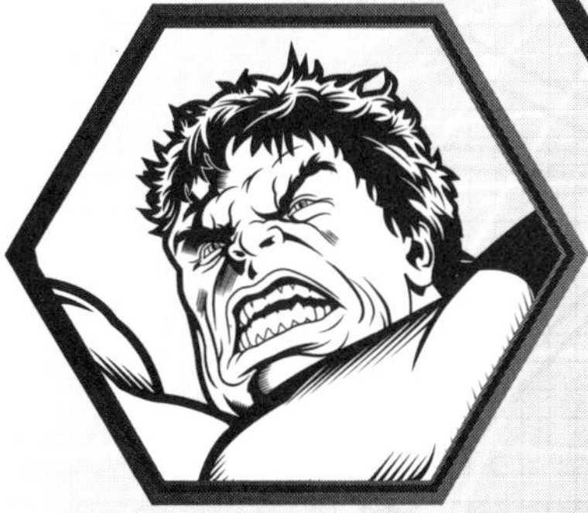

WDSWIO TSNIG

______ _____

Answers: Armor Up: Iron Man / Super-Soldier: Captain America / For Asgard: Thor / Hulk Smash: Hulk / Bull's-eye: Hawkeye / Widow's Sting: Black Widow

Can you find the following words?

AVENGER   **HULK**   **SHIELD**

BLACK WIDOW   **LOKI**   **TESSERACT**

CAPTAIN   **NICK FURY**   **THOR**

```
M D B T Q T T R T L Y P
B R Q L C J C B Q R T T
L R X M A A M Q U A V K
R L K T P C R F V Q R D
X Z Y T V G K E L M L J
B R A N M C N W S E L N
V I K Y I G M D I S M L
N T L N E H T H L D E Z
L Q M R U H S W J O O T
Y D Y L O Y B D D P K W
Q J K R L W B K L Y V I
```

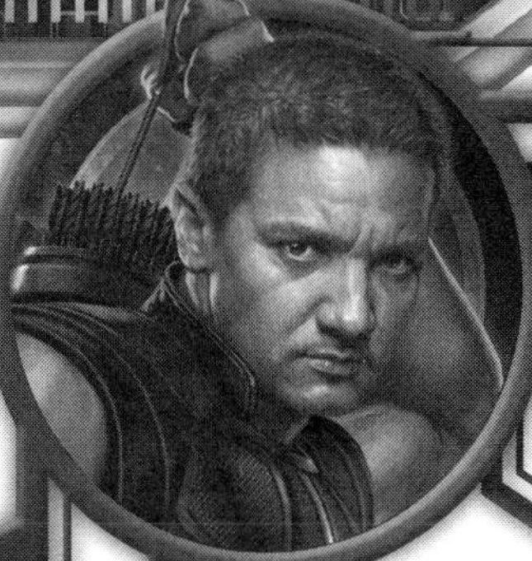

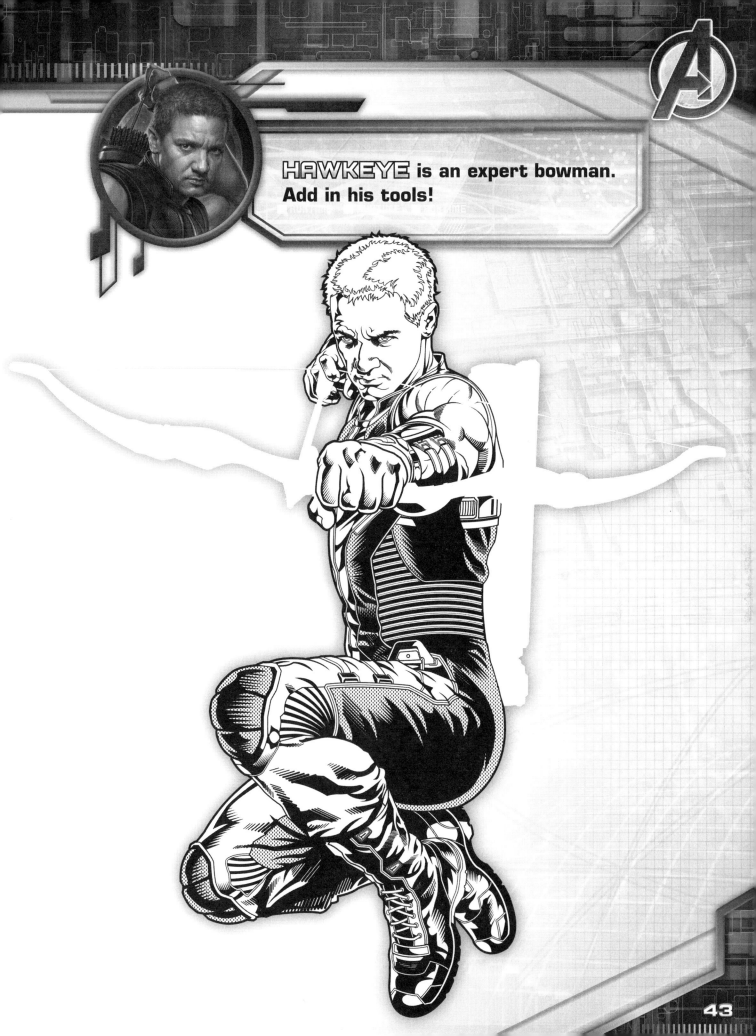

HAWKEYE is an expert bowman.
Add in his tools!

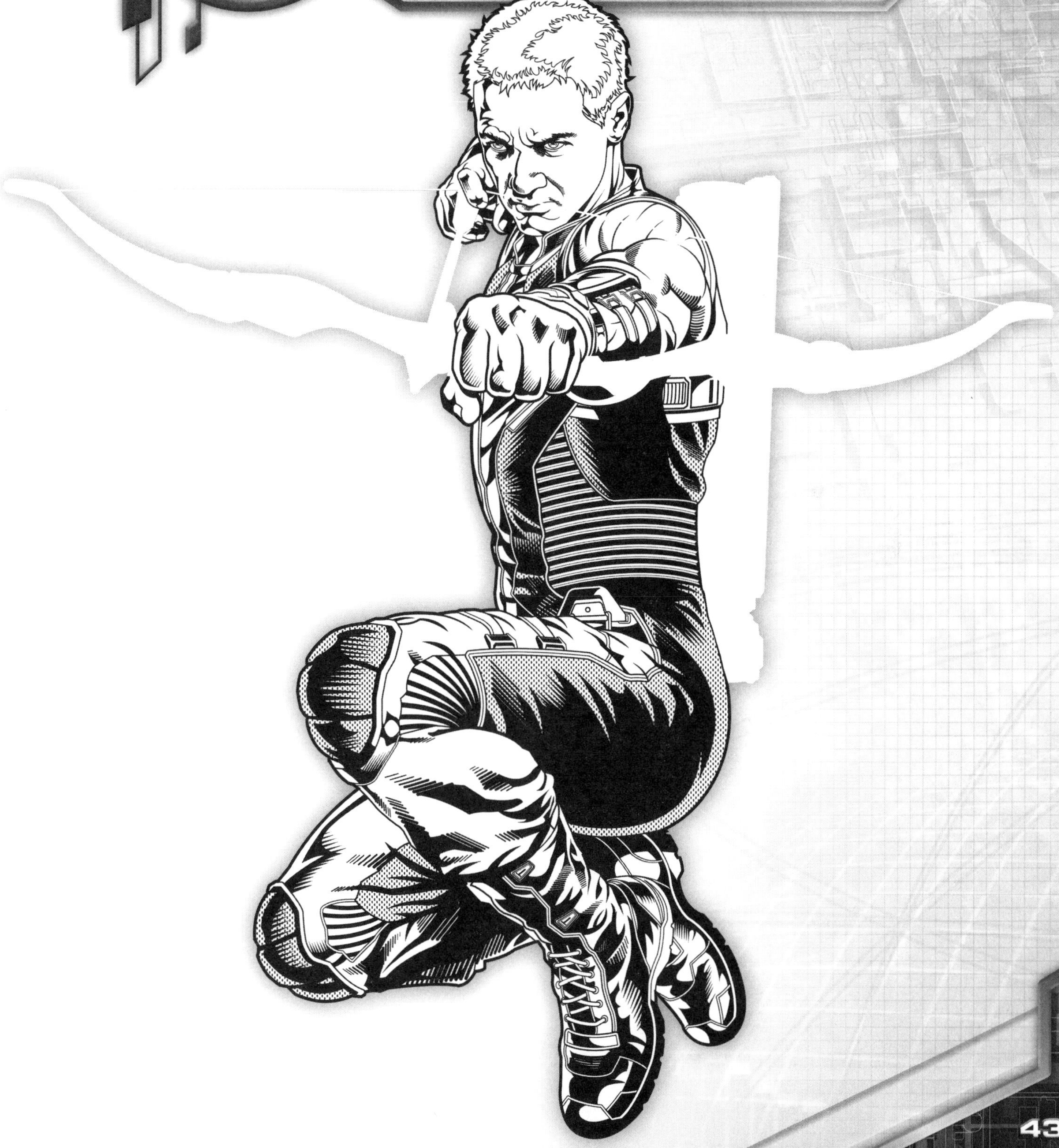

No one beats **CAPTAIN AMERICA** at hand-to-hand combat. Draw his opponent.

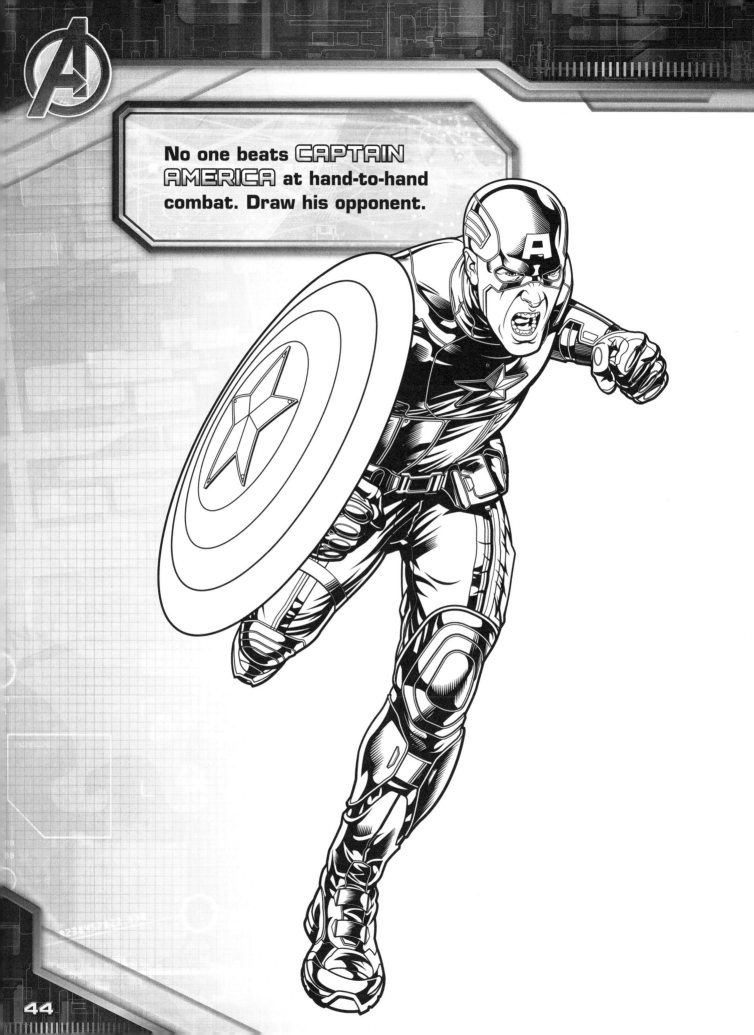

NICK FURY'S message is scrambled—better figure out what he's trying to tell you before he gets angry.

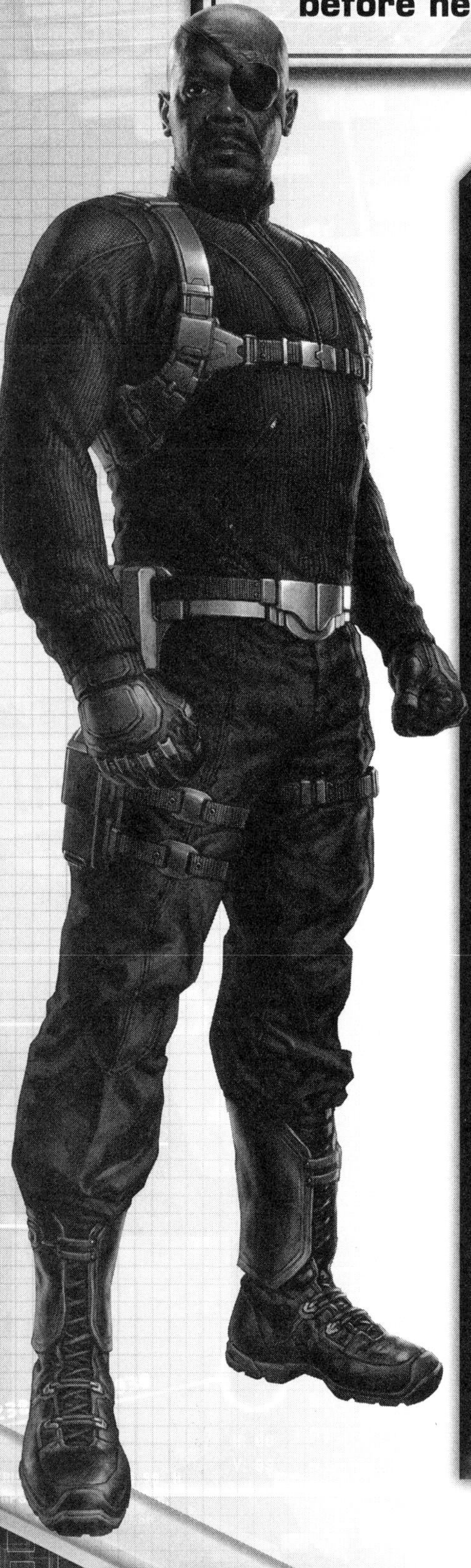

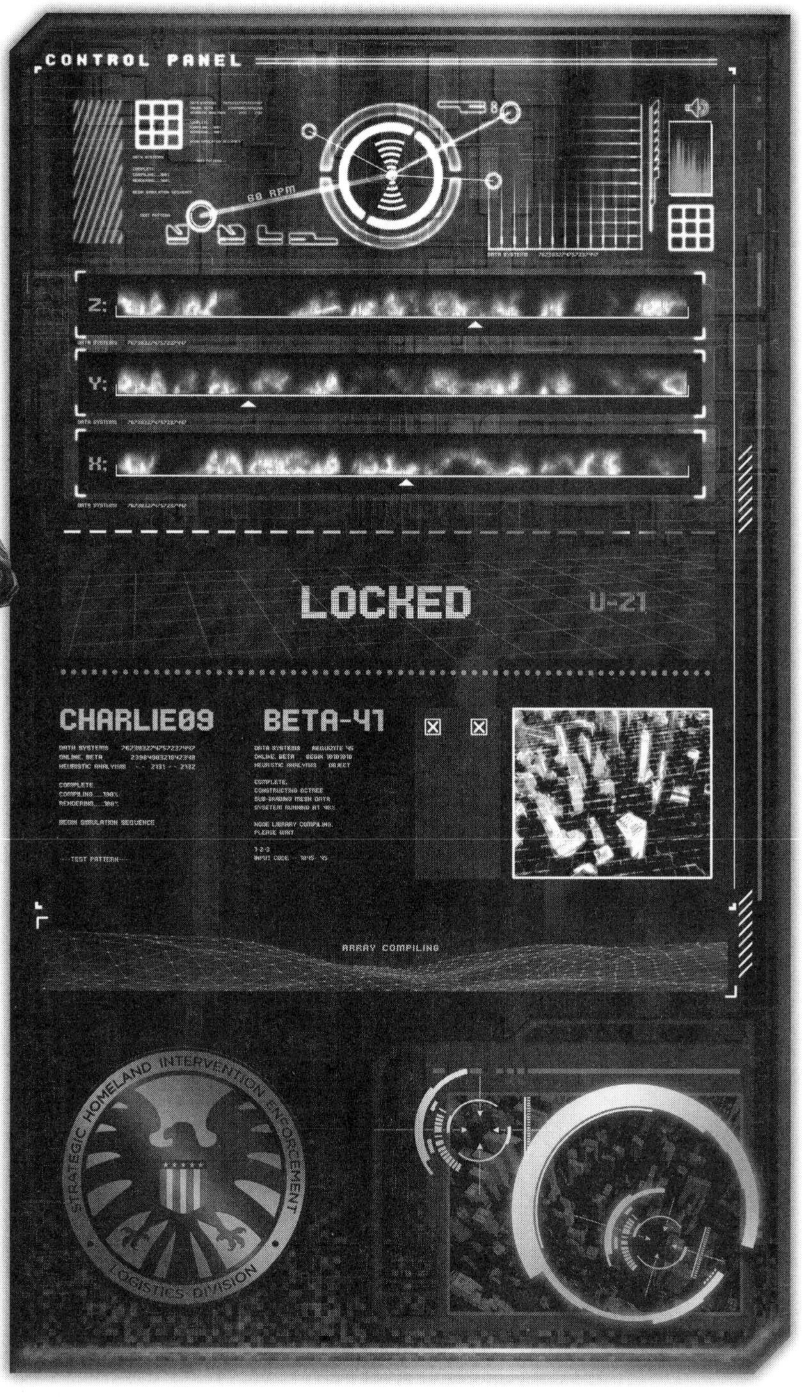
CONTROL PANEL
Z:
Y:
X:
LOCKED
U-21
CHARLIE09
BETA-41
ARRAY COMPILING
STRATEGIC HOMELAND INTERVENTION ENFORCEMENT
LOGISTICS DIVISION

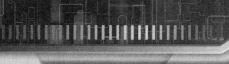

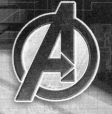

HET DAIE SWA OT RNGIB

___ ____ ___ __ _____

GHRTOEET A PRGOU FO

________ _ _____ __

KMABERAELR LPOPEE,

__________ ______,

NDA ESE FI YTEH LDCUO

___ ___ __ ____ _____

CMBOEE MHTGOESIN RMEO.

______ _________ ____.

Answers: The idea was to bring together a group of remarkable people, and see if they could become something more.

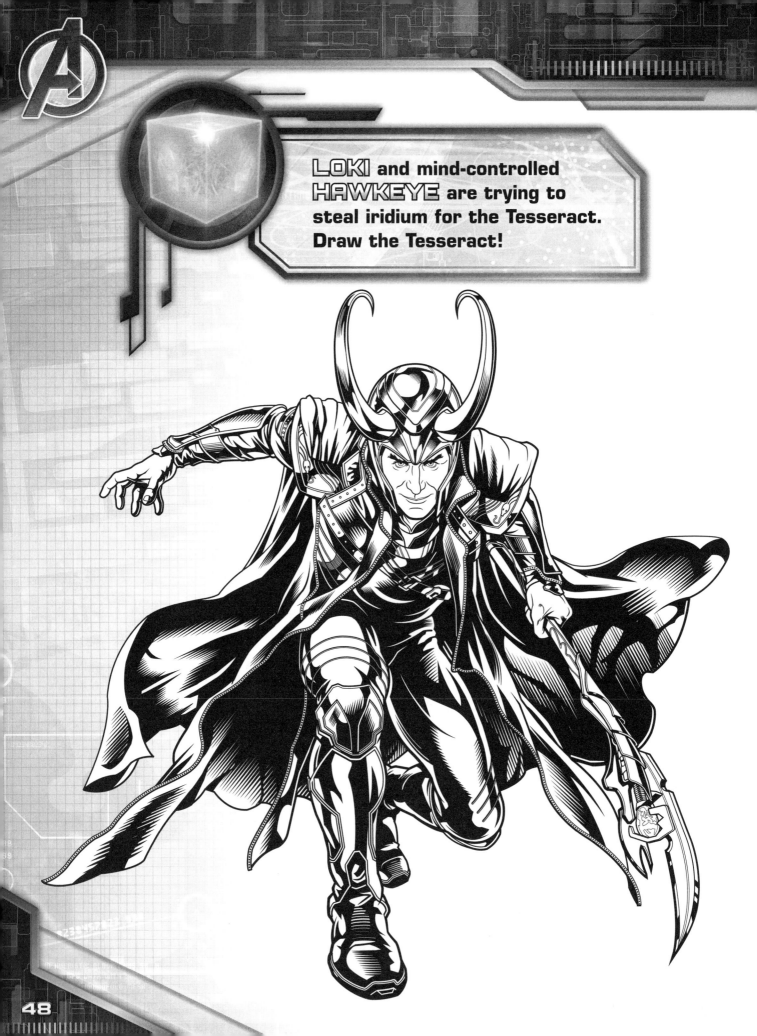

LOKI and mind-controlled HAWKEYE are trying to steal iridium for the Tesseract. Draw the Tesseract!

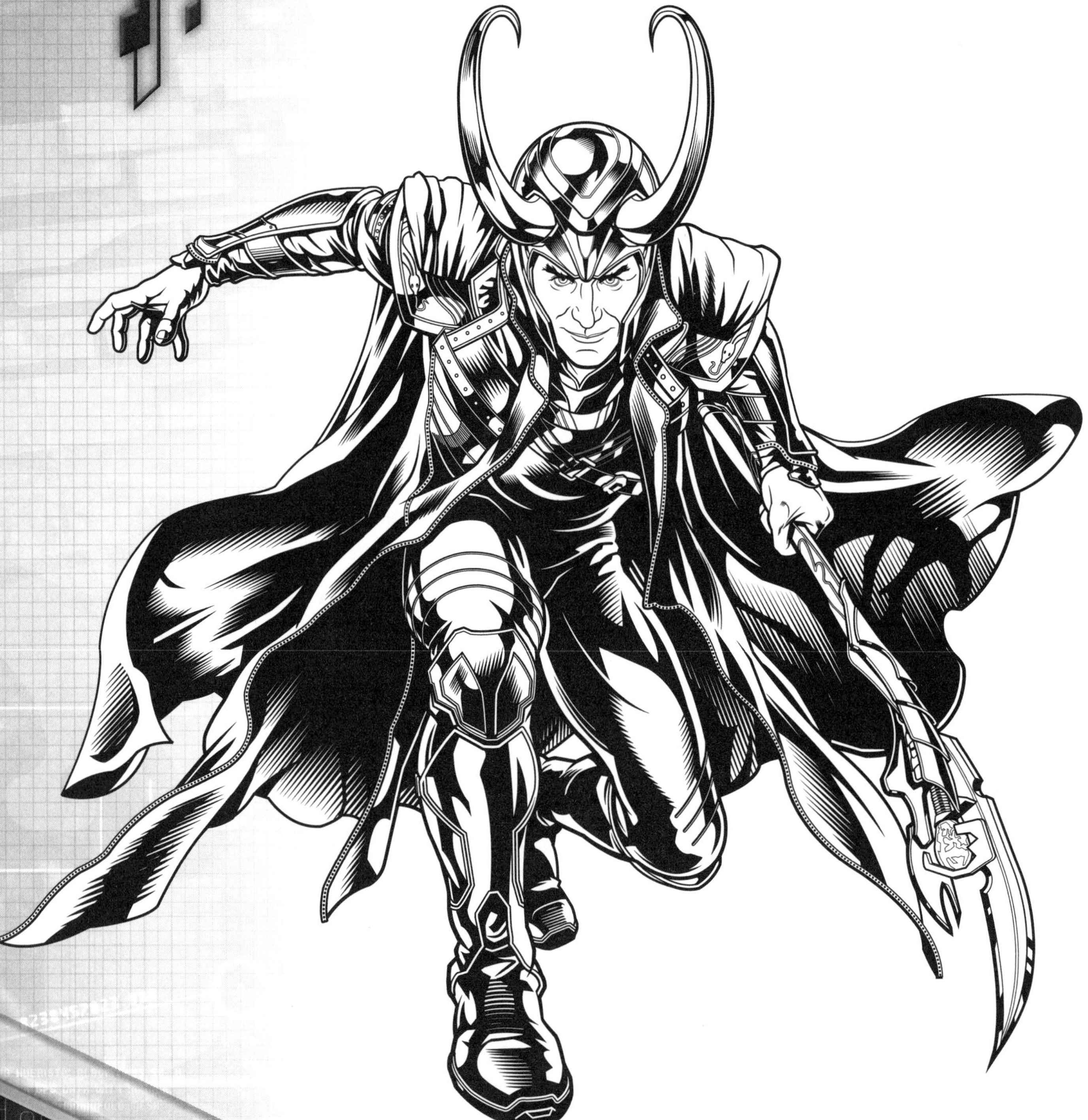

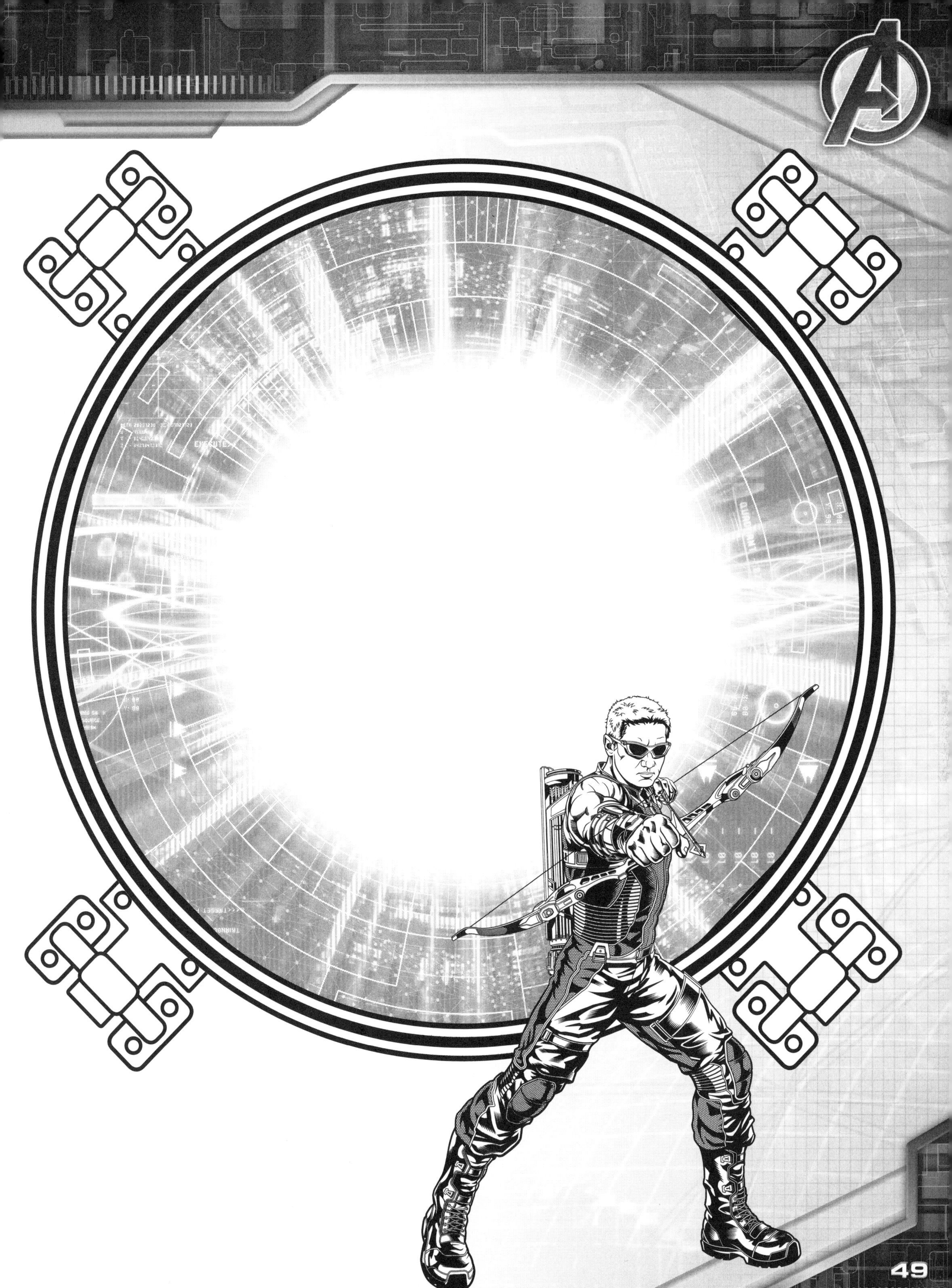

AGENT COULSON has a trading card of **CAPTAIN AMERICA**—draw it!

STEVE ROGERS/ CAPTAIN AMERICA

VITAL STATISTICS

What would your trading card look like if you were an Avenger?

VITAL STATISTICS

....

....

....

....

....

....

....

....

Now make trading cards for the rest of the Avengers.

NATASHA ROMANOFF/
BLACK WIDOW

CLINT BARTON/
HAWKEYE

TONY STARK/
IRON MAN

THOR

DR. BRUCE BANNER/
HULK

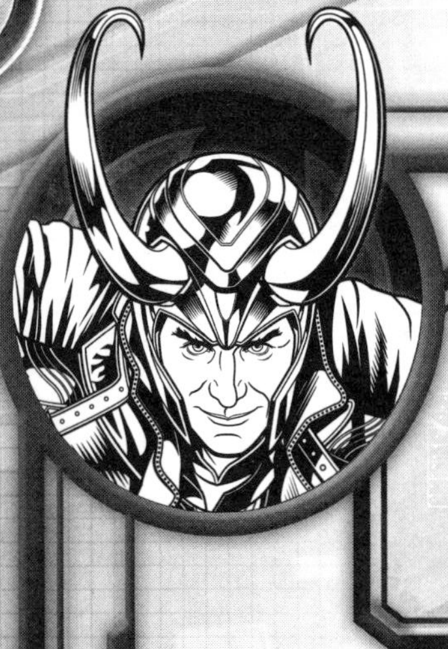

LOKI is imprisoned on the Helicarrier, and AGENT COULSON is guarding him with a very big weapon. What does it look like?

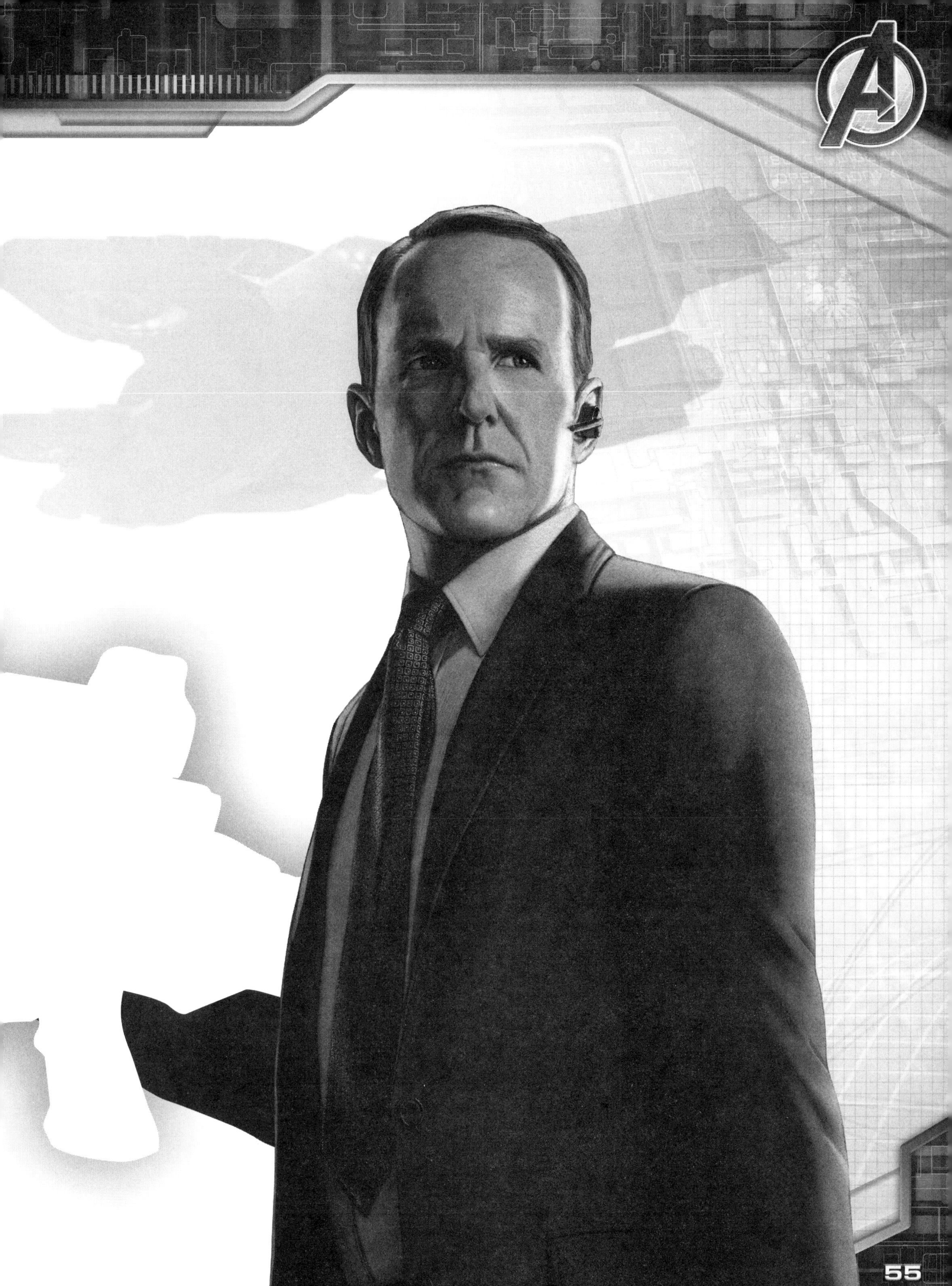

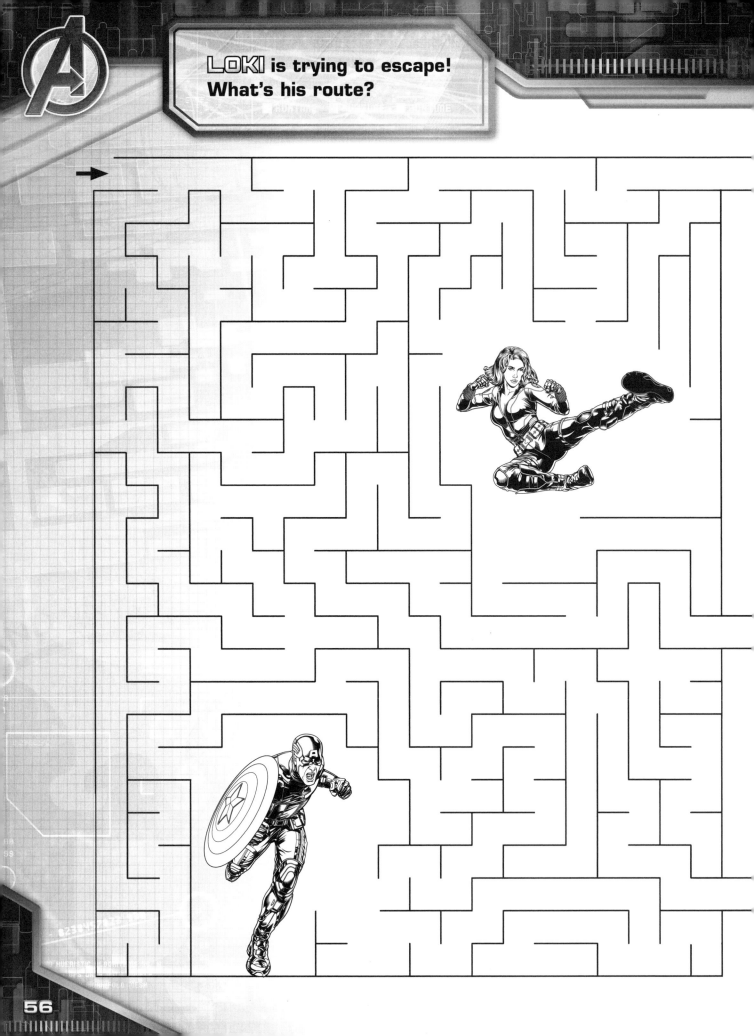

LOKI is trying to escape! What's his route?

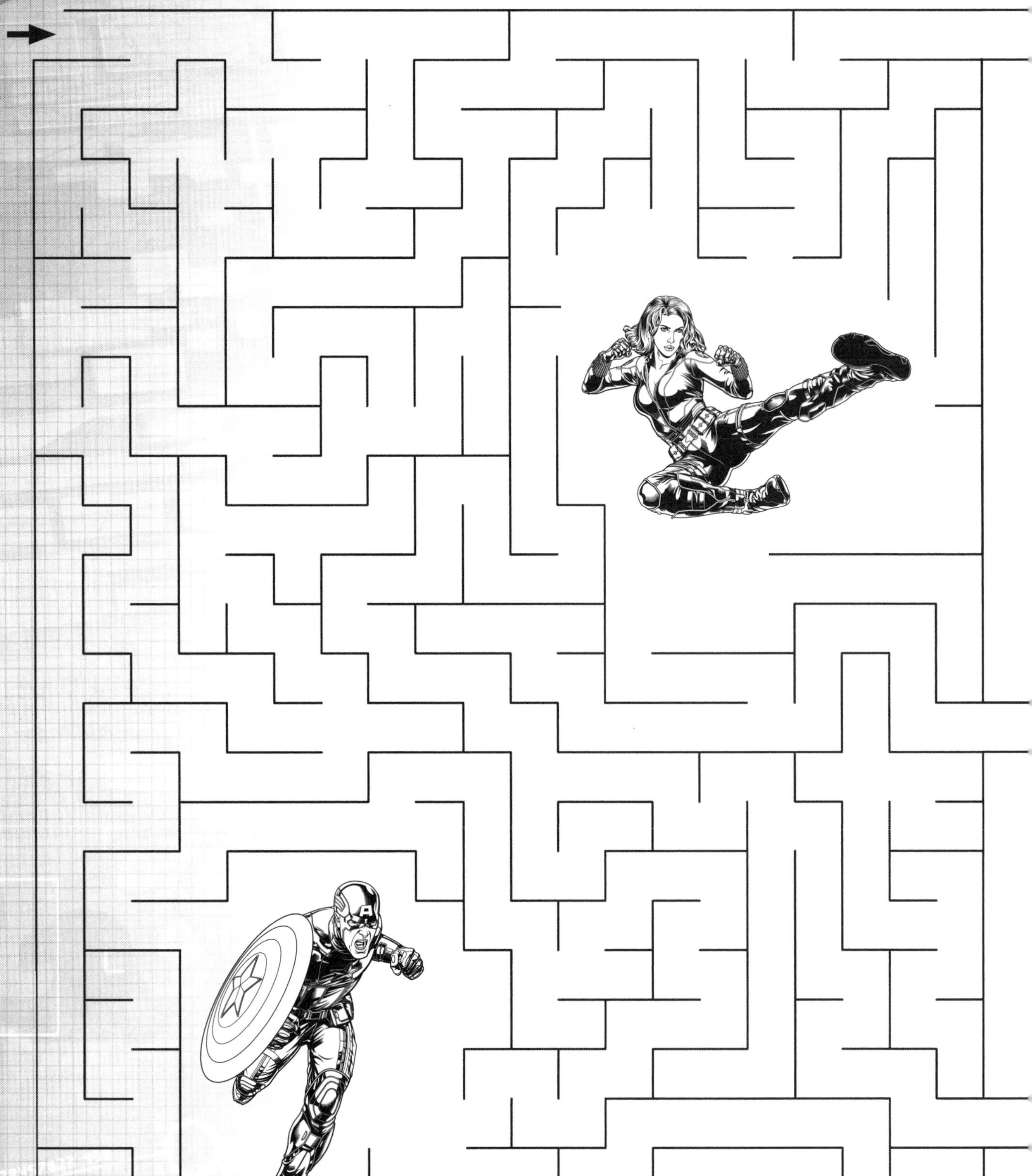

DR. BRUCE BANNER has turned into the **HULK!** Draw him smashing up the Helicarrier.

MARIA HILL is monitoring the situation on the Helicarrier. Draw her command station.

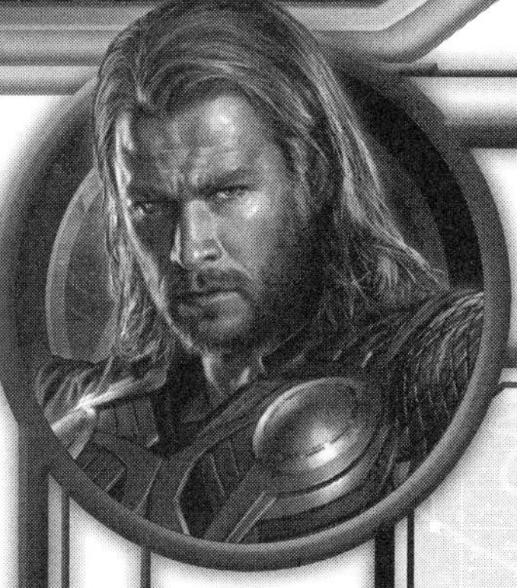

THOR is trying to stop the Hulk, but he drops his hammer! Where does it land?

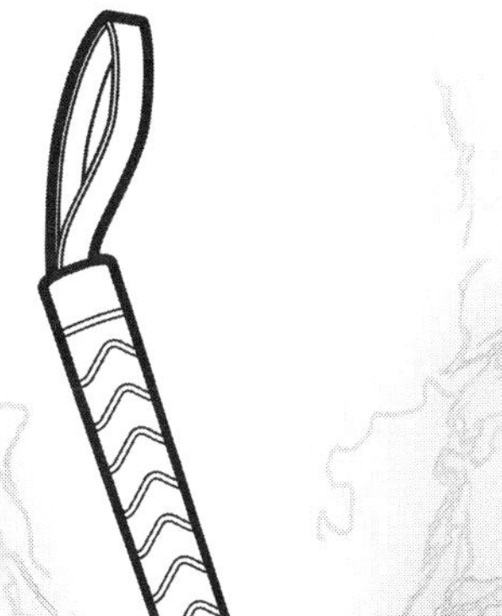

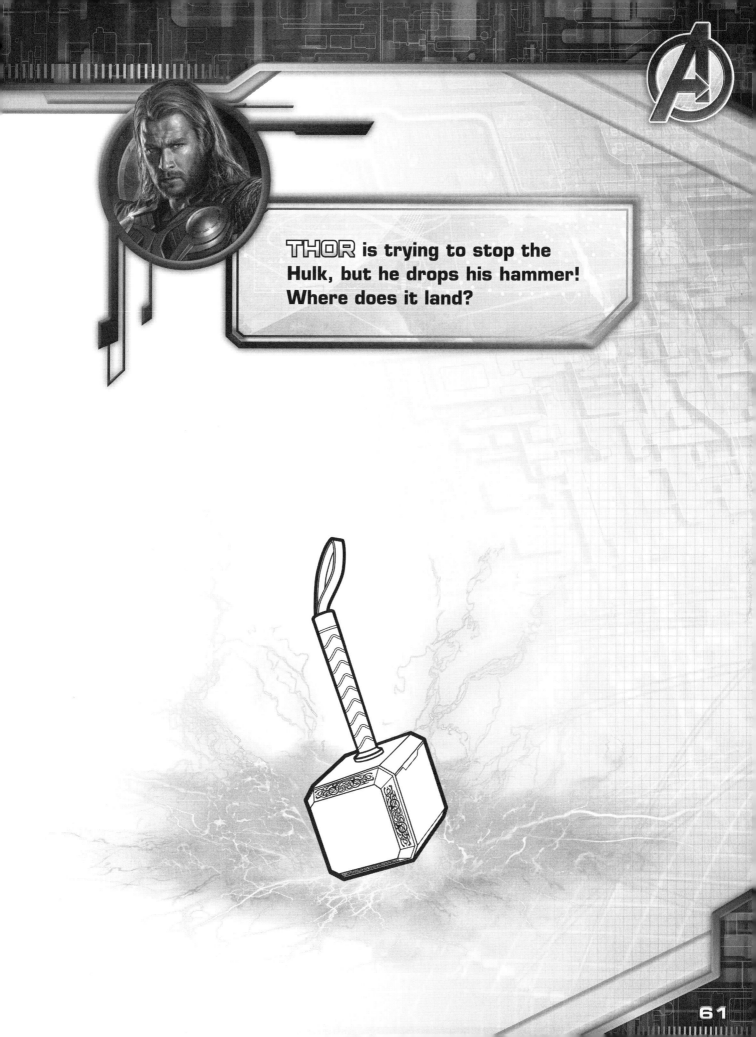

LOKI'S warriors are attacking the Helicarrier! What do they look like?

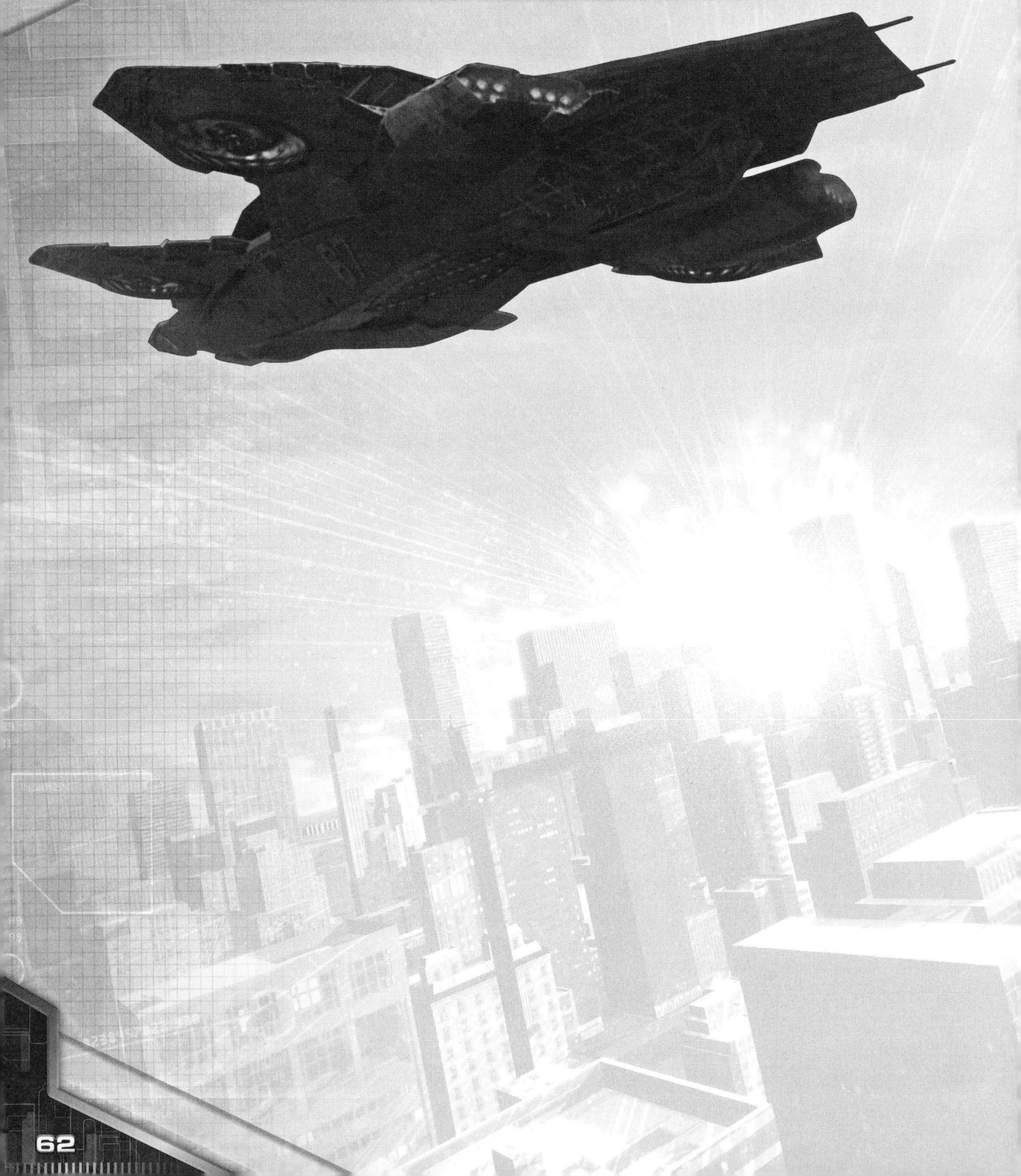

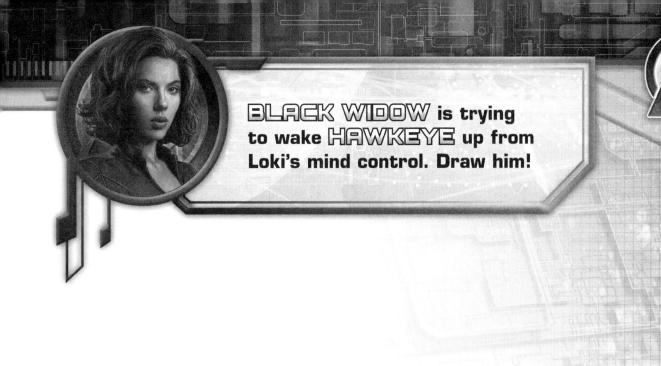

BLACK WIDOW is trying to wake **HAWKEYE** up from Loki's mind control. Draw him!

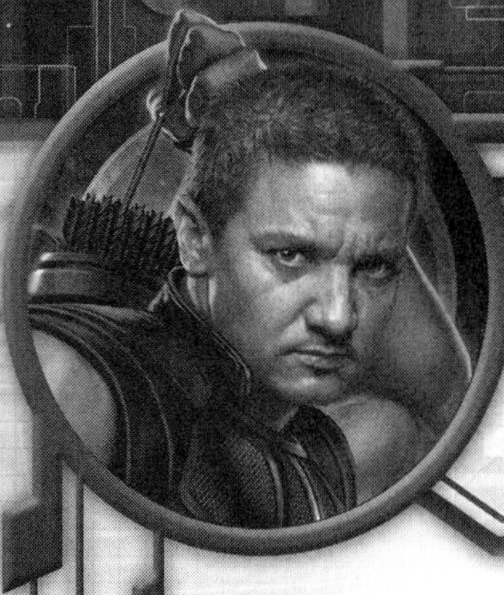

Toss a coin at the target to try to get the highest score. Practice makes perfect!

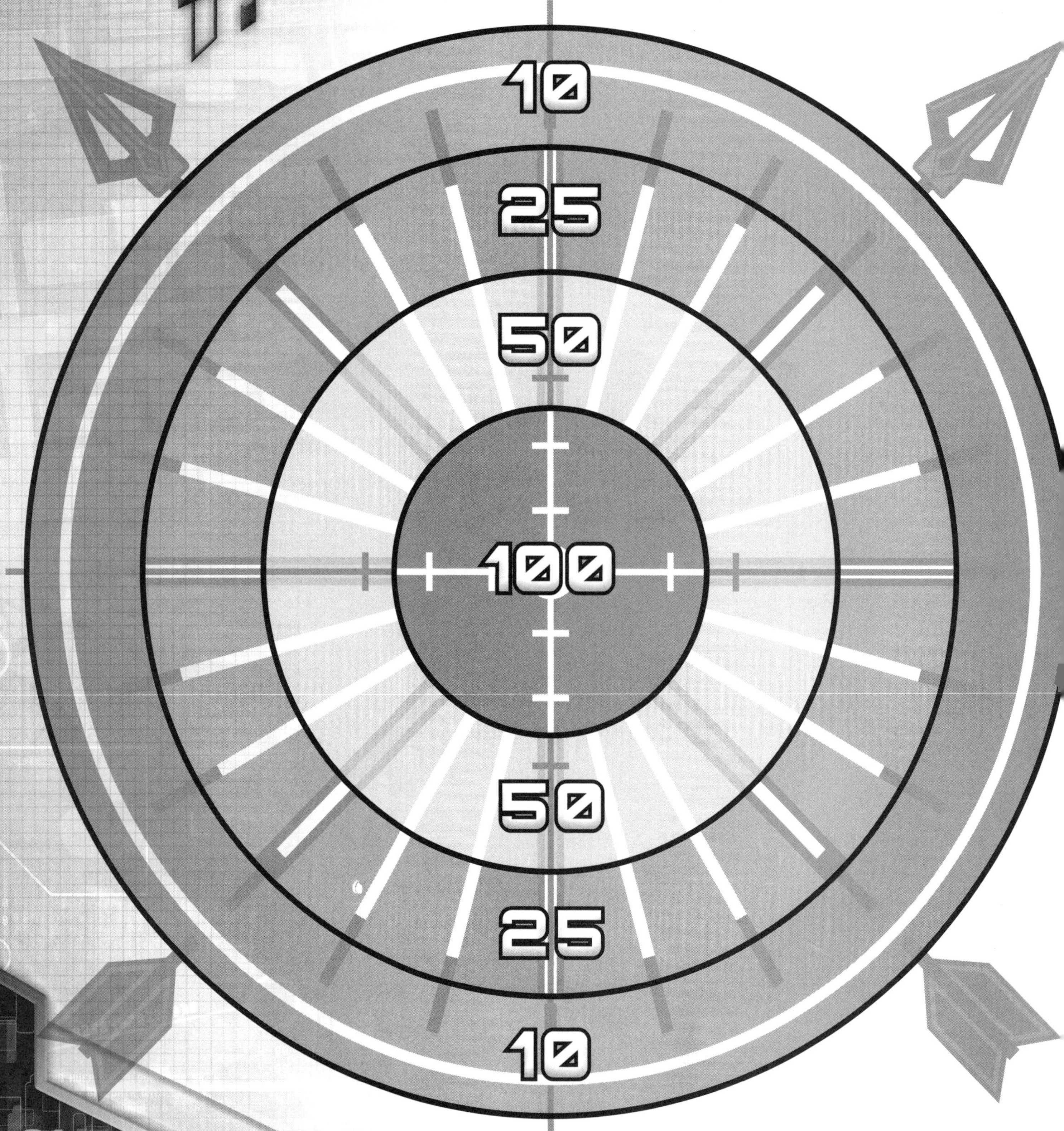
10
25
50
100
50
25
10

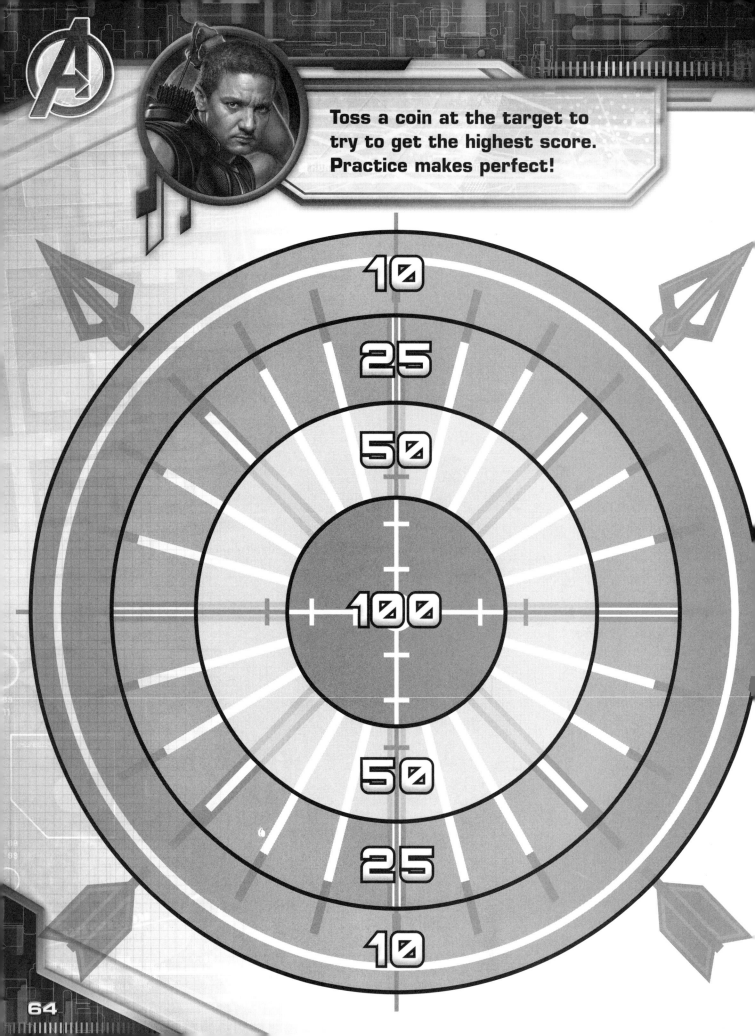

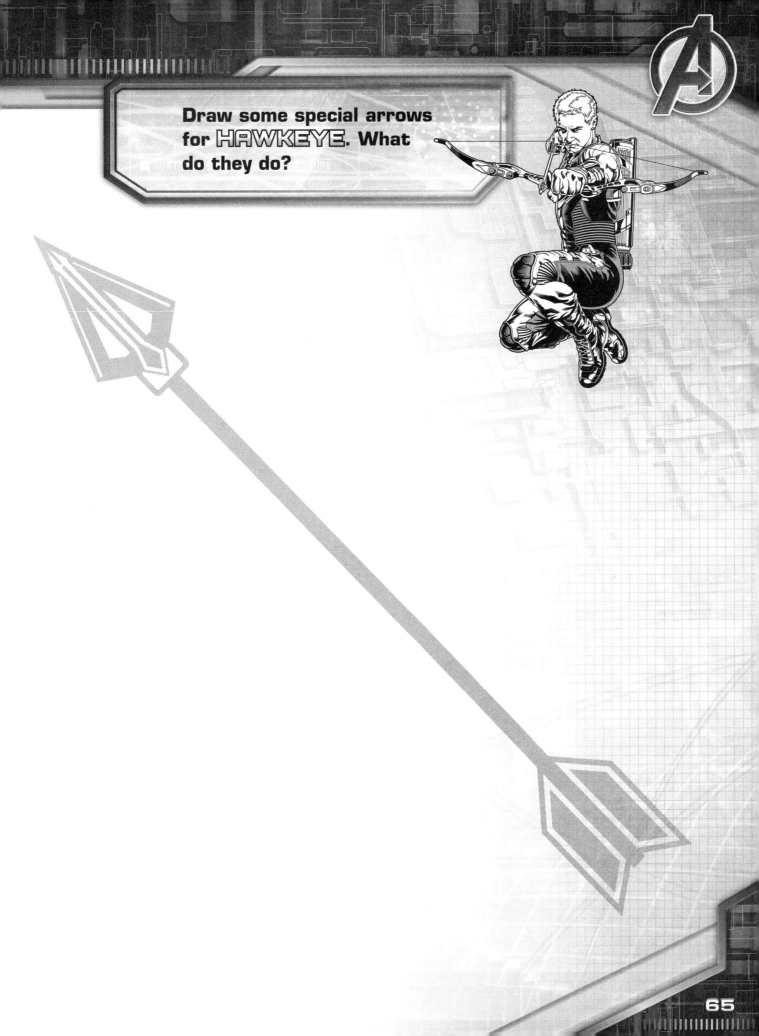

Draw some special arrows for HAWKEYE. What do they do?

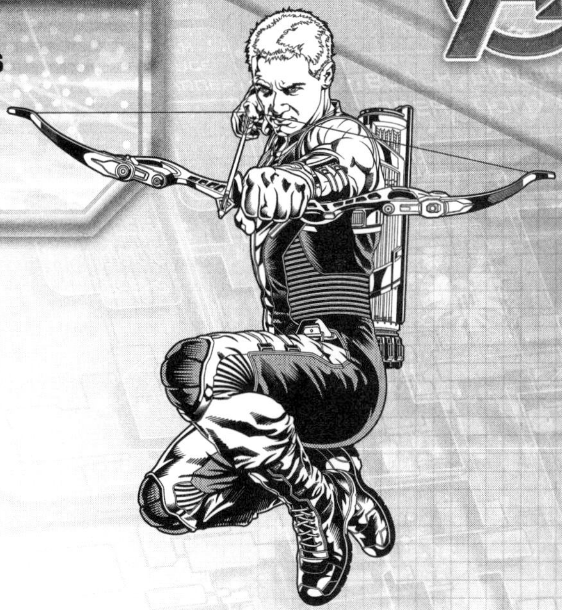

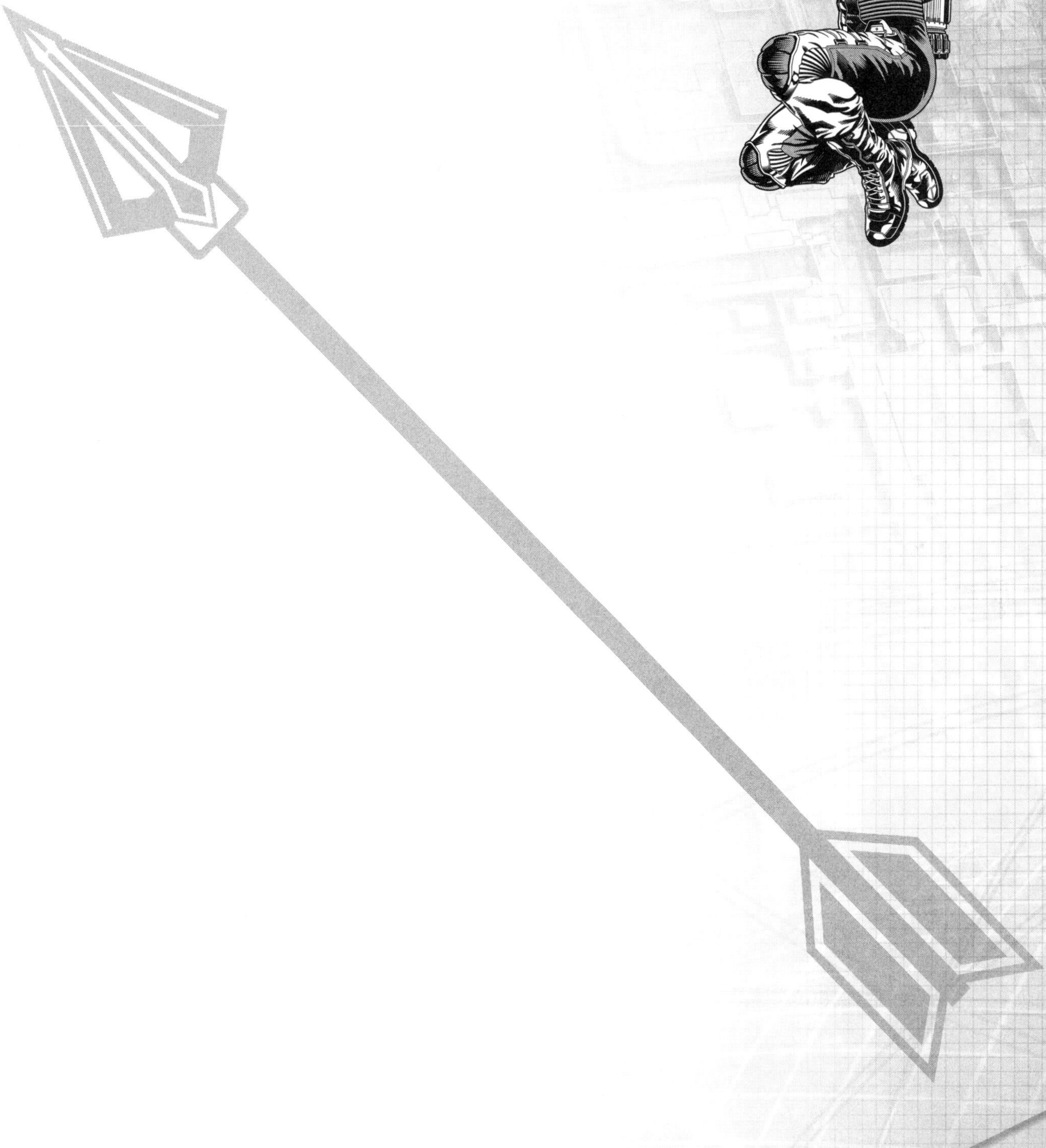

Finish drawing the HULK.

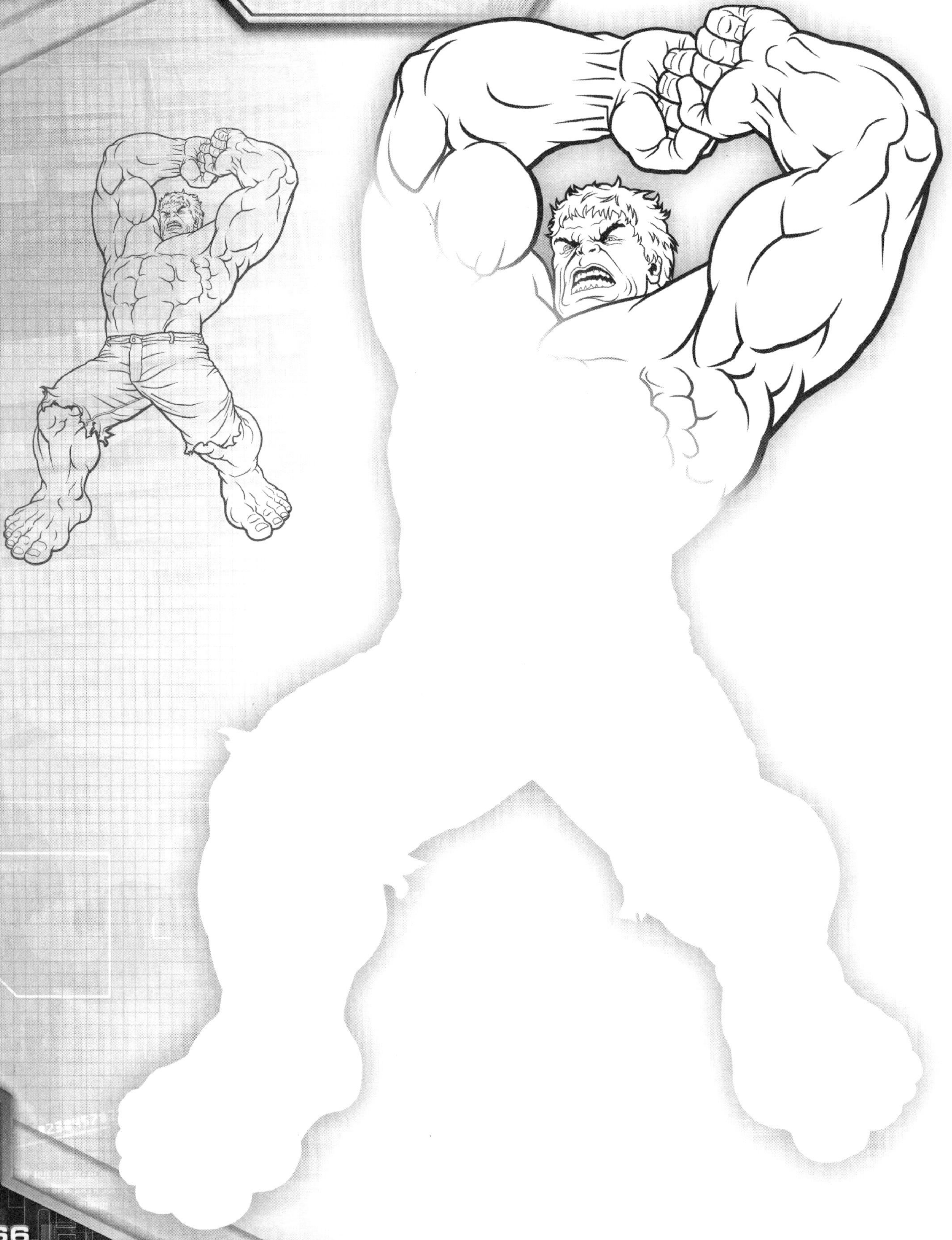

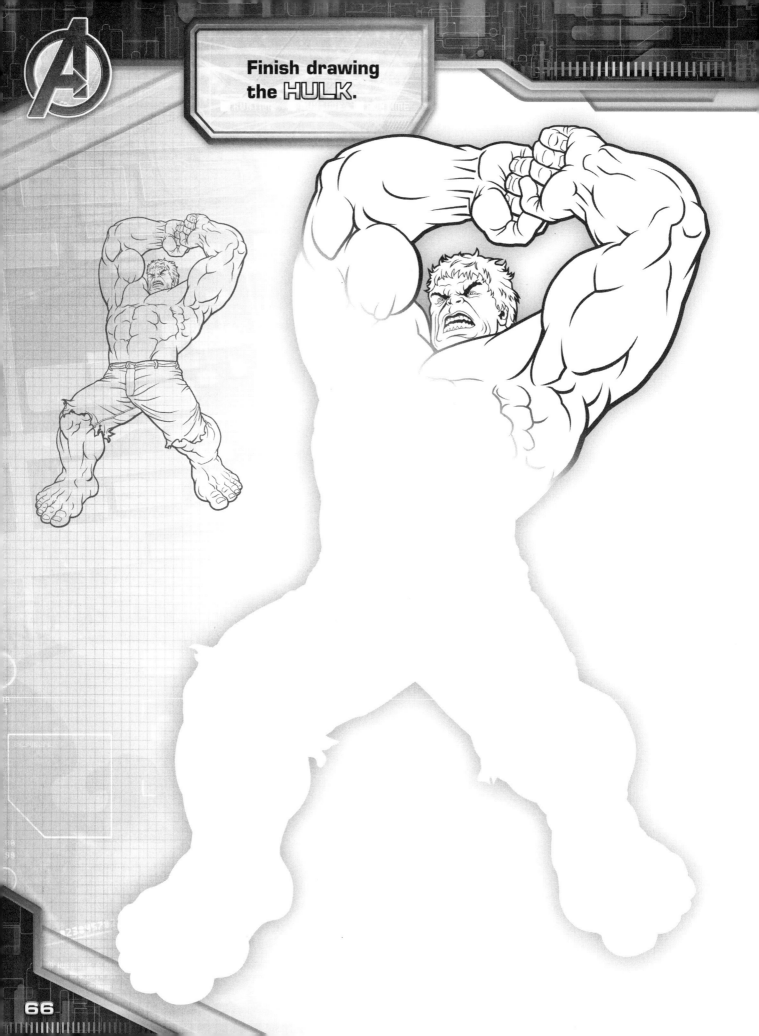

Help Cap reclaim his shield!

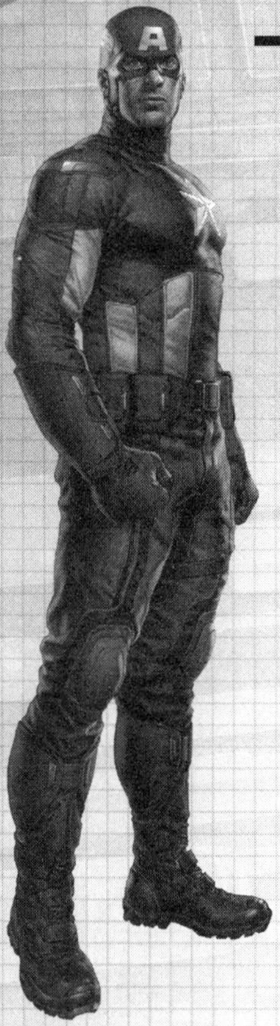

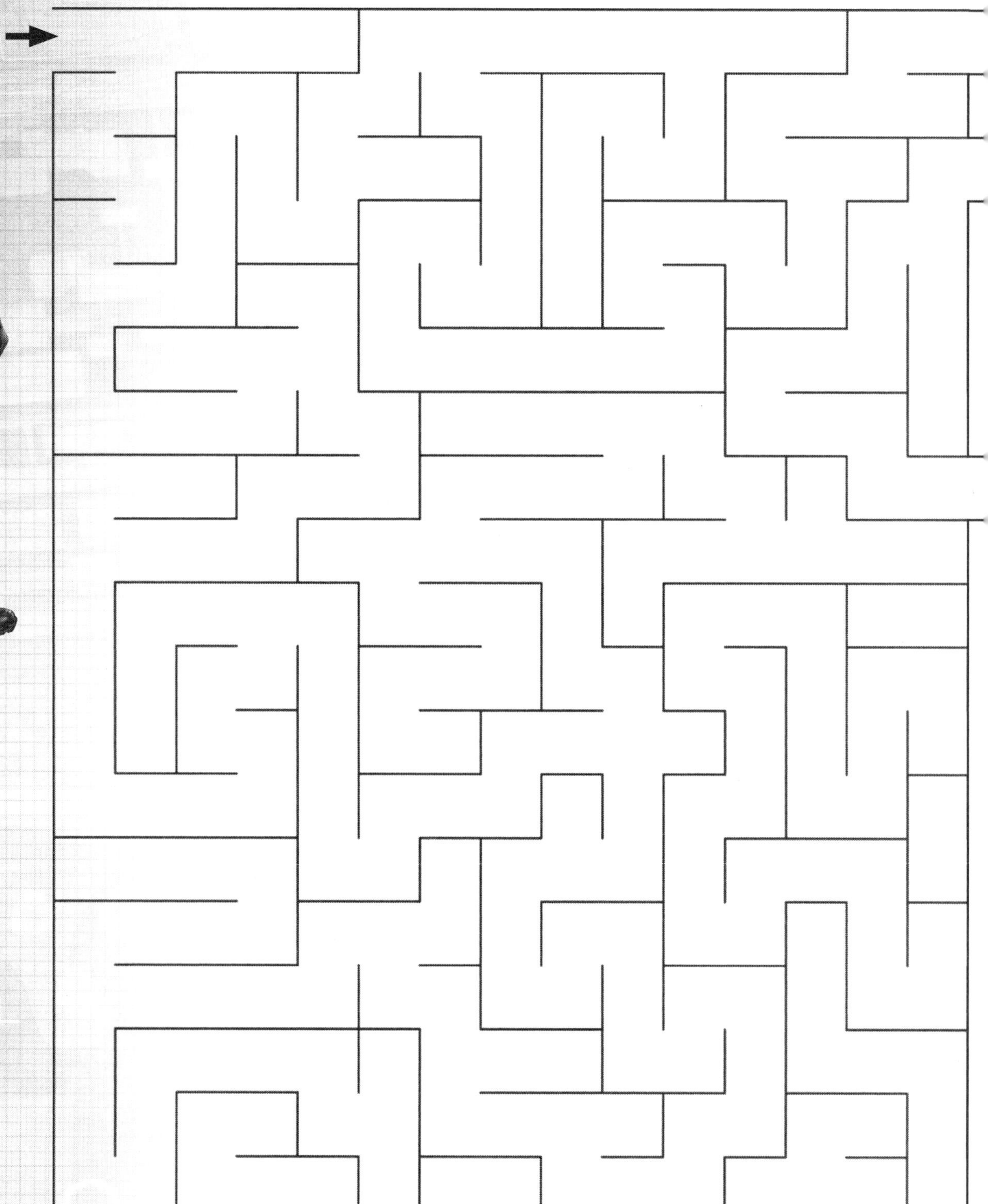

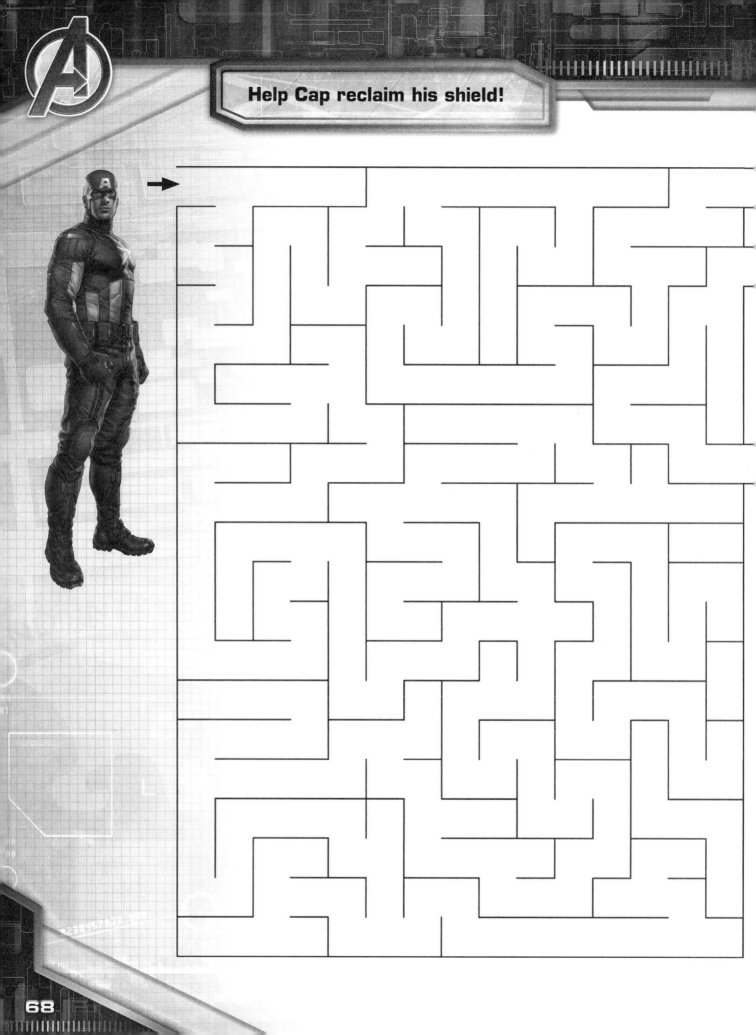

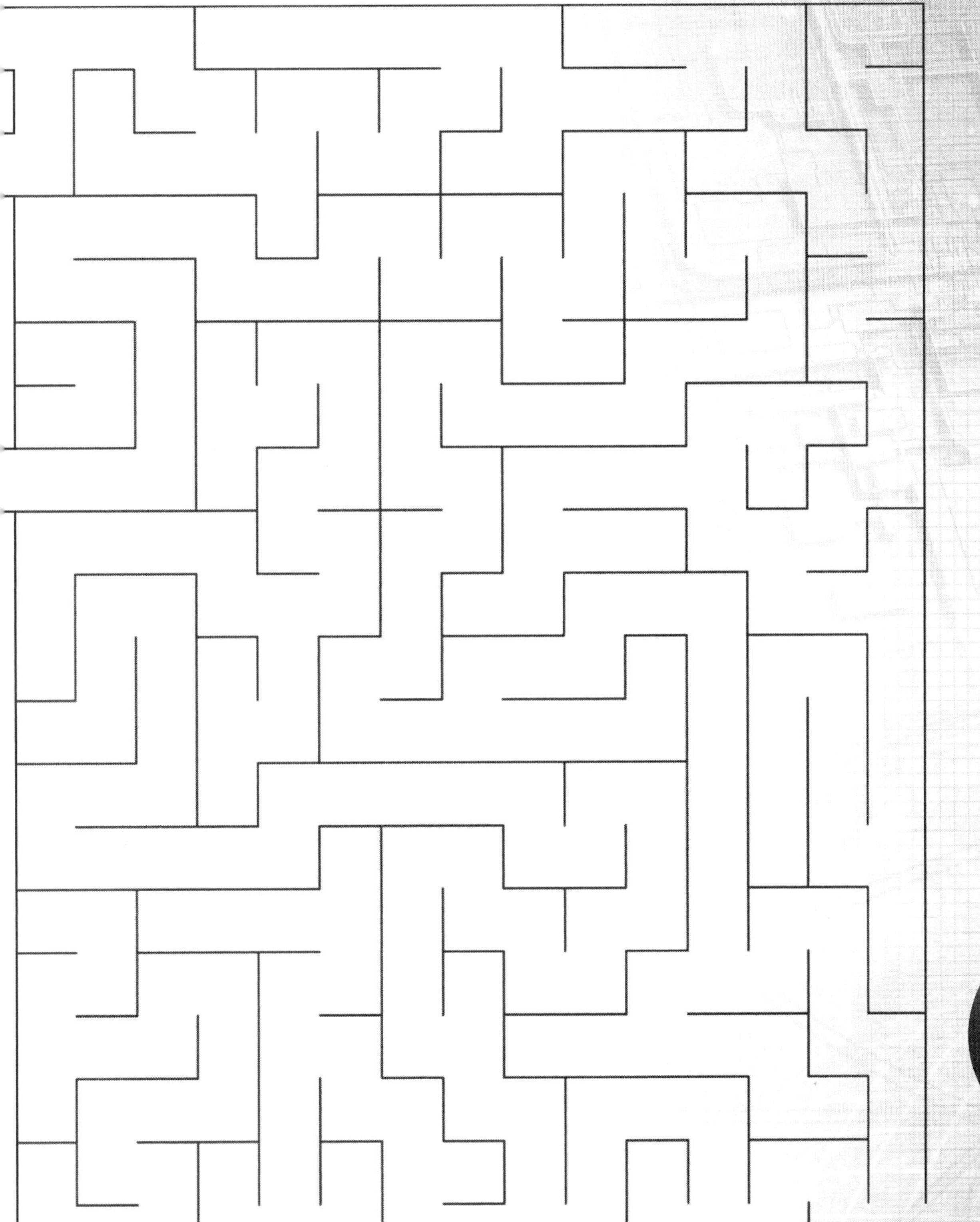

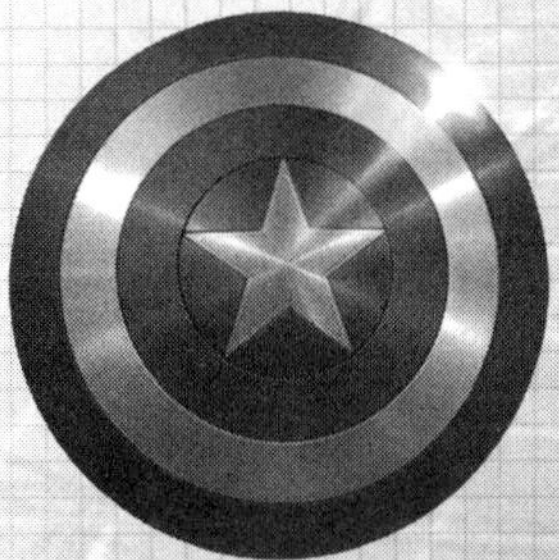

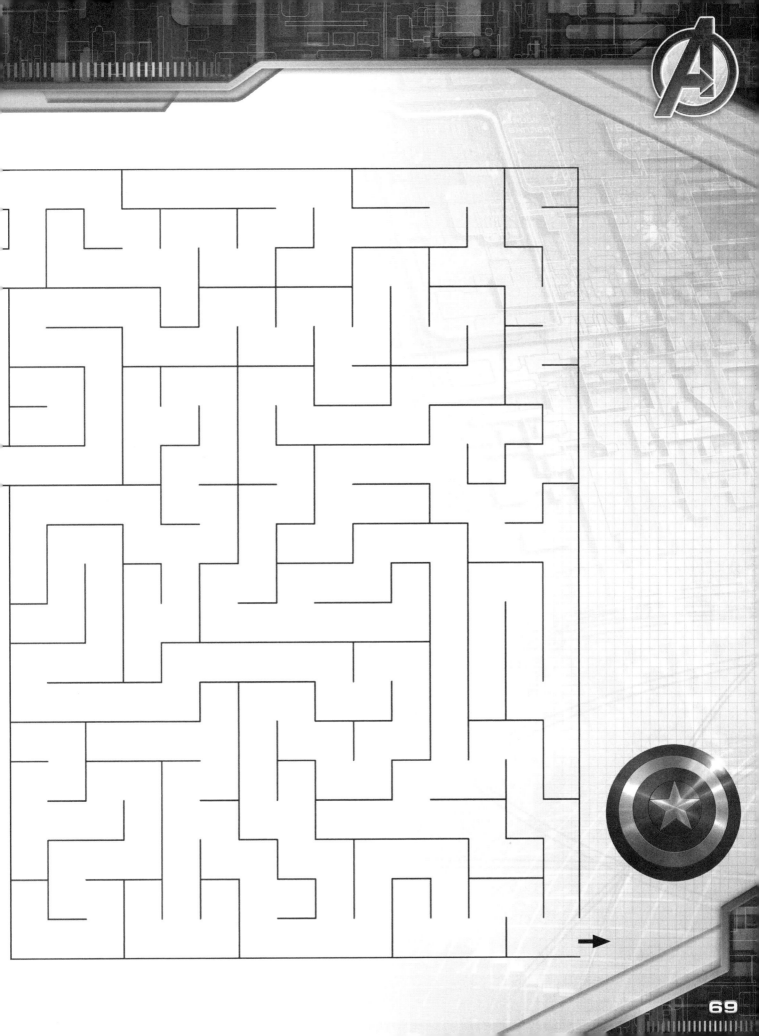

Stark Tower is the headquarters of Tony Stark's company. If you had a skyscraper, what would it look like? Turn the book and draw it as tall as you can!

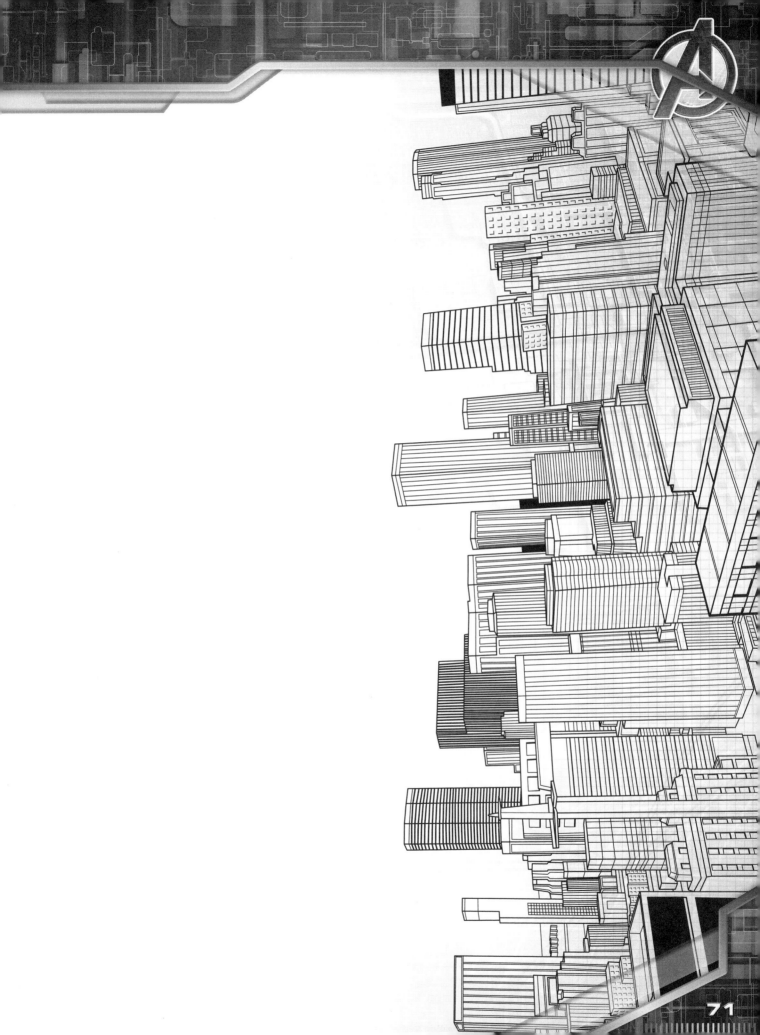

Jarvis is IRON MAN'S artificial intelligence assistant. If Jarvis worked for you, what would you have him do?

1. _____

2. _____

3. _____

4. _____

5. _____

6. _____

7. _____

8. _____

9. _____

10. _____

11. _____

12. _____

13. _____

14. _____

15. _____

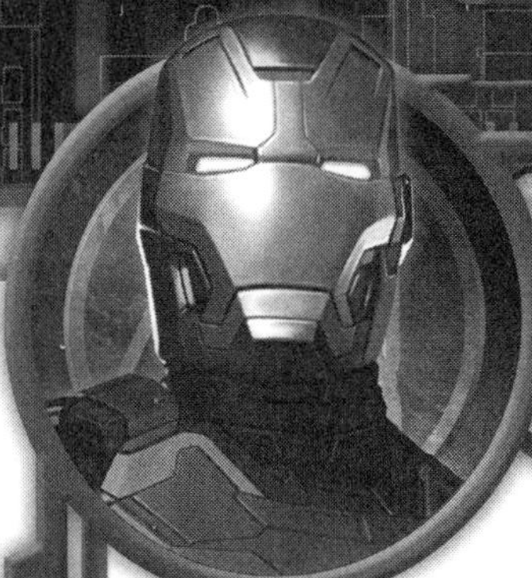

What does the world look like from inside IRON MAN'S helmet?

85%

Tony Stark has had many different IRON MAN suits. What do the old ones look like?

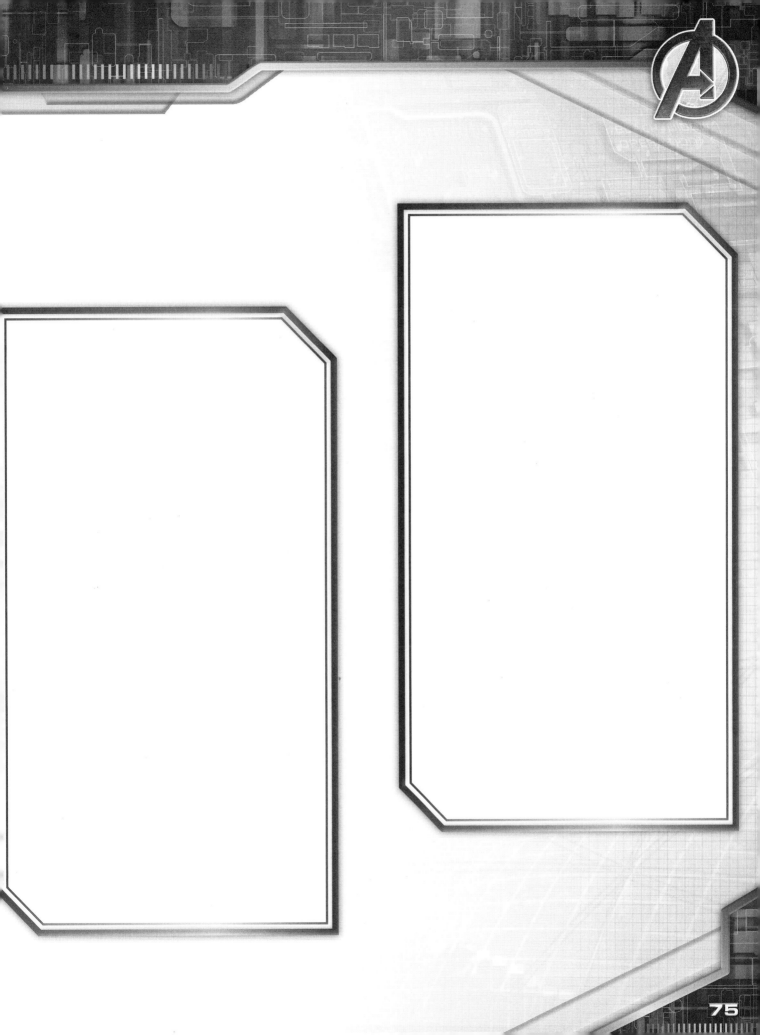

Can you find the following words?

ARROW   WIDOW'S STING   STAFF

VIBRANIUM   SMASH   QUINJET

MJOLNIR   HELICARRIER

```
M G M Y K N D Y L G K J X X Z T B T R
N K D L L W D N N R J J G V Z L N E X
W T J R J N F T G R T N T B J J I J R
V Y T L V F Y R T J I B Y J J R K R P
X R W Q A Q P Y T T W B D Z R B V Z T
V D Q T D K Y M S X D B R A T R K R N
B K S Y R R J S M R D B C V W W T B M
D N M Q M P W T T Y V I B R A N I U M
K N L M P O T S W L L P M W W M Q N Z
T J X R D E L T M E L P N X Z P B J R
Y J Q I J N V B H A T Y B J X W M V N
D V W N T A W R L Y S D R N J W M J R
D R I G R Q I R N Q J H D T G B D R M
B U Y R R N M Y Y T Z V D B T J Z Z R
Q J O B L Y Y J R B N G L L D D W W T
Q W M O W X T R T L X V L X M L R G R
M T J Z G B M R G R R N P N J G K D D
M M Y G R X D L V Y R J G G X G D D N
```

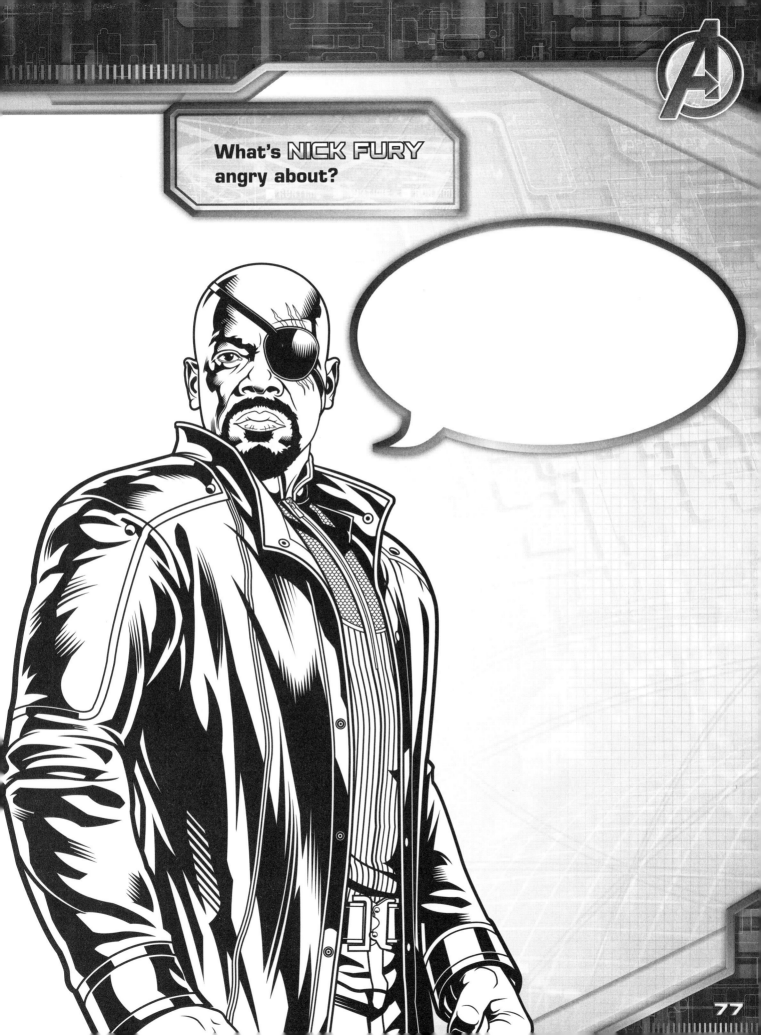

What's NICK FURY angry about?

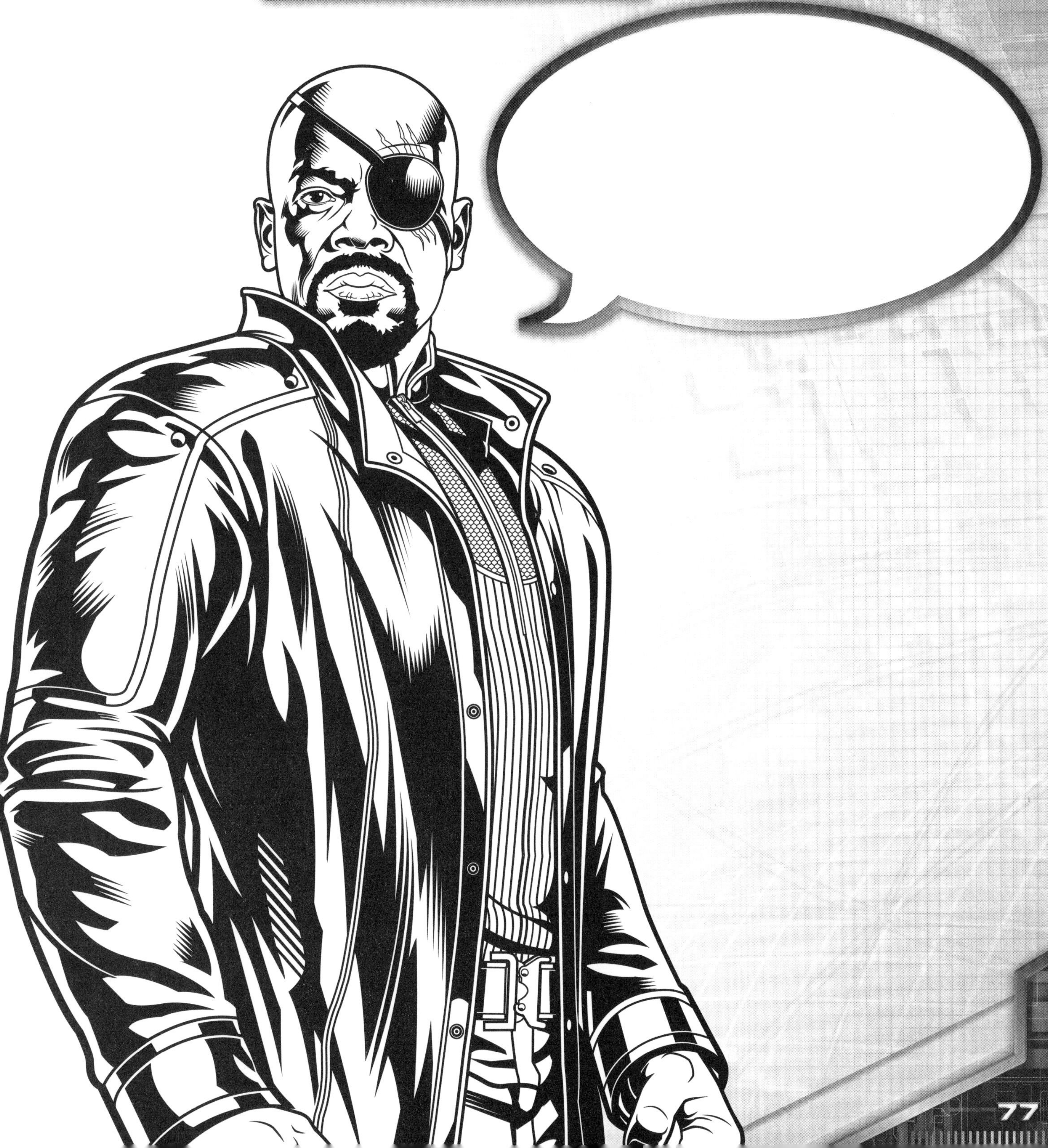

Draw the Avengers making NICK FURY happy.

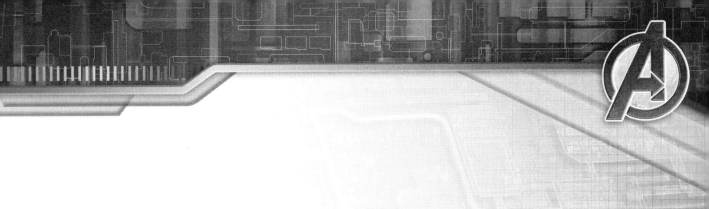

If you were an Avenger, what would your powers be? What would your name be?

Every Super Hero needs an outfit—design yours.

Now draw yourself fighting with the Avengers. Who are you fighting?

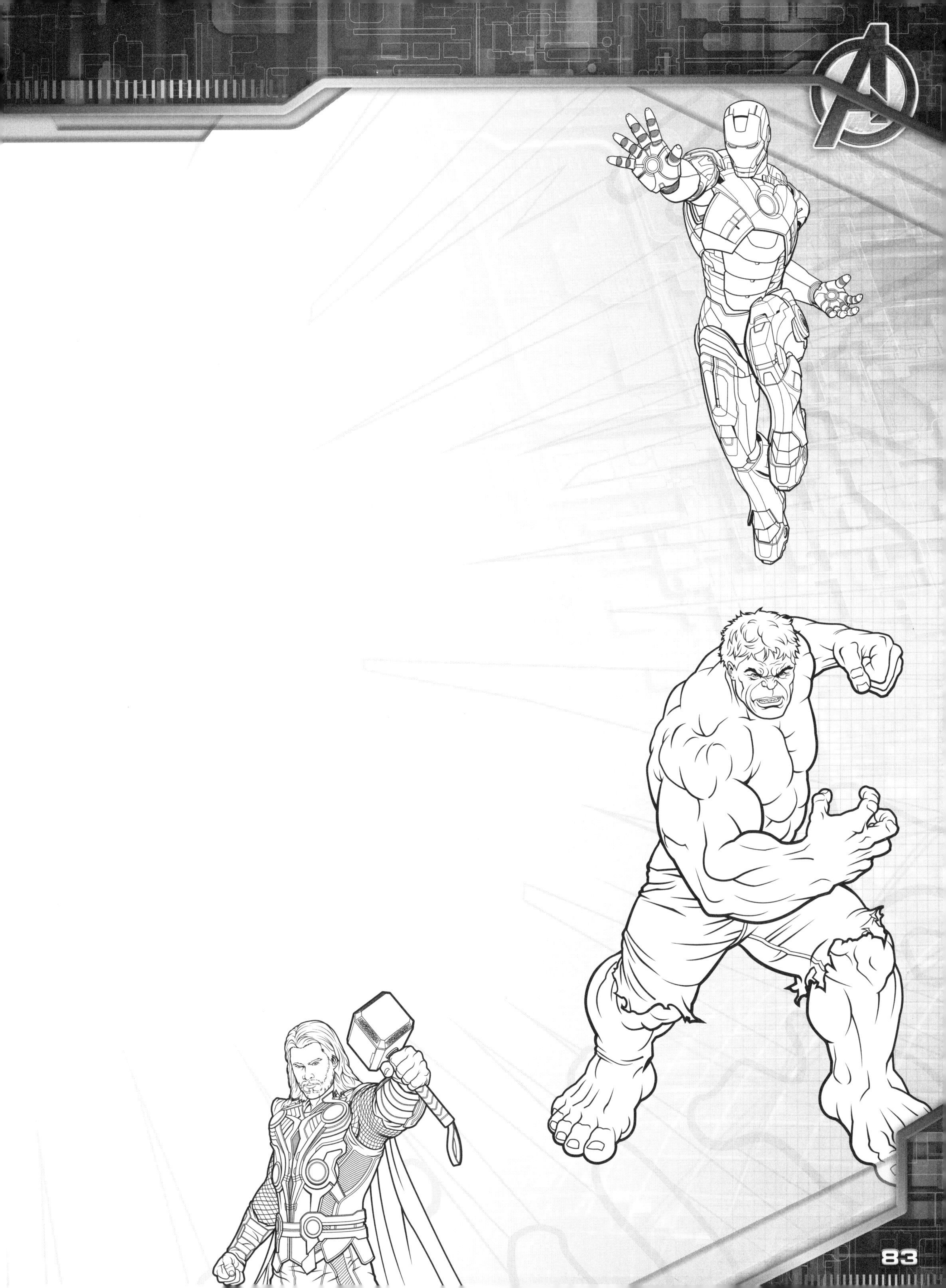

What's your greatest strength as a Super Hero?

What's your greatest weakness as a Super Hero?

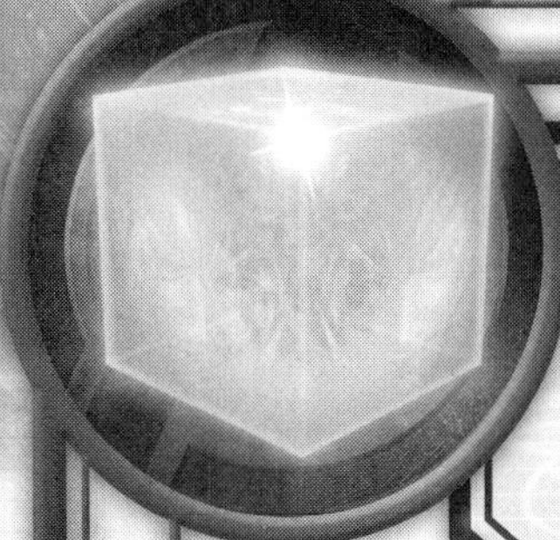

LOKI has used the Tesseract to open a portal to another planet. What do the alien visitors look like?

The city is under attack! Show what the Chitauri are doing to the city.

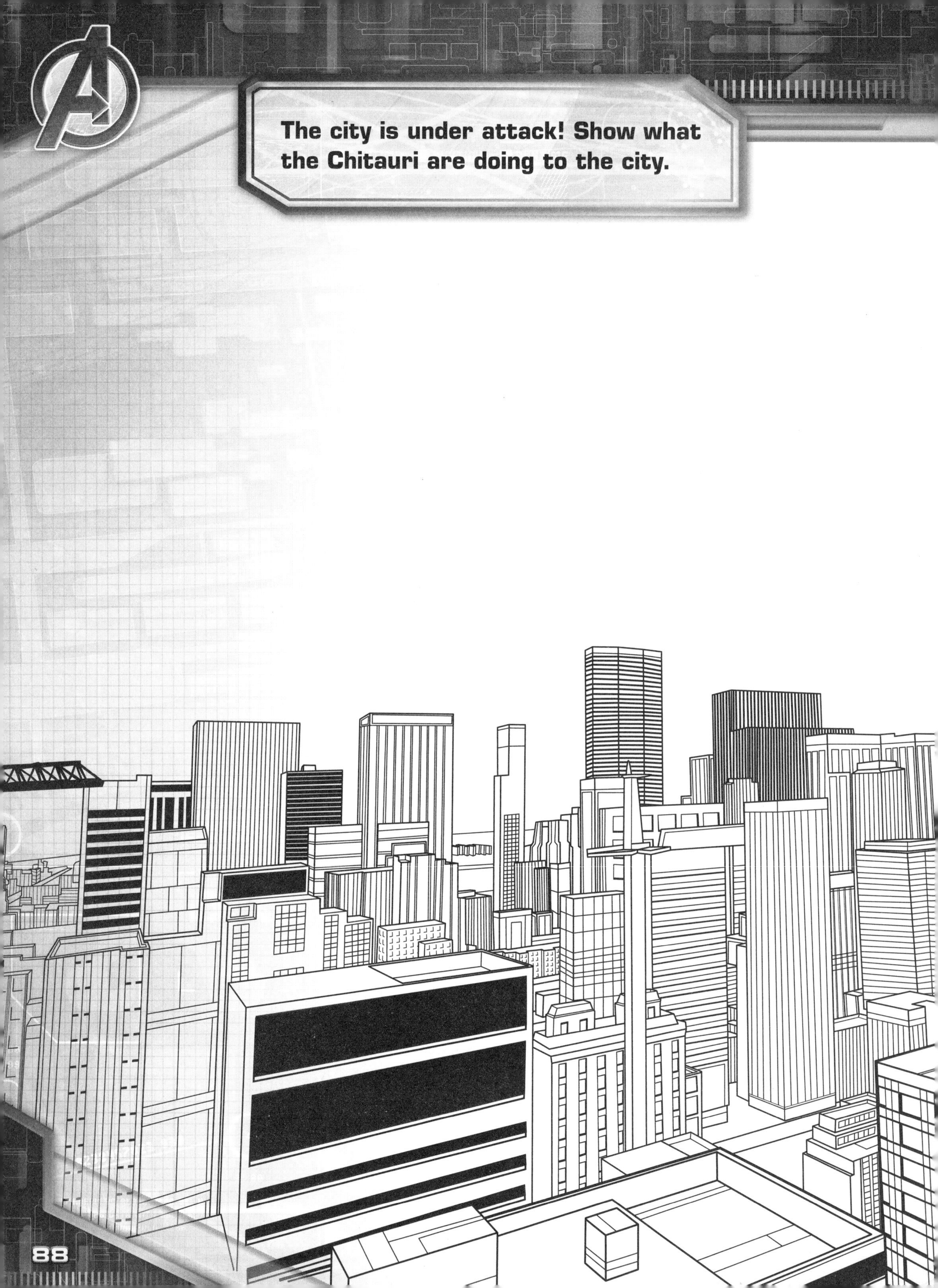

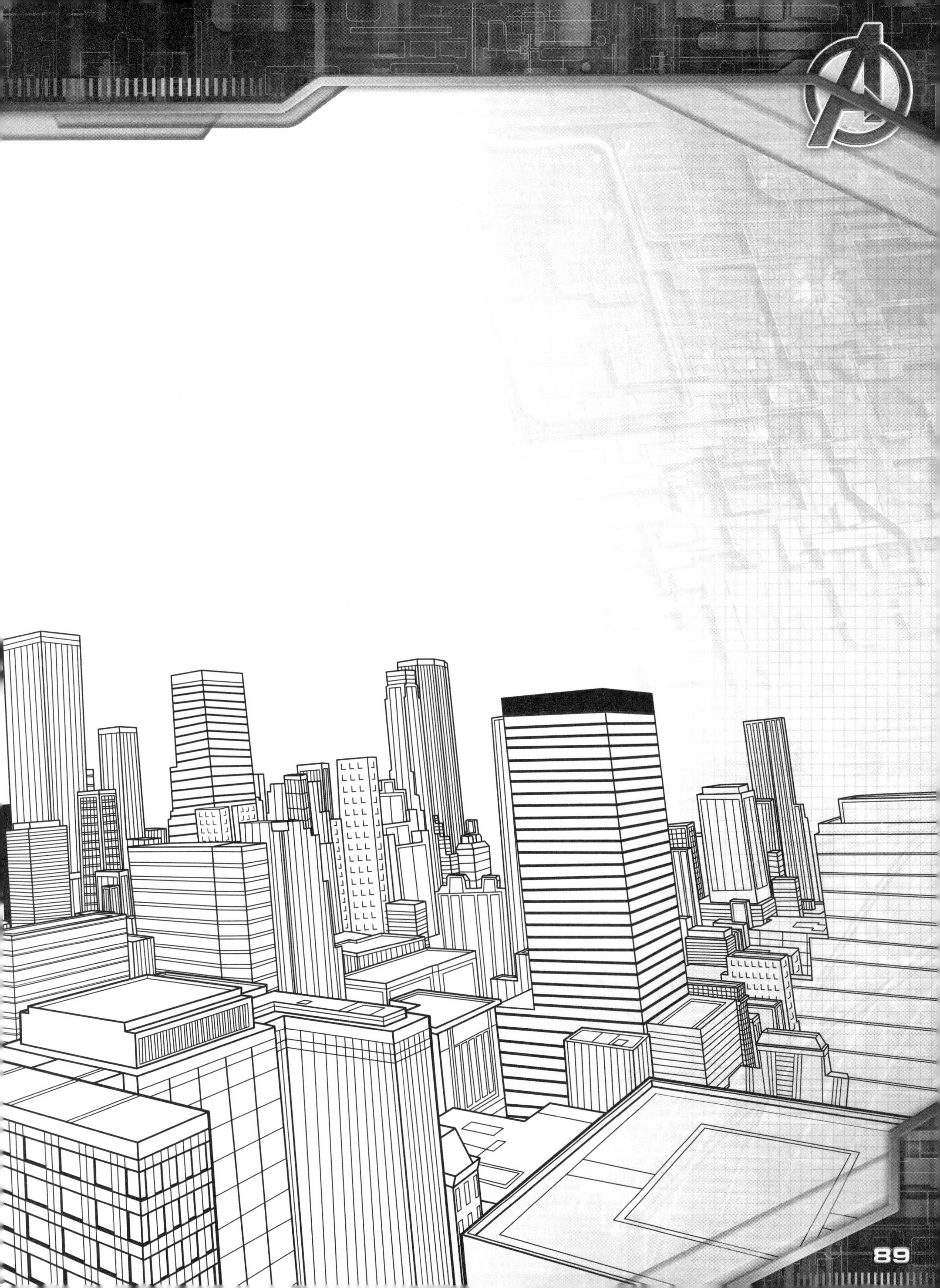

What is the HULK smashing?

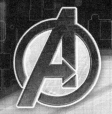

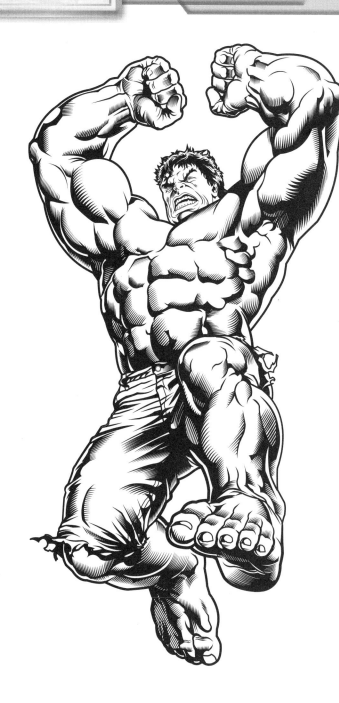

Draw what you would look like if you had the **HULK'S** gamma powers when you were angry.

Find the following words

ASSEMBLE
REPULSOR
GAMMA
HELICARRIER
SUPER-SOLDIER
COVERT
JARVIS
ASGARD
BULLSEYE

S	U	P	E	R	S	O	L	D	I	E	R
R	E	I	R	R	A	C	I	L	E	H	R
S	R	E	P	U	L	S	O	R	B	J	Y
Q	I	D	L	B	C	D	W	U	Y	Z	R
X	Z	V	K	B	R	O	L	L	J	N	T
A	Y	P	R	A	M	L	V	R	R	T	W
M	G	N	G	A	S	E	D	E	N	Z	R
M	Y	S	Z	E	J	W	S	T	R	D	Z
A	A	R	Y	D	Z	Z	G	S	R	T	V
G	R	E	W	G	B	Y	Y	Y	A	R	R

CAPTAIN AMERICA is using his shield to protect himself from an explosion. Draw the explosion.

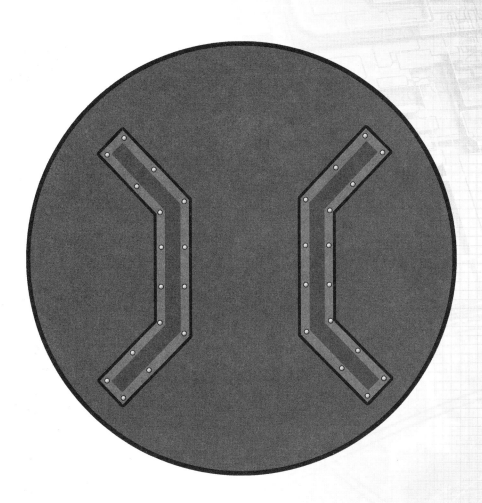

The HULK is surrounded by tanks! Draw more tanks to challenge him!

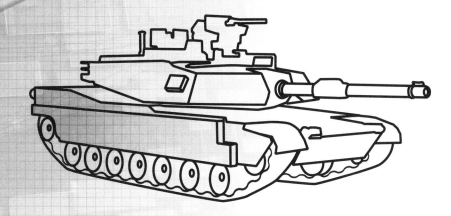

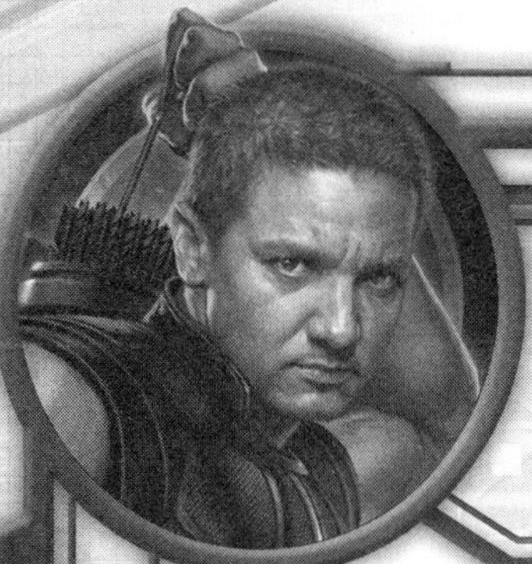

HAWKEYE is targeting enemy fighters from the roof of a building. Draw his targets!

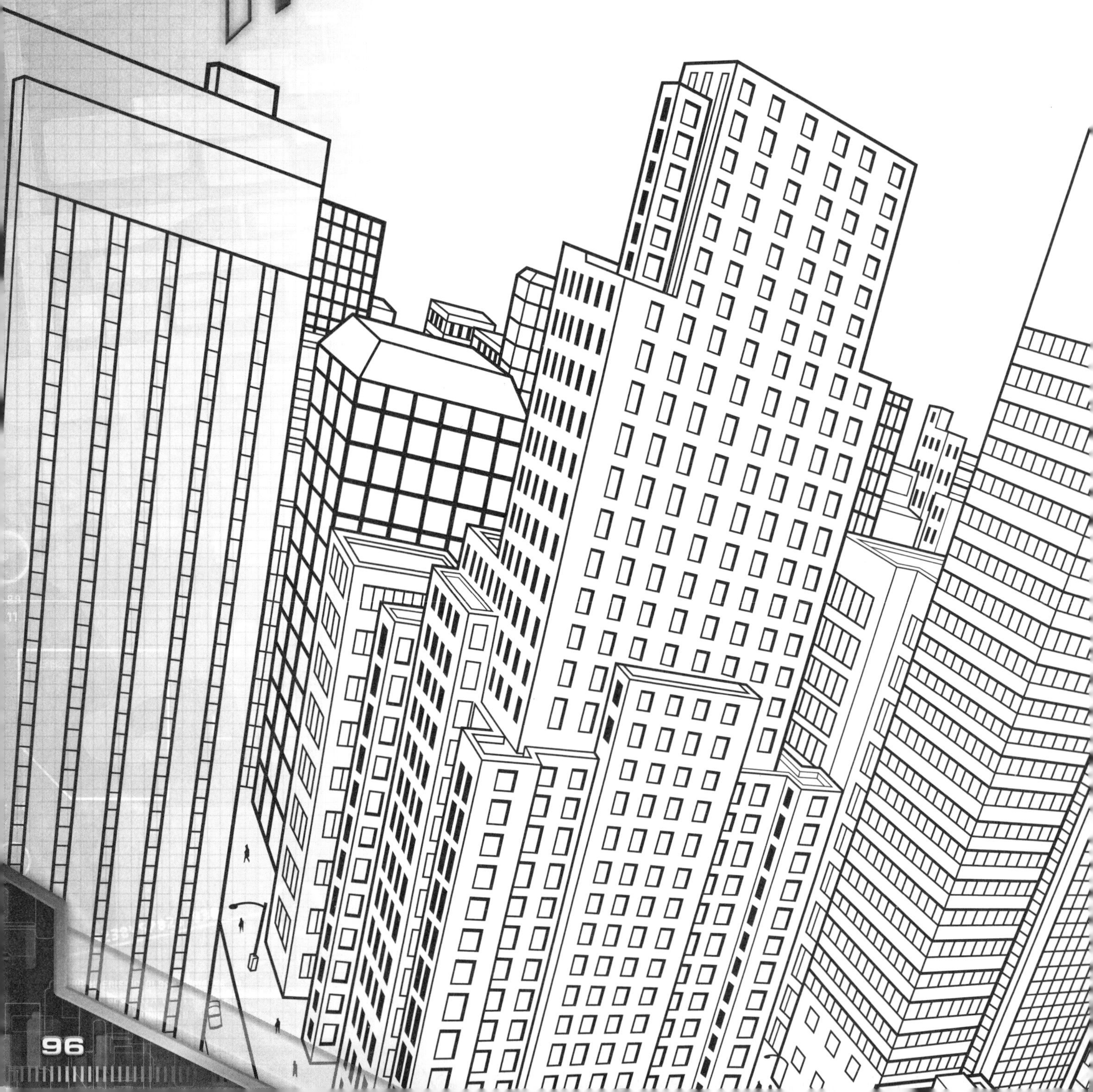

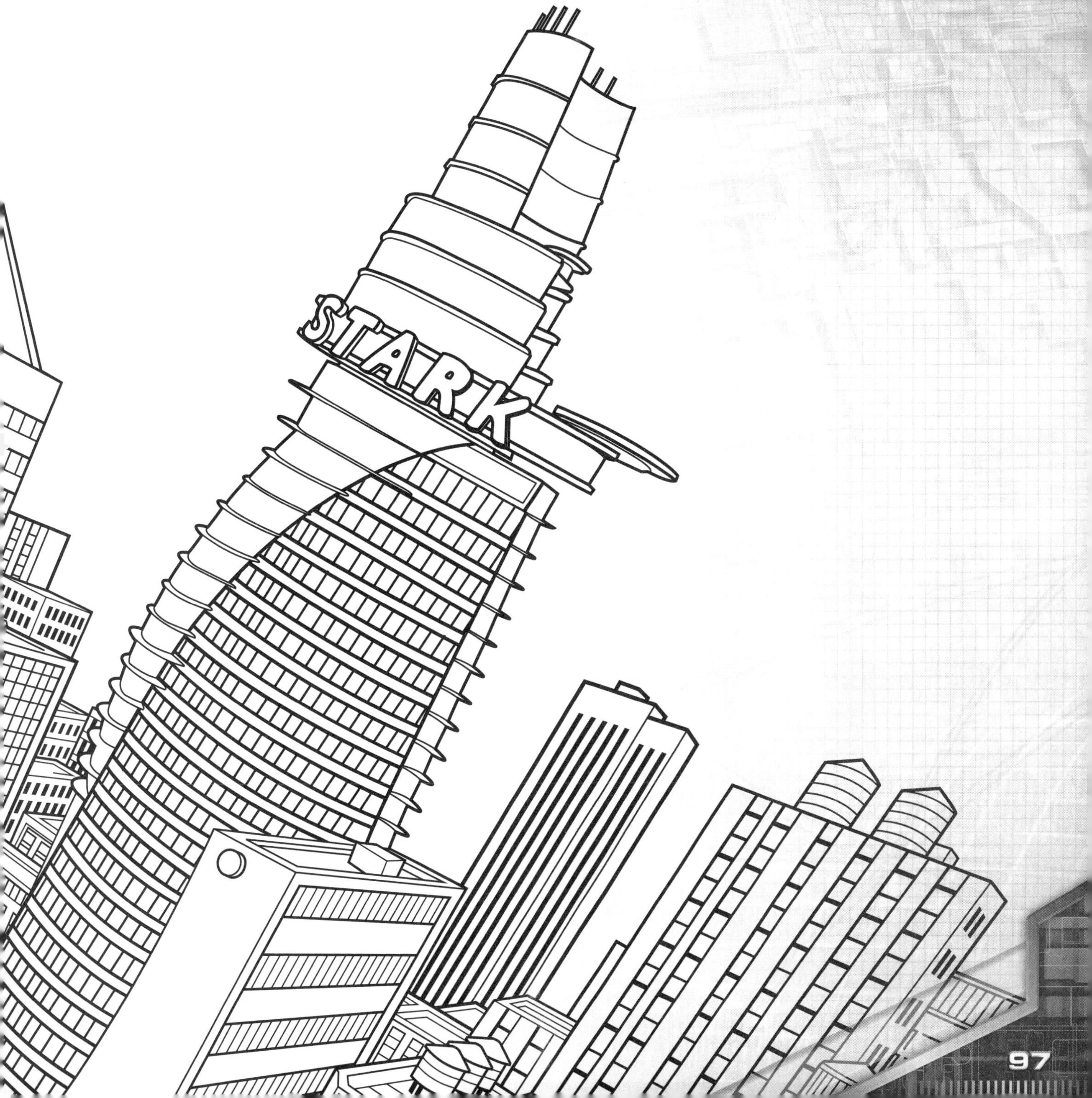
STARK

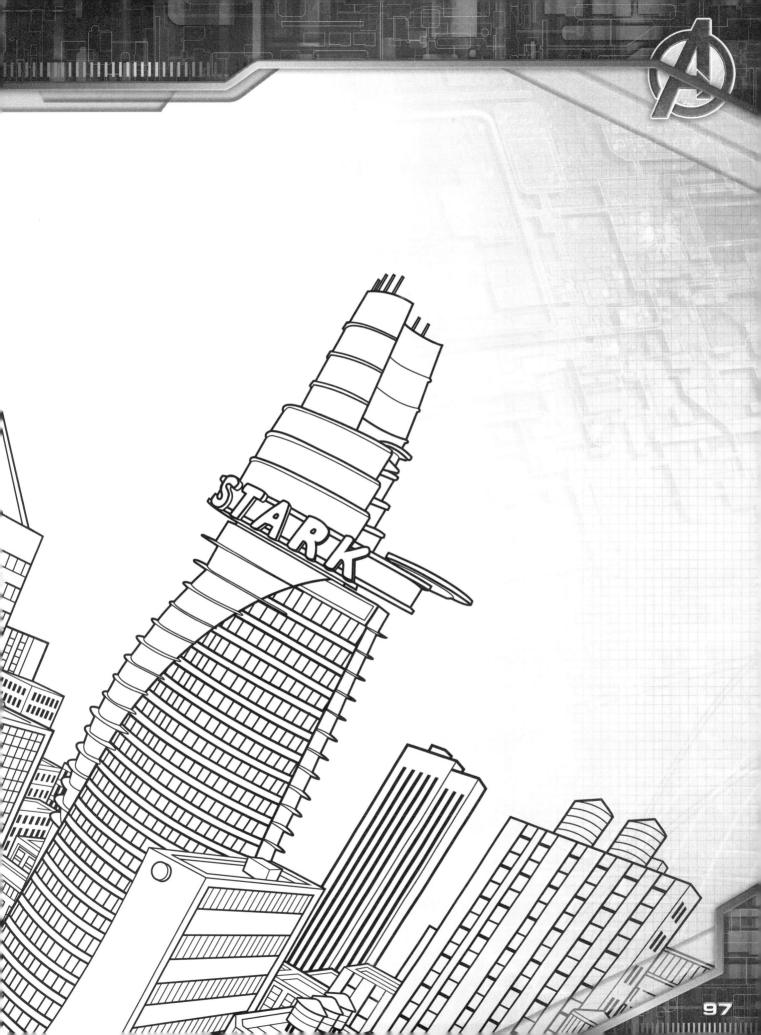

Uh-oh! IRON MAN is lost in the rubble of the battle. Help him get back to Stark Tower!

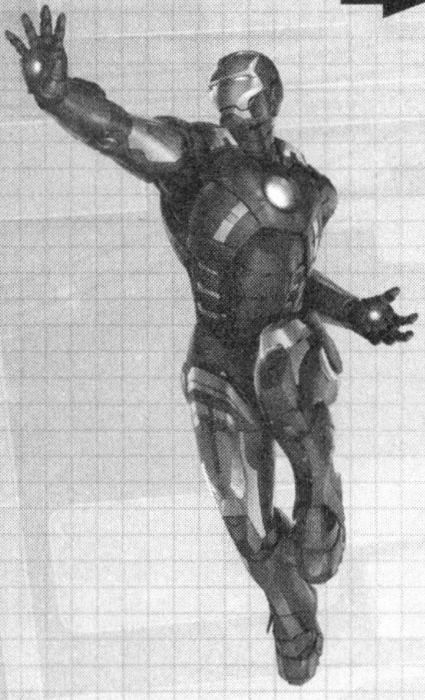

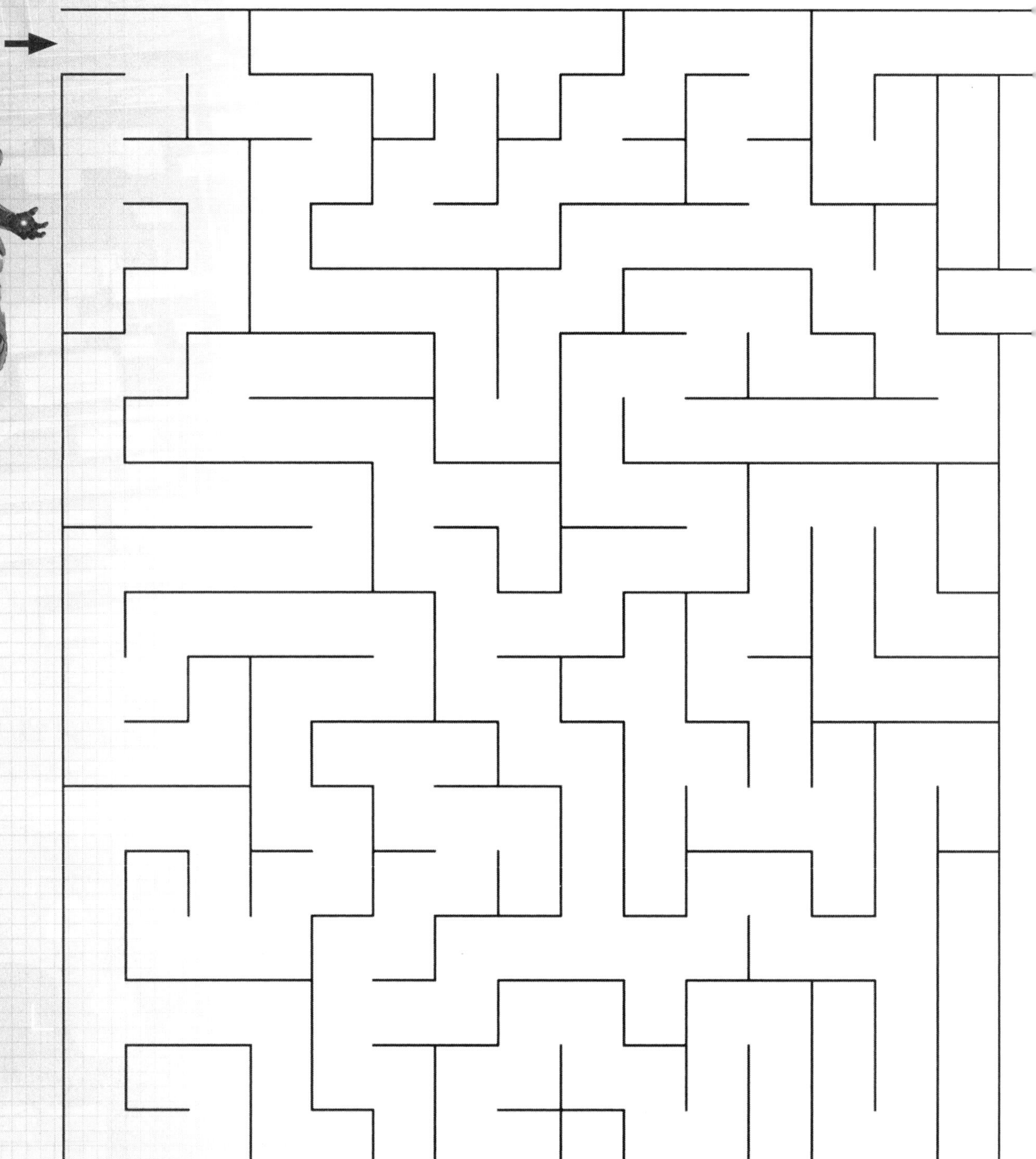

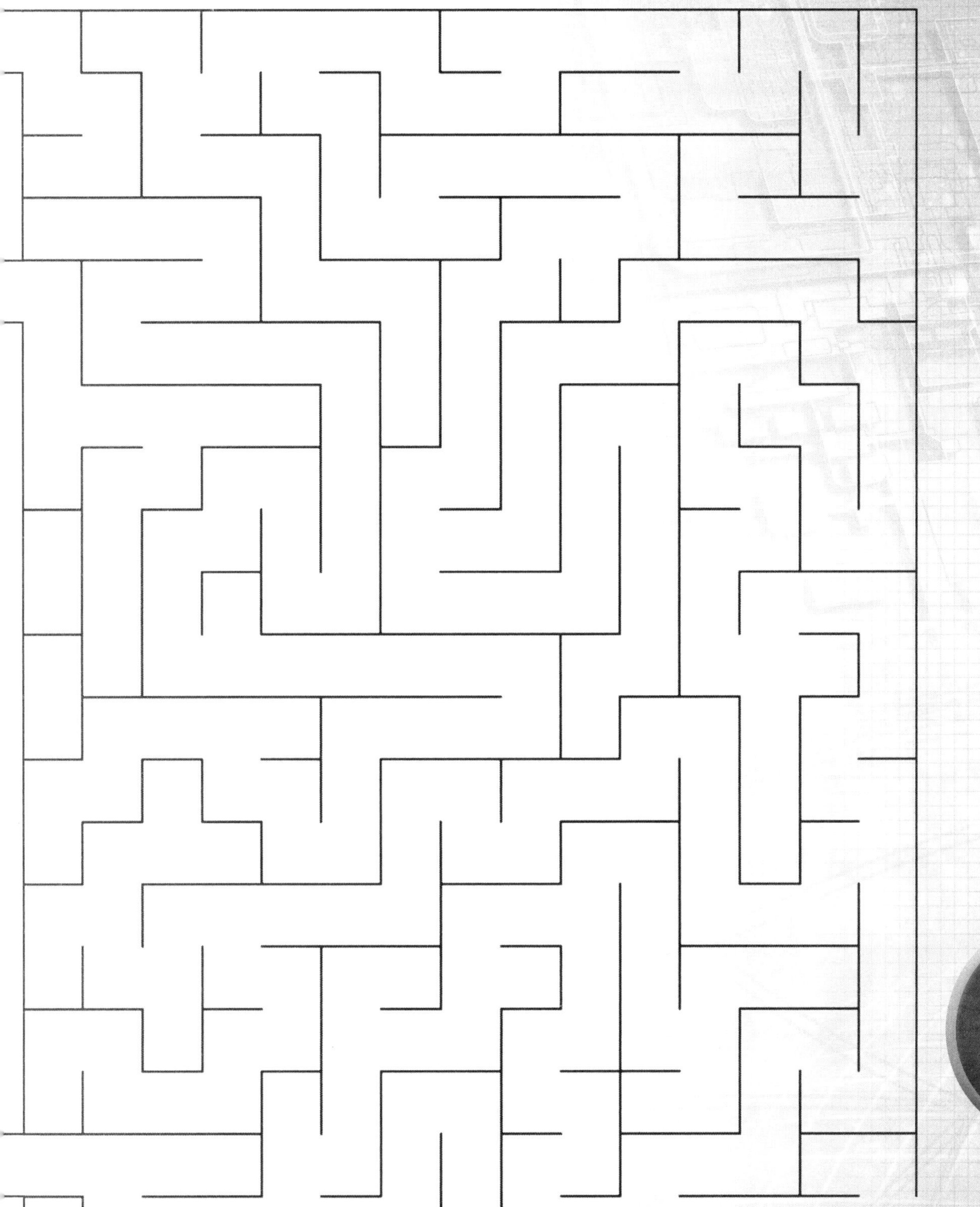

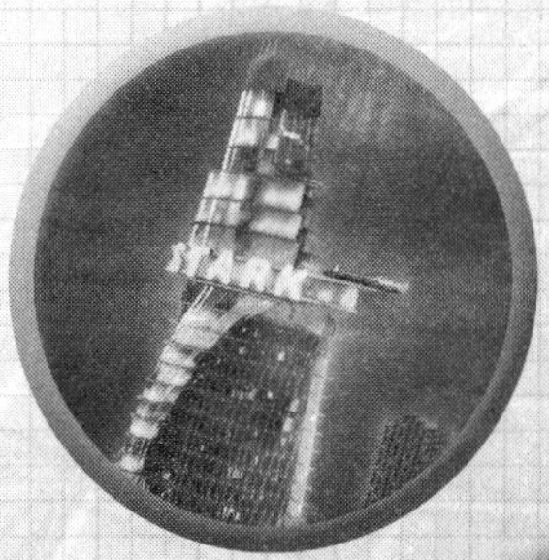
STARK

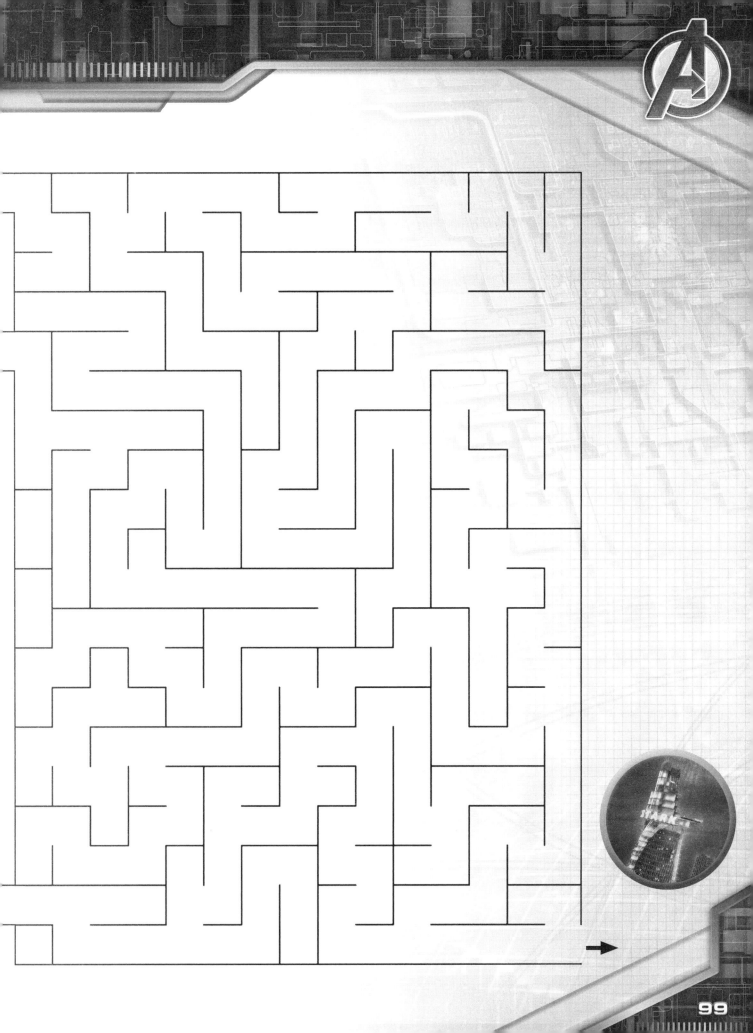

Who is attacking IRON MAN?
Draw his repulsor blast!

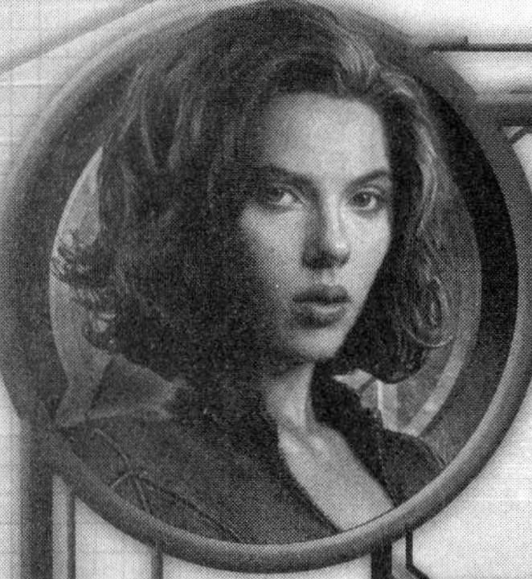

BLACK WIDOW must try to destroy the wormhole generator to stop the Chitauri and help defeat LOKI! Draw the wormhole generator.

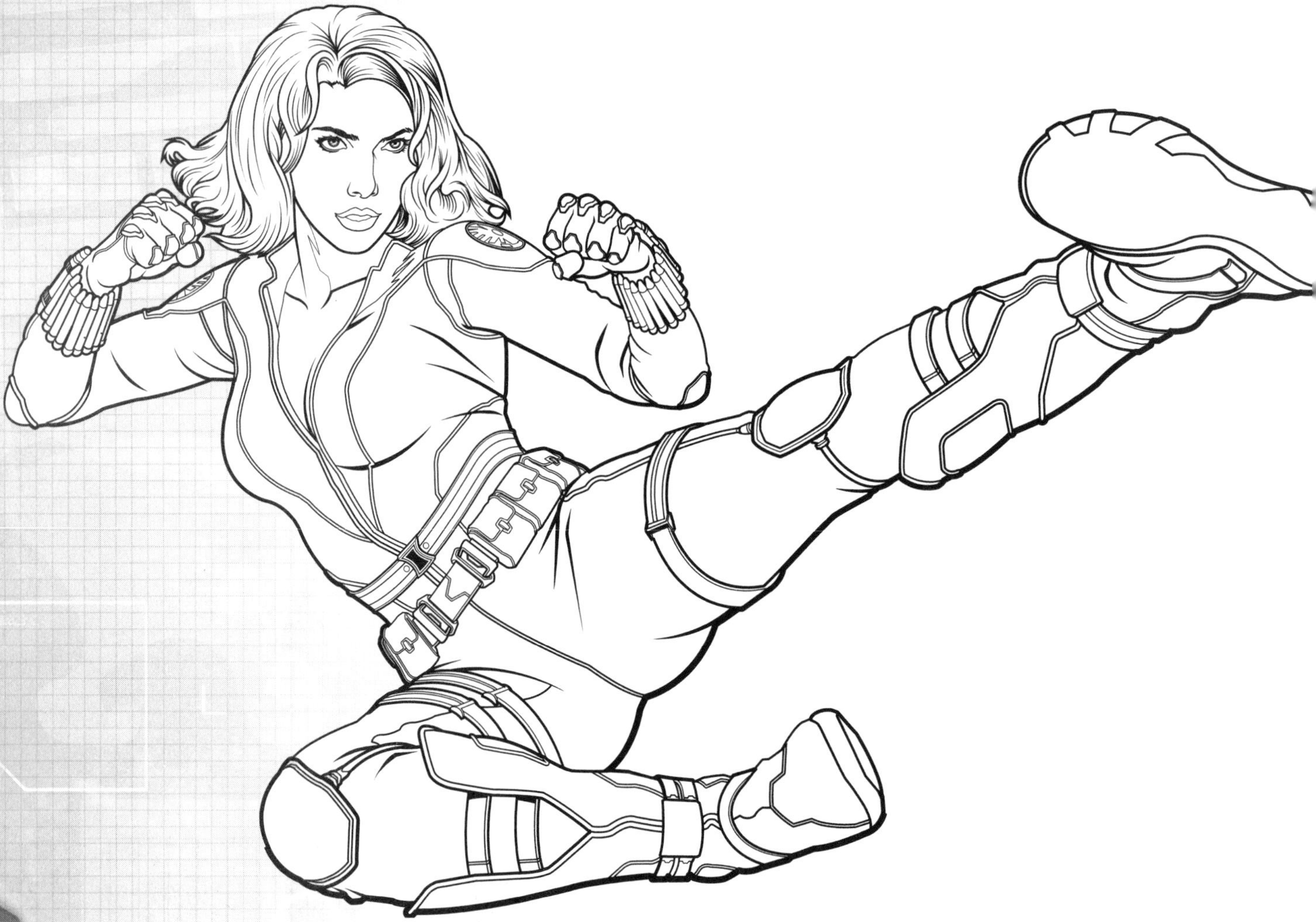

The Quinjet is surrounded by bogies! Draw enemy aircraft to challenge the Avengers.

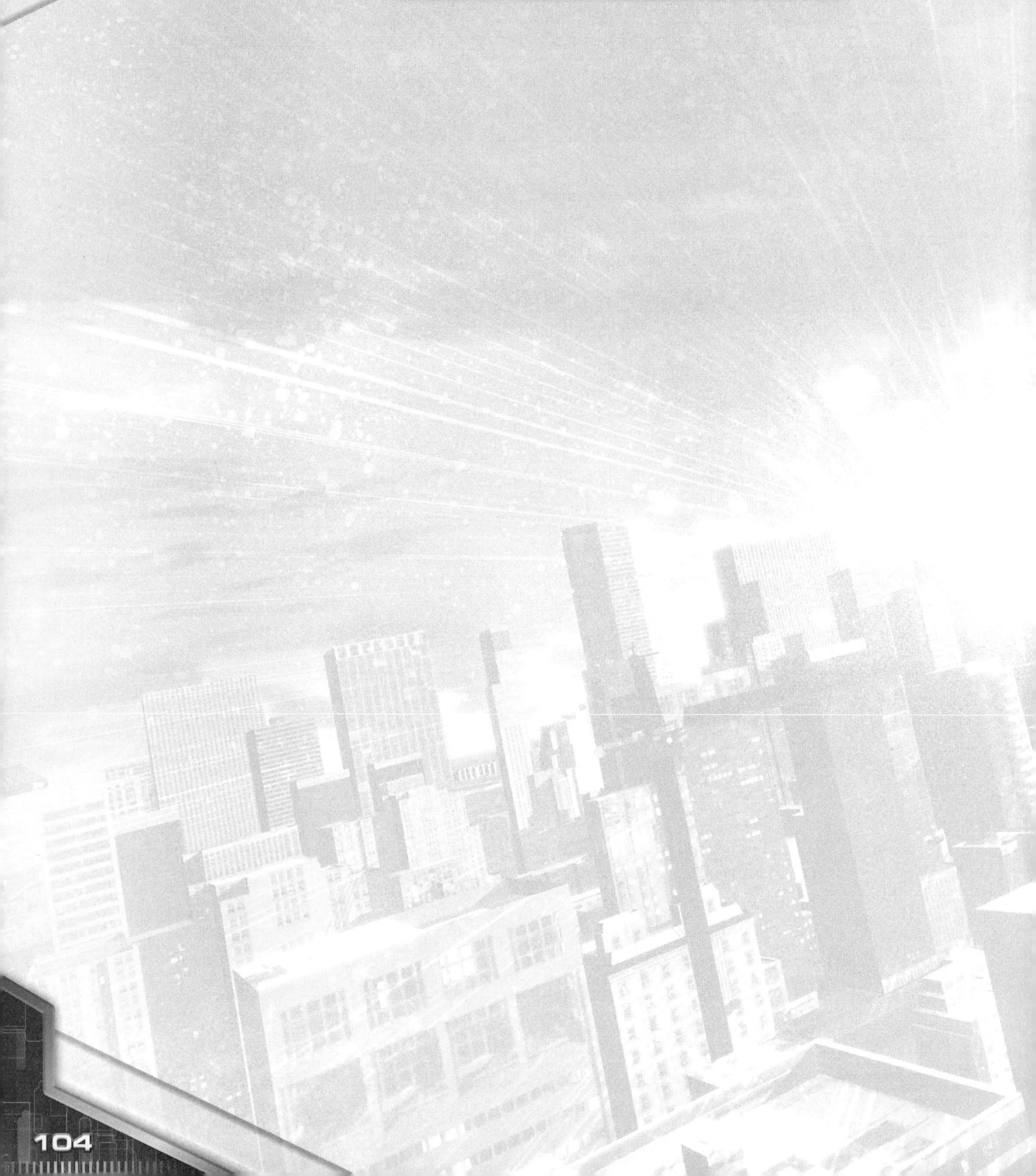

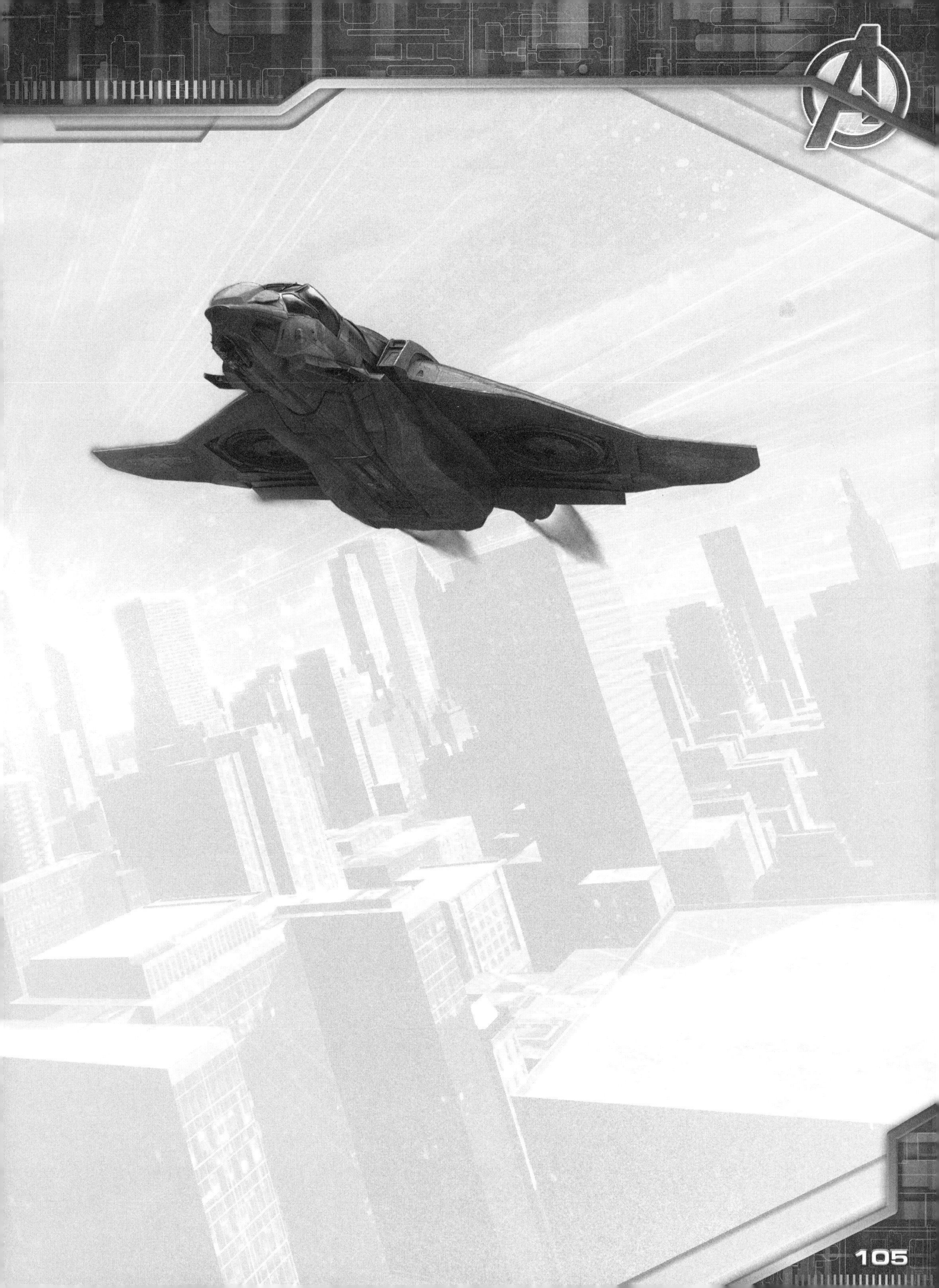

A giant enemy fighter is on its way to challenge the Avengers. What does it look like?

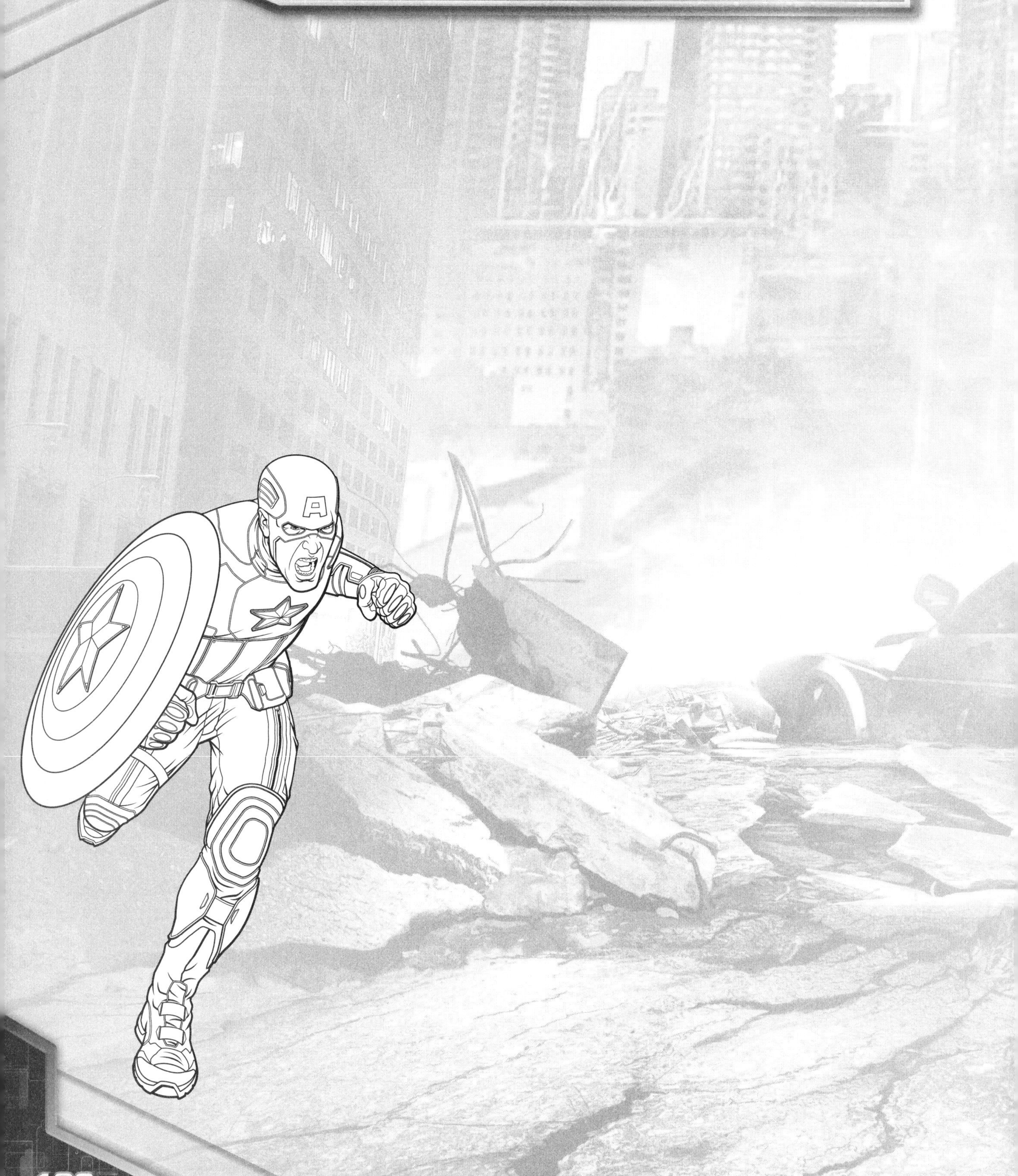

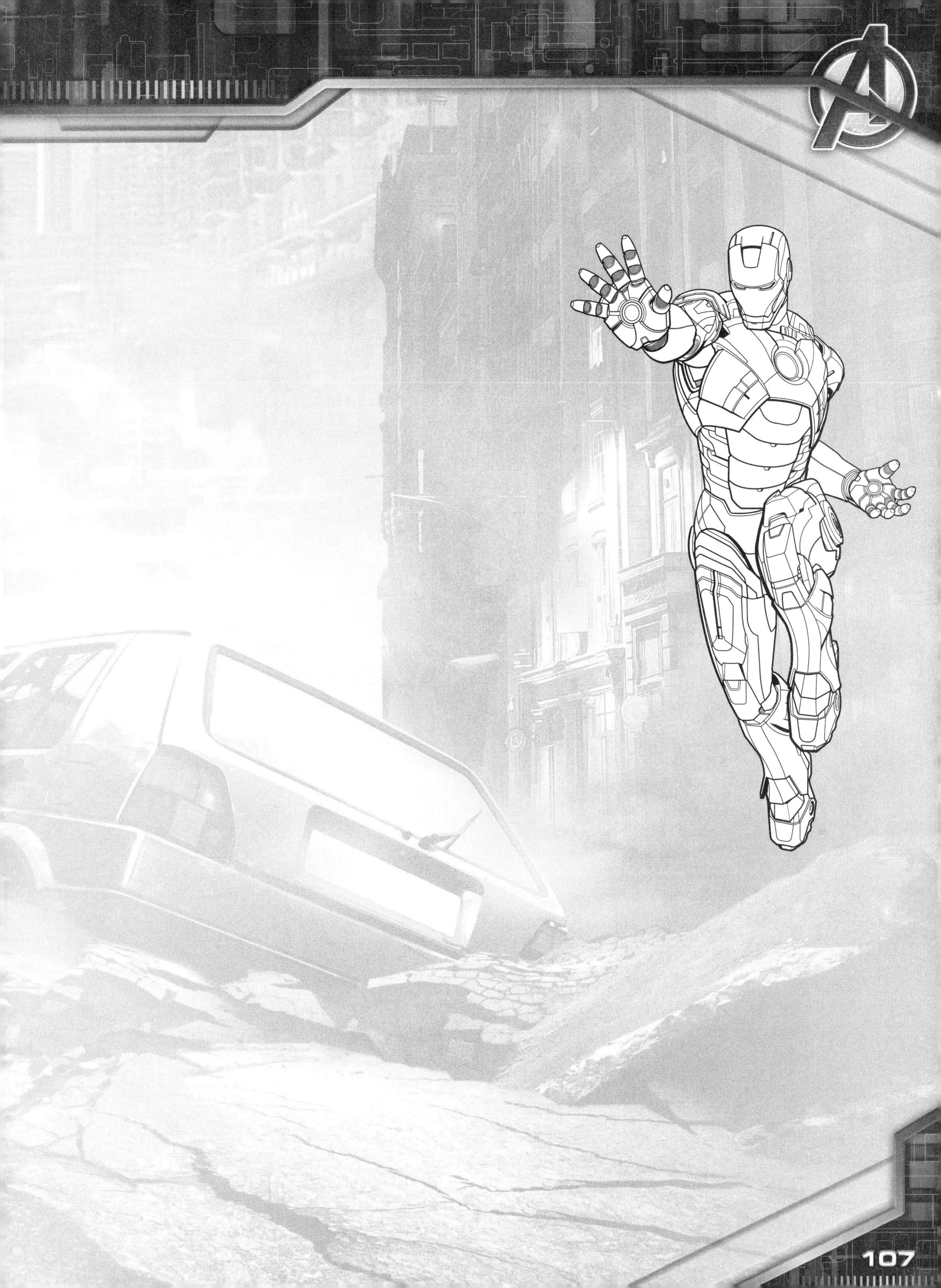

THOR and Mjolnir are fighting off enemies by the dozen. What do they look like?

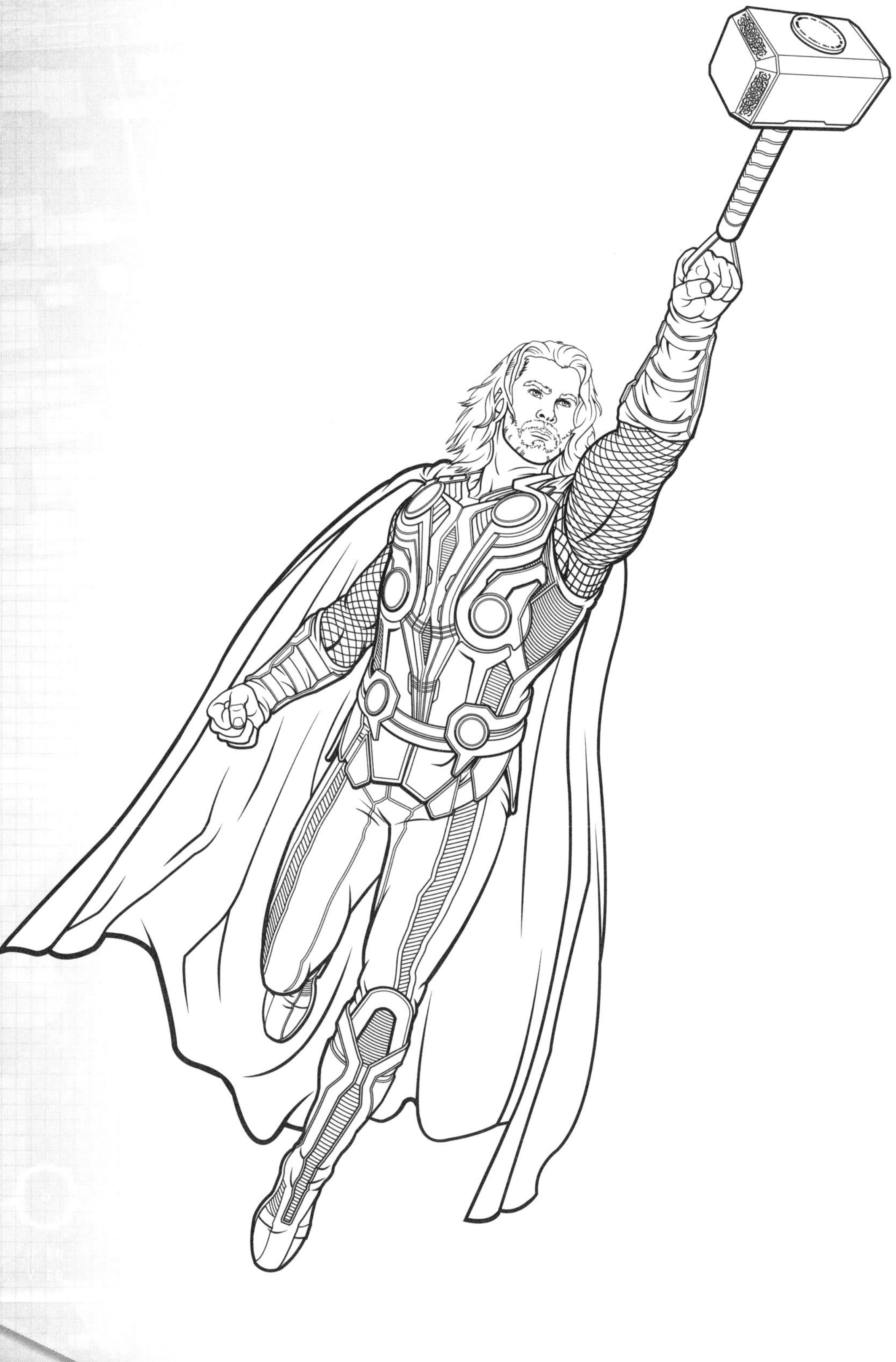

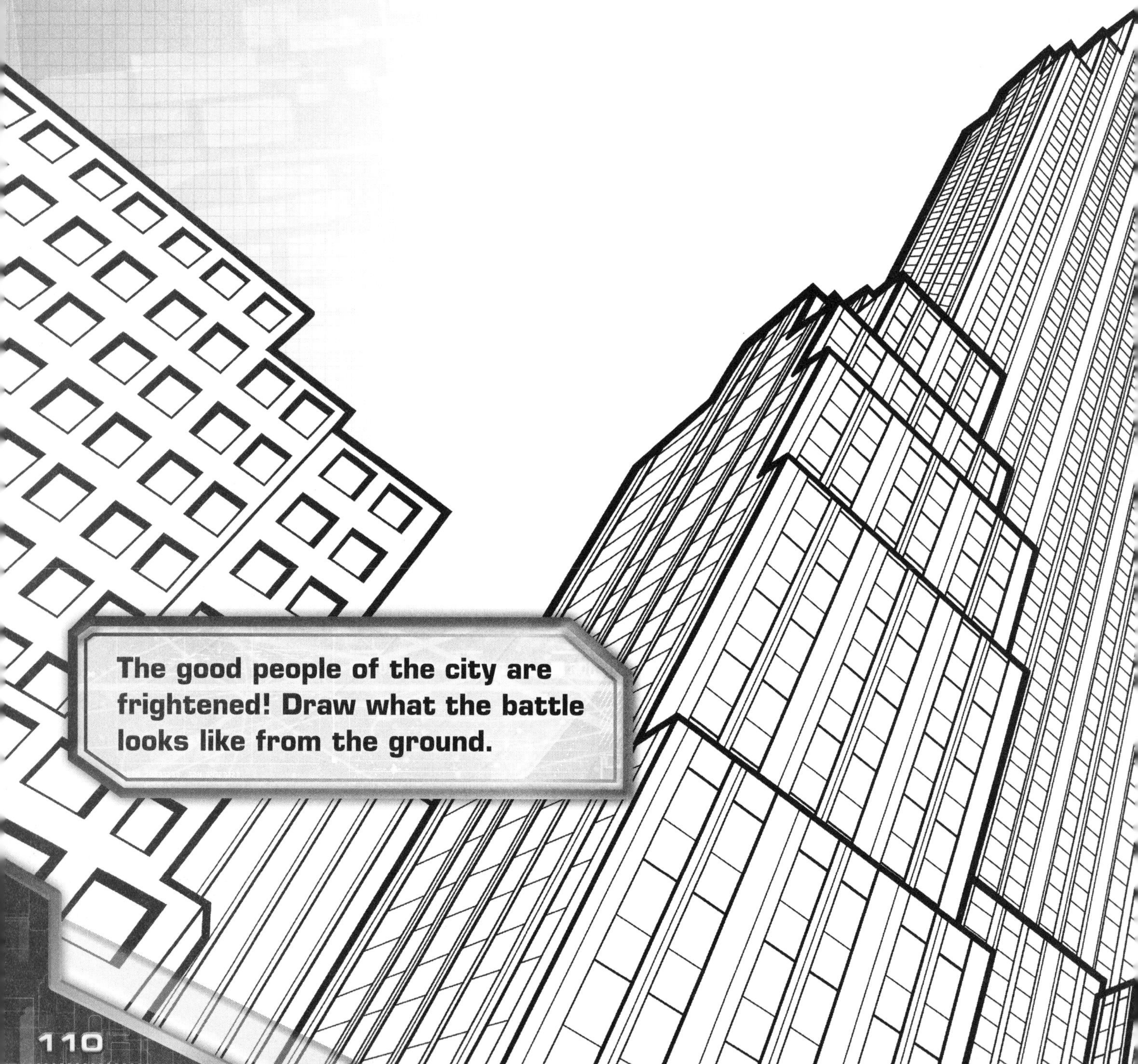

The good people of the city are frightened! Draw what the battle looks like from the ground.

IRON MAN is facing off with **LOKI**. Draw their fight!

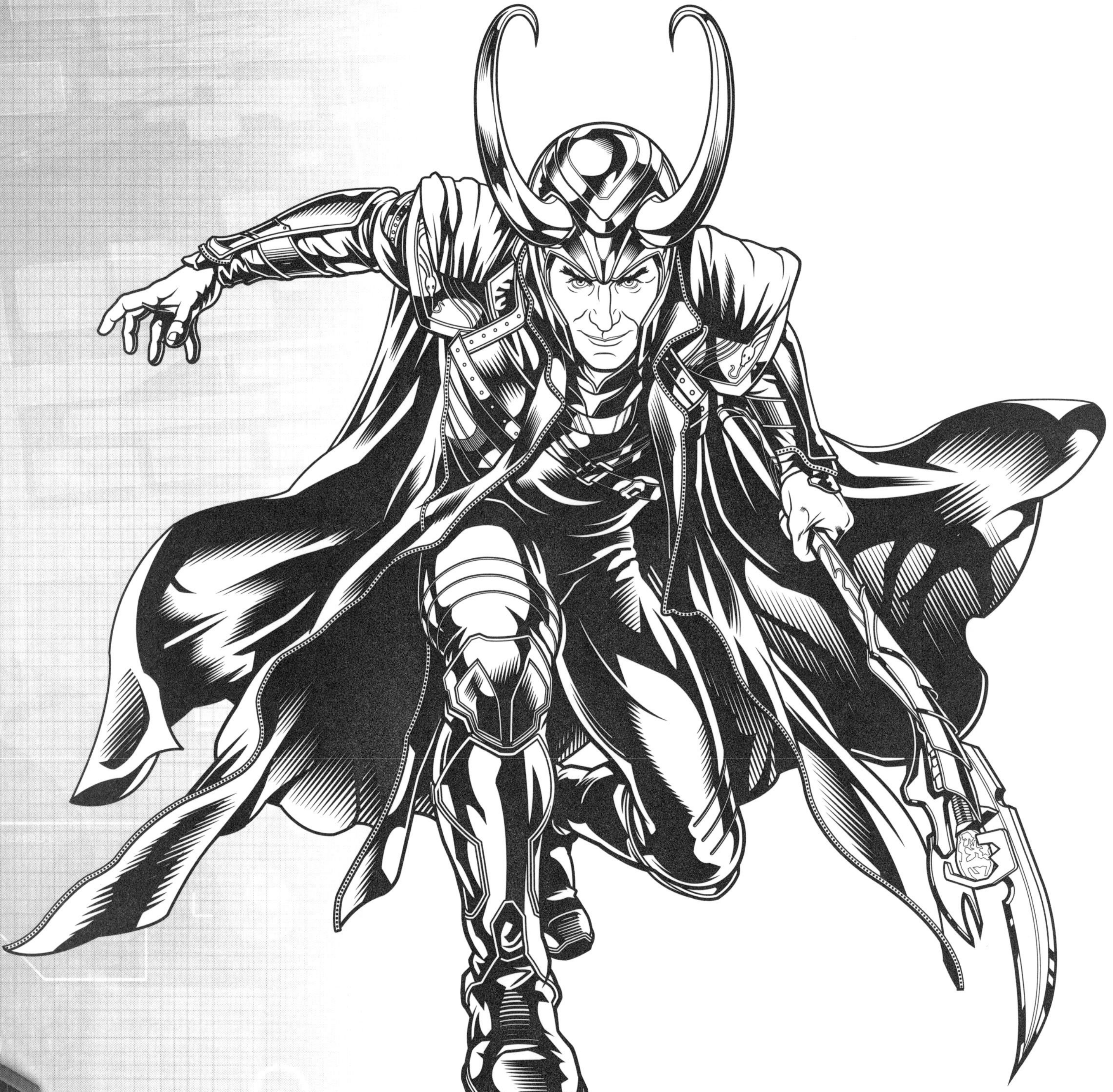

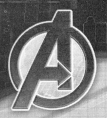

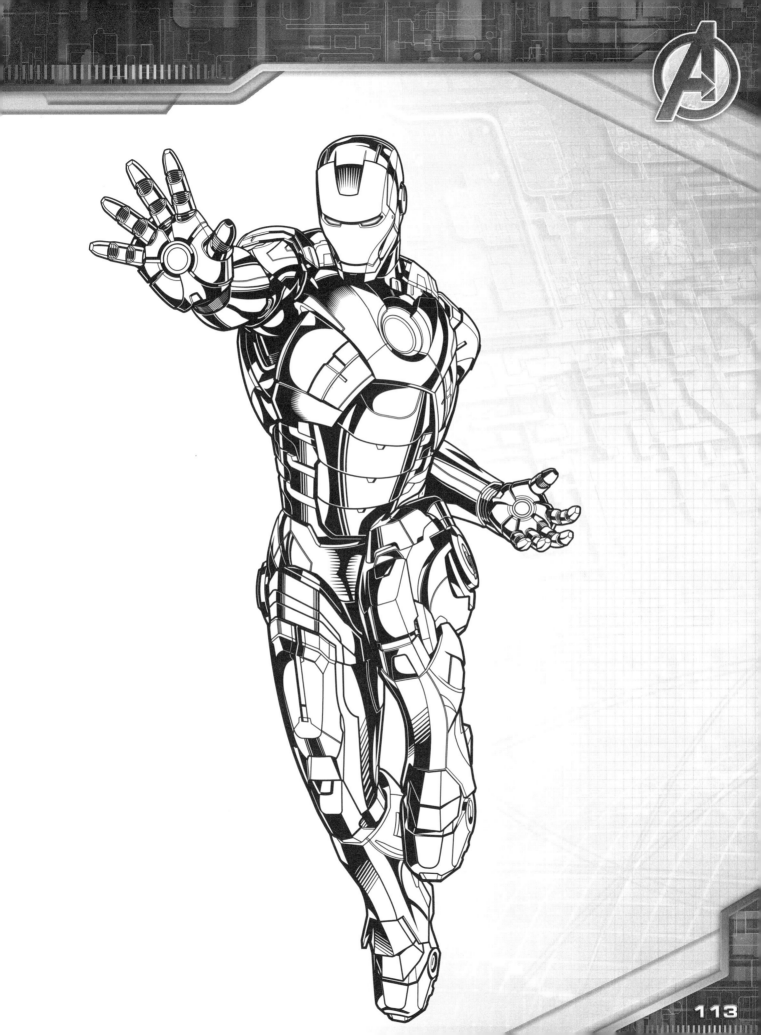

A missile is headed straight for the city! Draw the city skyline.

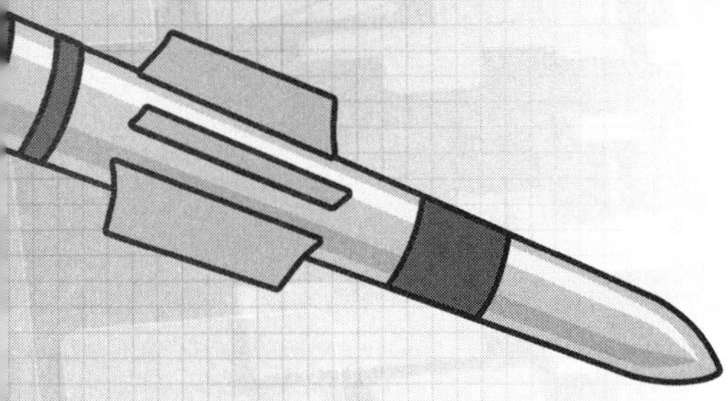

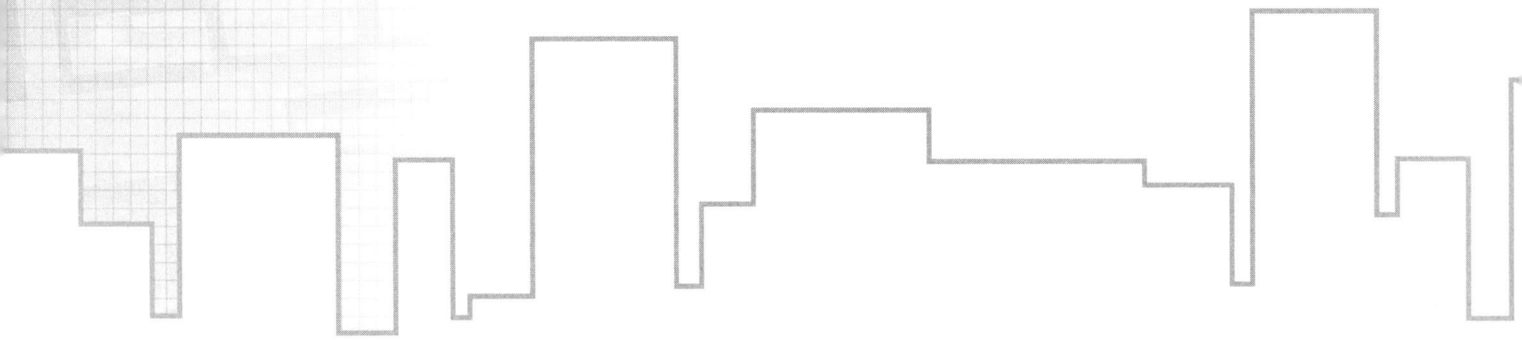

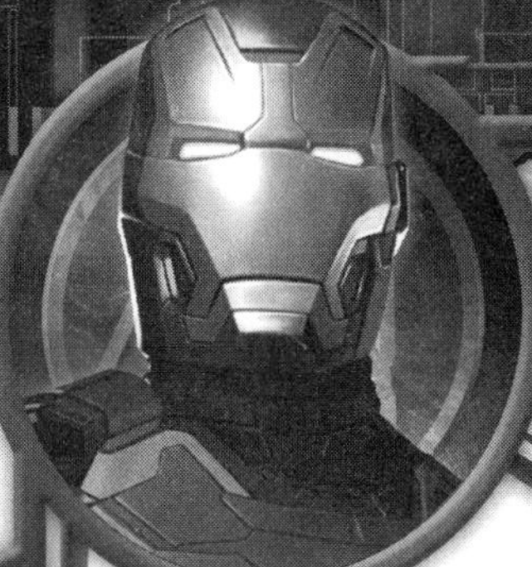

IRON MAN intercepts the missile and sends it through the wormhole. Draw what he sees!

85%

Oh no! IRON MAN'S suit has lost power. HULK, catch IRON MAN before he falls!

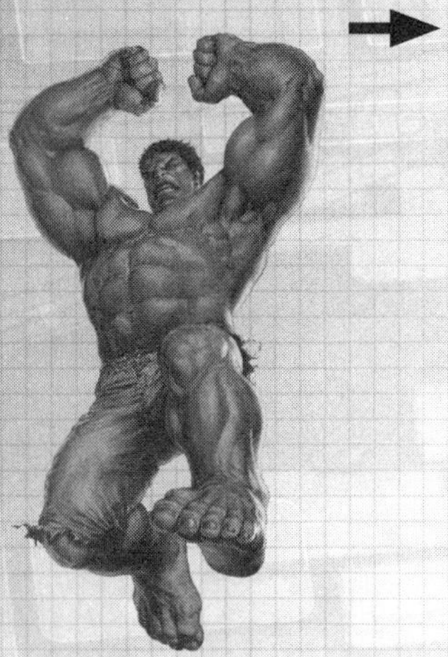

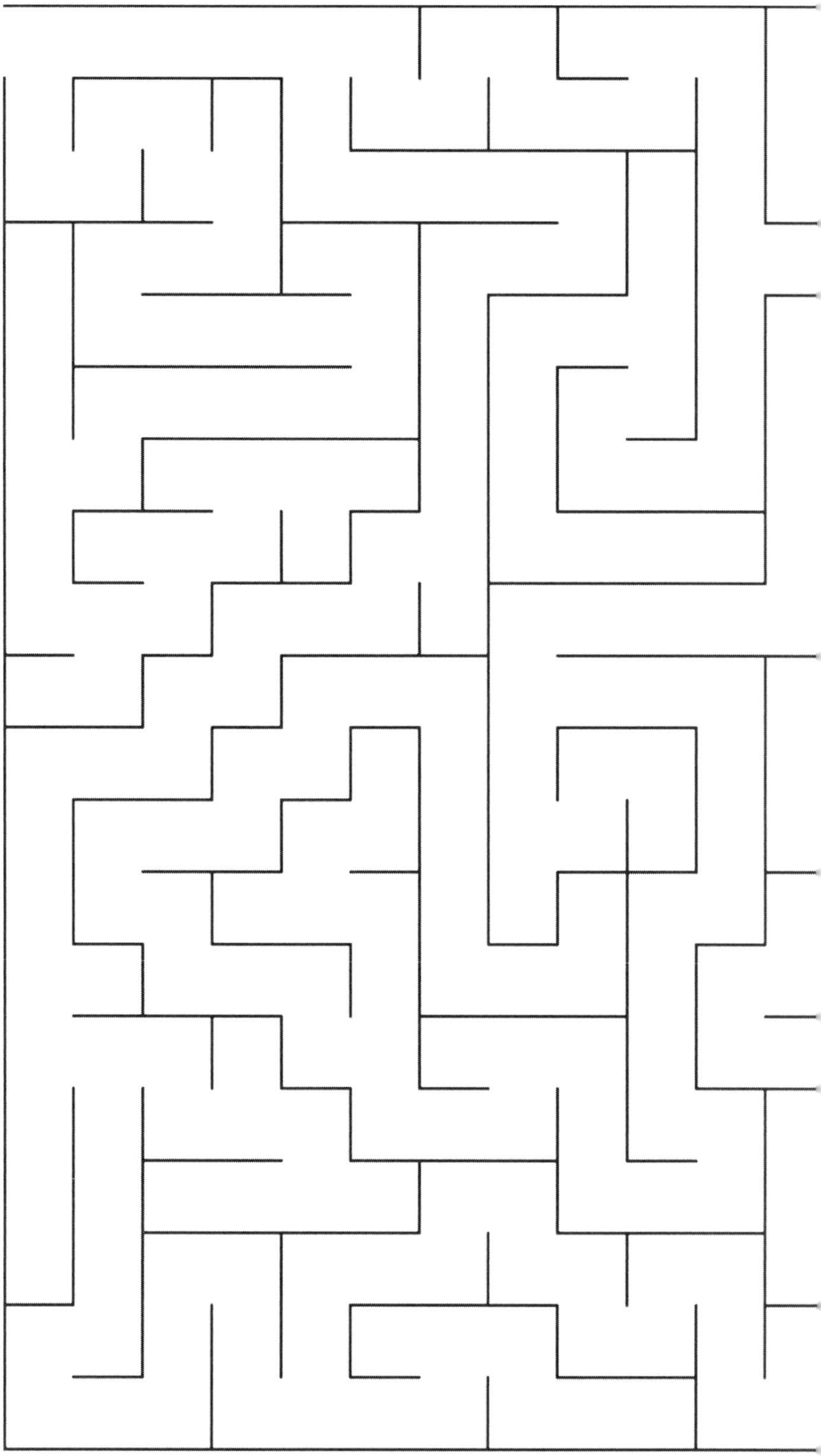

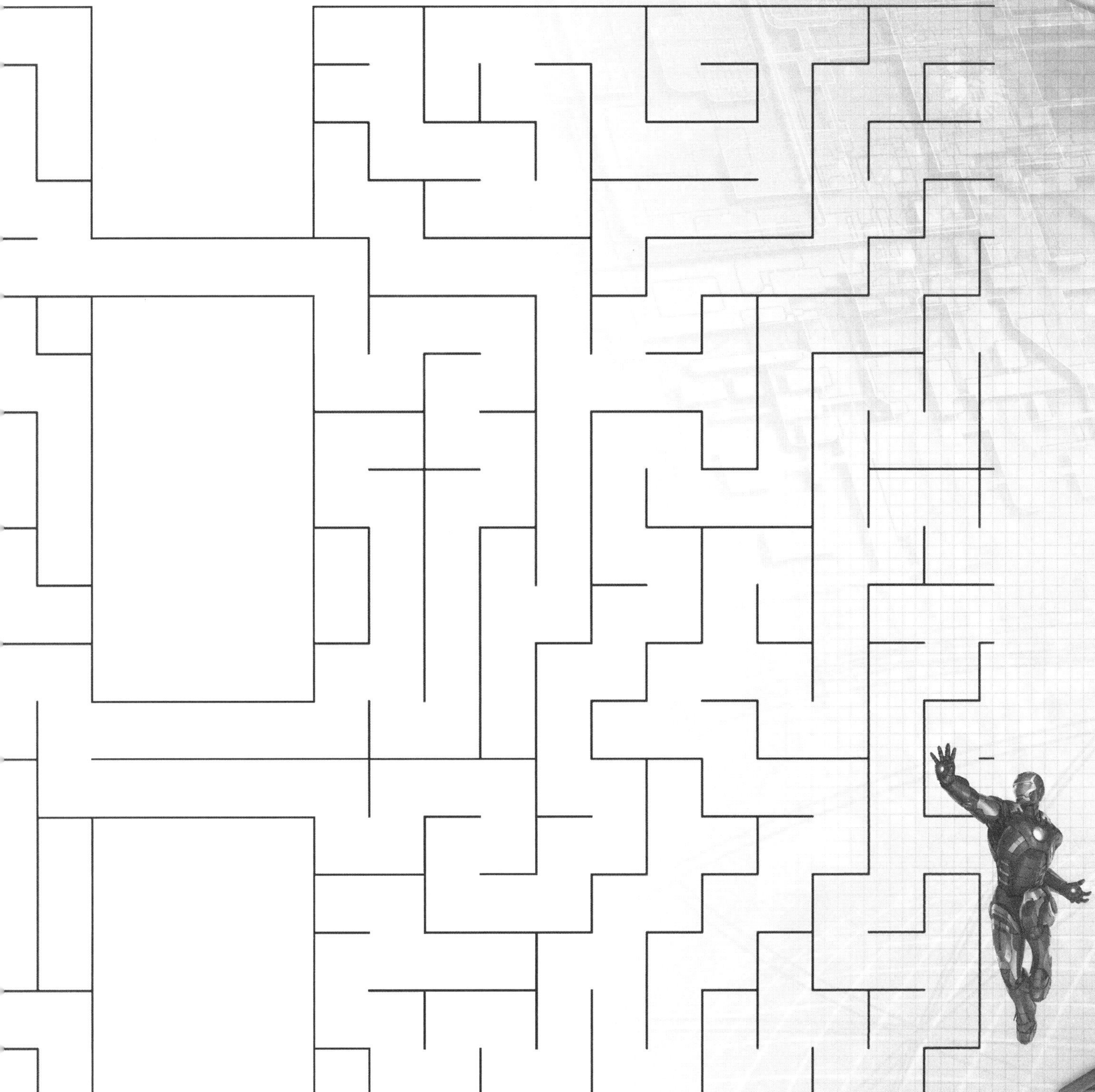

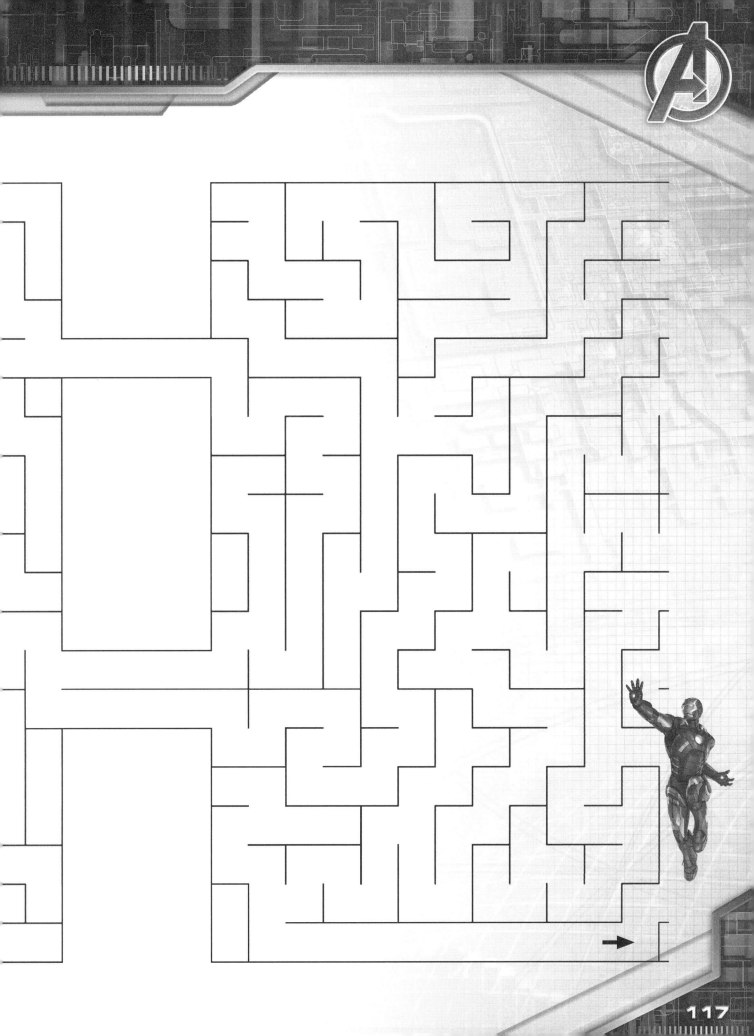

The city is safe, and THOR is taking LOKI back to Asgard. What does Asgard look like?

Build LOKI a prison from which he can't escape!

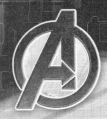

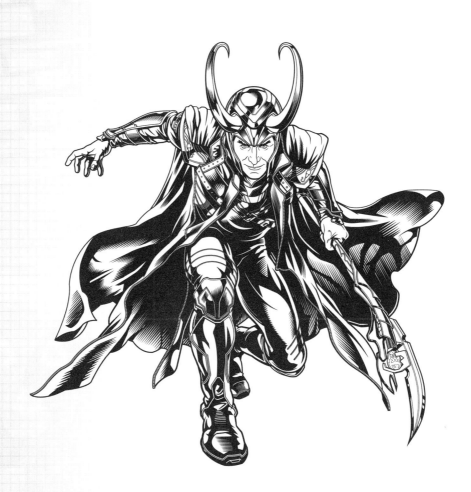

How would you destroy LOKI'S staff?

Help HULK rebuild these buildings he smashed!

The Avengers go out for food after a victory. What would you eat after a battle?

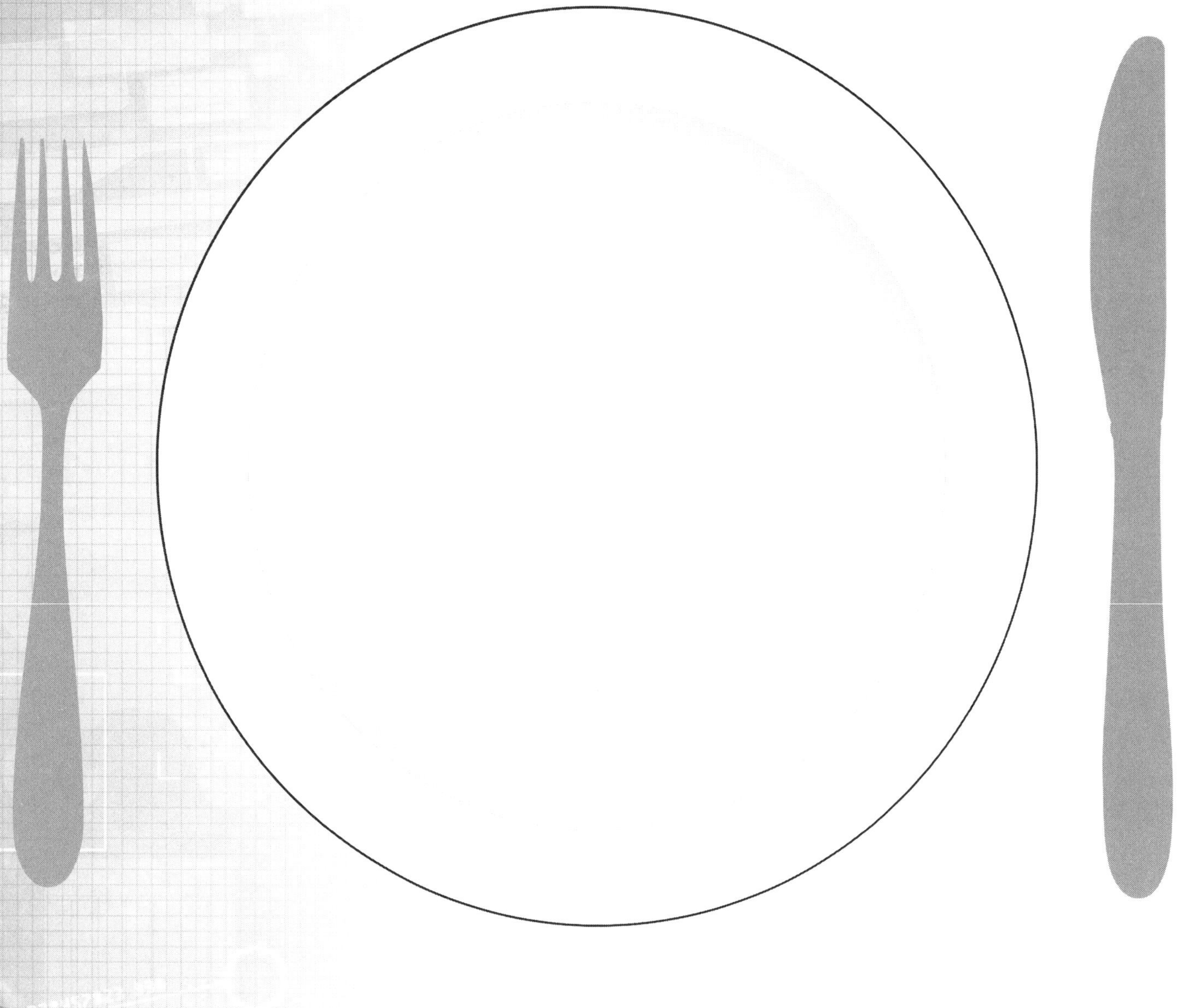

The Avengers have triumphed and peace is restored. What's on the front page of the newspaper today?

The Avengers are disbanded—for now. But they'll return if and when they are needed!

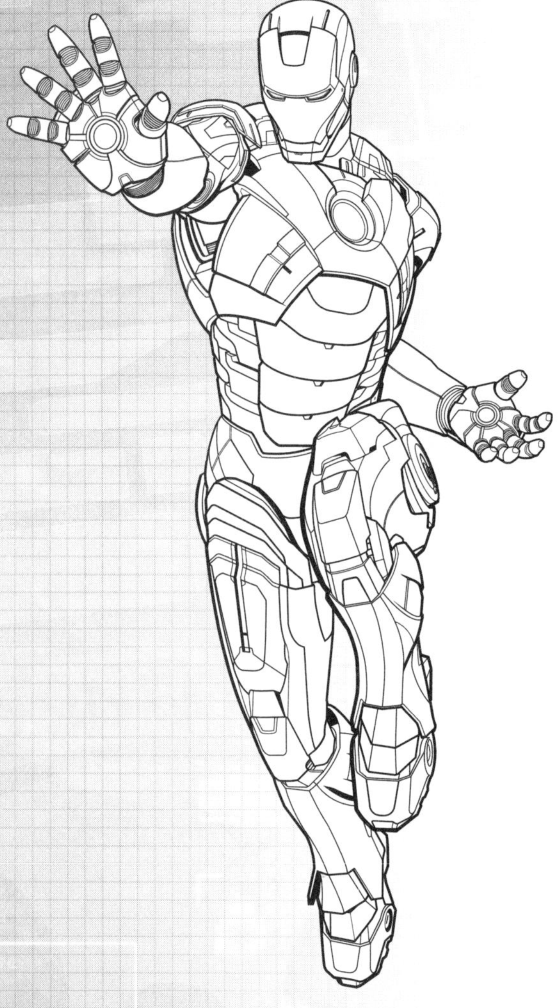

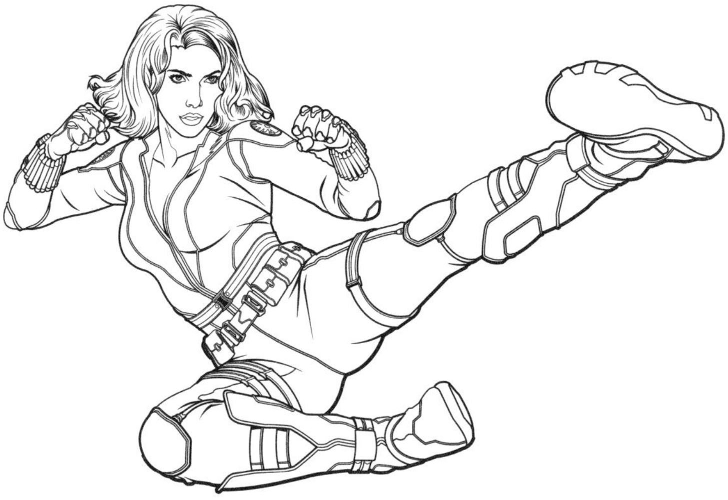

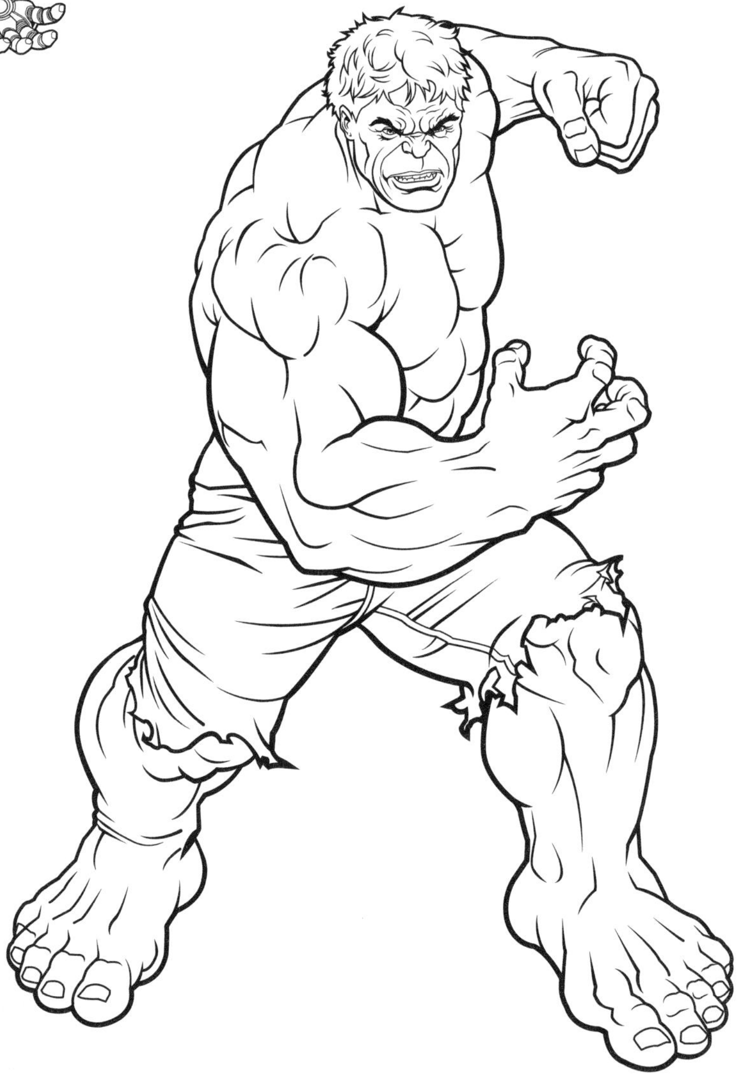

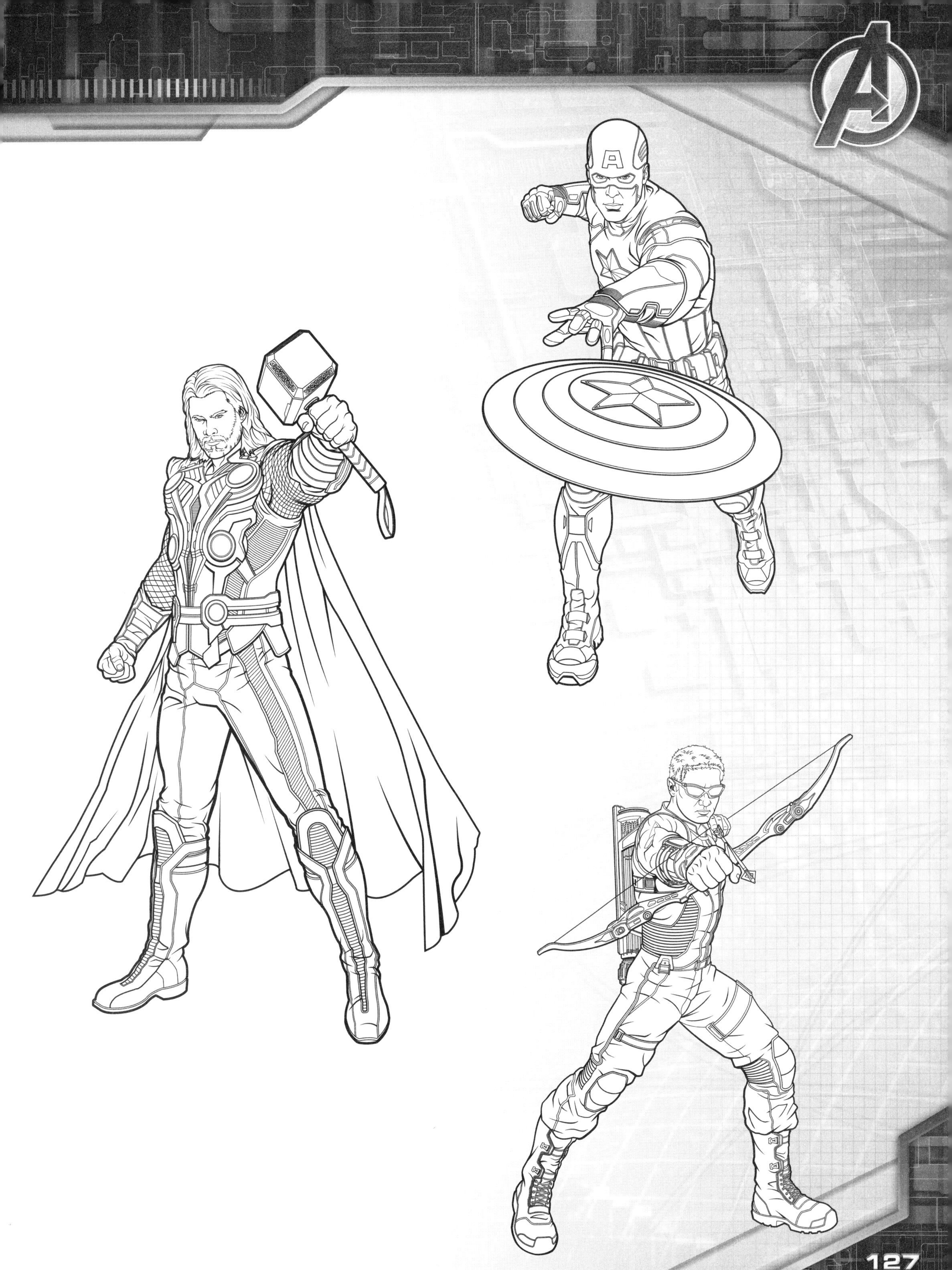

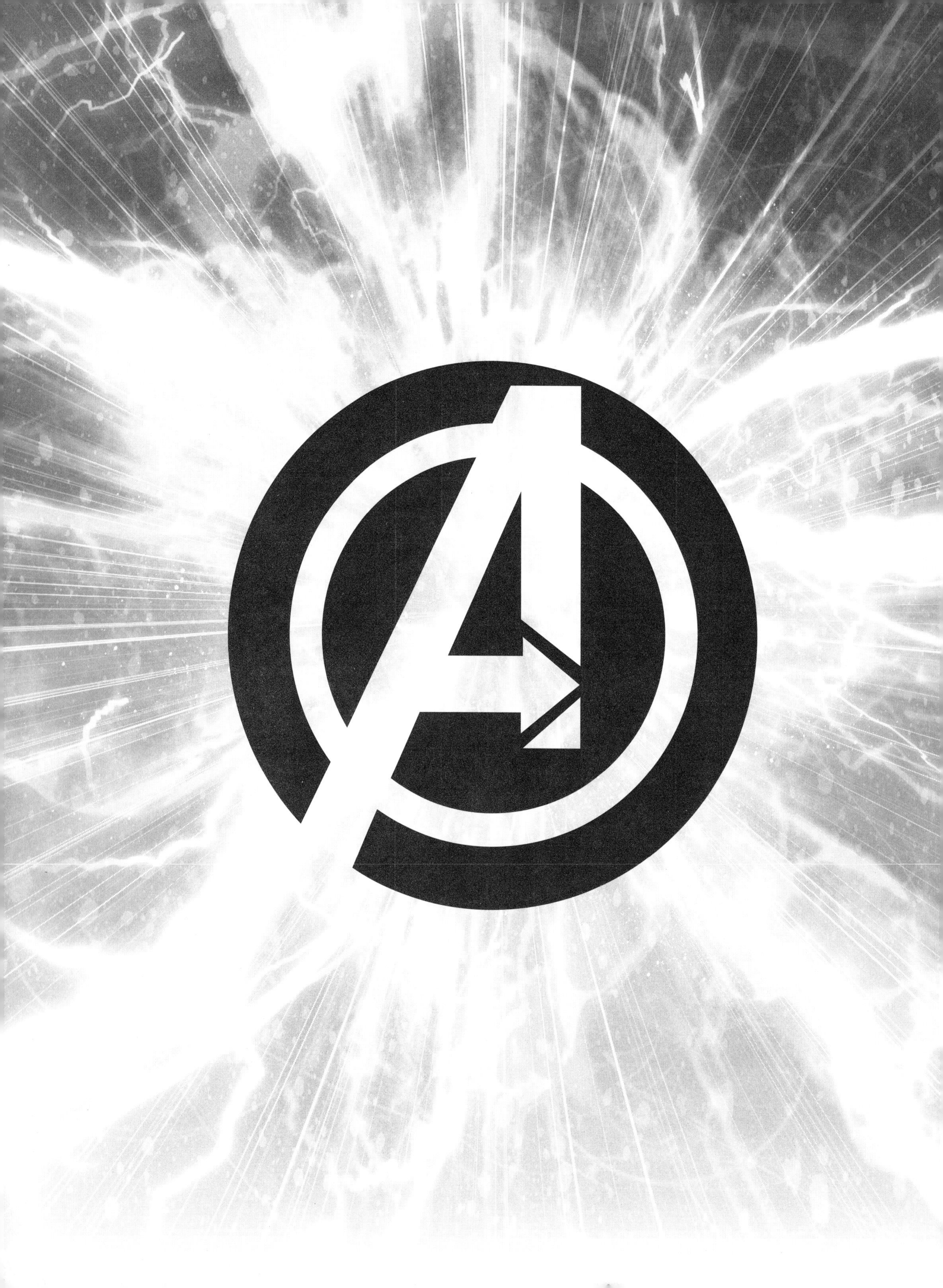